"Just so we understand each other," he said ominously, "I have no interest in staying with you, but I'm not going to be responsible for Sterling and Chloe canceling their honeymoon."

"Oh, darn," she teased with a sultry pout, "I'm heartbroken. I thought you were about to rip off that leather jacket to reveal a tuxedo, whip out a bouquet of wild pink roses, then propose." She stamped her foot. "Damn."

"Funny."

"Do you think?"

For reasons she couldn't imagine, his eyes suddenly sparked with humor.

"What I think," he said, "is that you're the only woman I know who'd rather have wild pink roses than the standard red."

Her laughter was deep and sensual. "I'd think you'd know by now that I'm anything but standard—and I'm certainly not shy about it."

"I'll show you shy."

It happened so fast that she barely had time to register what he was doing. By the time she had, she was lying flat on her back, Ben on top of her. And when his gaze drifted to her lips, all she managed was a breathless "Oh" before he leaned forward, and she was certain he was going to kiss her.

Also by Linda Francis Lee
Published by Ivy Books:

DOVE'S WAY
SWAN'S GRACE
NIGHTINGALE'S GATE
THE WAYS OF GRACE
LOOKING FOR LACEY
THE WEDDING DIARIES
SUDDENLY SEXY
SINFULLY SEXY

Simply Sexy

A Novel

Linda Francis Lee

IVY BOOKS • NEW YORK

An Ivy Book
Published by The Random House Publishing Group

Copyright © 2004 by Linda Francis Lee

www.ballantinebooks.com

ISBN 0-345-46273-4

Manufactured in the United States of America

First Edition: November 2004

OPM 9 8 7 6 5 4 3 2 1

Acknowledgments

There are several people I would like to thank, all of whom helped me in different ways while I wrote the Sexy trilogy.

Charlotte Herscher, for understanding the trilogy and providing valuable insight to make it better. Amy Berkower, as always, for her kindness and guidance. Officer Robert Giannetta, for answering all my undercover and police questions when I dove into *Simply Sexy*. Amelia Grey, Lorraine Heath, Nicole Jordan, and Michele Jaffe, for laughter, friendship, and a willingness to read and offer their thoughts. Travis Rutherford, for lots of laughs and great marketing ideas. Sally Cato, for the amazing covers. And, as always, Michael, for everything.

To: Julia Boudreaux <julia@ktextv.com>
    Katherine Bloom <katherine@ktextv.com>
From: Chloe Sinclair <chloe@ktextv.com>
Subject: Proud

Julia, I'm so glad that you're going to stay on at KTEX even after you sold the station. I know you are going to do a great job. And to think, now that I've stepped aside as the station manager, I'll be working alongside you in the trenches. At least I will once I get back from my honeymoon!

What kind of programming are you thinking of creating?

Chloe

Chloe Sinclair
Former Station Manager
Award-winning KTEX TV, West Texas

To: Chloe Sinclair <chloe@ktextv.com>
    Katherine Bloom <katherine@ktextv.com>

From: Julia Boudreaux <julia@ktextv.com>
Subject: Confessional

Actually, I'm having second thoughts about staying on at the station. I mean, really girls, me creating some sort of television show? There are plenty of things I can do outside of TV. I could be an artist's muse. I could be an artist myself. Or maybe I'll find some nice, rich man who I can wrap around my finger. I might actually like being a kept woman. <g>

xo, j

Julia Scarlet Boudreaux
Former Owner
Award-winning KTEX TV, West Texas

To: Chloe Sinclair <chloe@ktextv.com>
    Julia Boudreaux <julia@ktextv.com>
From: Katherine Bloom <katherine@ktextv.com>
Subject: Shows

Julia, I know you don't mean that—about being kept. You always talk big, bold, and brassy, but you would no more take money from a man than I would. So start thinking about a show. You will make a wonderful producer. And once you create a huge West Texas hit, you won't have to worry about money.

Kate

p.s. Chloe, when are you and Sterling finally going on your honeymoon?

Katherine C. Bloom
News Anchor, KTEX TV, West Texas

To: Julia Boudreaux <julia@ktextv.com>
    Katherine Bloom <katherine@ktextv.com>
From: Chloe Sinclair <chloe@ktextv.com>
Subject: Forget men. Think sex.

Jules, Kate is right. *You* and *kept* don't go together. You can't commit to a monthly subscription to the local newspaper. You certainly couldn't commit to having one man in your life. And if you're being kept, that's exactly what you'd be expected to do. So start creating a show. Just think SEX. As you told both Kate and me, sex and sexy always sell.

As to the honeymoon, we fly out the first week of November. Now that my darling Sterling has bought KTEX, he doesn't want to leave until he has the new station manager secured to take my place. But then we're leaving! For a month! I can't wait!

Lots of love,
C

To: Chloe Sinclair <chloe@ktextv.com>
    Katherine Bloom <katherine@ktextv.com>
From: Julia Boudreaux <julia@ktextv.com>
Subject: re: Forget men. Think sex.

Sugar, it's easy for you to dish out *forget-men* advice since you are now happily married with a full-time husband sleeping next to you. But more than that, how do you expect me to think sex and not include a man in that scenario? Chloe, you naughty girl, who knew you had turned so modern-day-woman on us? What have you been hiding in your bedside drawer all this time?

As to my own show, I guess I'll have to give it some thought. In truth, you're both right. I doubt I could take being at the beck and call of any man. Hopefully I'll have something to present to Sterling by the time you return. For now, I'm off to think about sex. <g>

xo, j

chapter one

Standing so close, he could smell the hot, sweet scent of her. Desire hit him like a hard kick to the chest. He told himself to get the hell out of there. He didn't need the complication. Instead he reached out and touched her.

Her lips were full and meant for sin as they parted on a slow shivering inhalation that made her eyes widen ever so slightly. His hand slid around her waist, his gaze fastened on her mouth, and he pulled her close. He pressed his other palm to her thigh, heat racing through him, the shimmering material of her clinging dress gathering against his wrist as his hand moved higher. Then he kissed her. A brush of lips against her forehead, then trailing across to the delicate shell of her ear. But never her mouth.

If she noticed, she didn't let on. Her body trembled. She wanted this. She wanted him in any way she could get him. She had told him as much when she took his hand and led him to the bedroom.

All he wanted was release.

He tugged the slip of a dress over her head, felt a low growl of appreciation deep in his chest at the sight of the gossamer-thin strip of panties. She wore no bra, her breasts were full, her nipples already taut peaks. Yes, she wanted him.

Pulling her to him, he wrapped her in his arms. Her murmur rumbled as she kissed his naked chest, her hands working his belt with ease. When she tugged his zipper down, there was no turning back.

He drove her back against the wall, their slow sultry dance changing to a panting tangle of need. In seconds, what remained of their clothes was gone. Lifting her, he wrapped her bare legs around his naked hips as he entered her in one hard thrust. She cried out and clung to him, arching to take more. Their bodies slammed together, demanding what they knew the other could provide. They gasped and thrust, she vocal and encouraging, he silent and forceful.

Their bodies came together, each lost, desire thundering through his veins until he felt her convulse. But just as his body sought satisfaction, craved that moment of shuddering oblivion, the world turned upside down when a gunshot exploded, overwhelming everything with light and fire.

"No!"

The single word was wrenched from him, the sound echoing, yanking him out of a deep tormented sleep.

Ben Prescott jerked up in his bed, adrenaline cranking through him as he looked around the room. For the woman. For the gun.

His body was covered with sweat, his heart raced, his pulse pounded in his ears. There was no woman. There was no gun.

He'd been dreaming. Again. The same dream that had plagued him since his undercover partner had been shot and killed a little over a month ago. The only reprieve he'd had was for the two short weeks he had spent as a bodyguard of sorts for his brother Sterling's crazy bachelor TV show—*The Catch and His Dozen Texas Roses,* which they had taped in Julia Boudreaux's house.

Staying in her home had offered a refuge of sorts from the dreams, though only because Julia, despite her sexy, southern heat, was a bigger nightmare than the one in his head.

Just remembering the way she would look him in the eye and drawl his name made his body burn to touch her.

Hell.

Rolling his legs over the side of the mattress, he planted his hands on his thighs. He tried to get a grip by concentrating on the cardboard boxes that lined the small room. Mentally, he listed the things he needed to do before he moved out at the end of the month. Put the deposit down in the morning to secure the new apartment or he'd lose it. Finish packing.

But the tension and impotent fury wouldn't lessen. He still couldn't believe Henry was dead. The final report listed that he had been shot in an alleyway while making an undercover drug bust. Ben knew he should have been there with him. But he hadn't been.

As much as Ben wanted to, he couldn't rewrite the past. He couldn't turn back time. Though night after night that was just what he tried to do.

Muttering an oath, he glanced at the clock. Midnight. The alarm was set to go off in another thirty minutes. So he flipped the switch and got up, thankful for an excuse not to go back to sleep.

He dressed in jeans, high-polished boots, and a black leather jacket. As one of El Paso's top undercover cops, he didn't play the part of the typical small-time drug dealer. He posed as a major supplier, a man who had high-quality weight to move. Large quantities of cocaine and heroin. No chump change for him.

His street name was Benny the Slash—frequently shortened to Slash. With the exception of a select few people in his immediate family, no one knew he was a cop. No wife, kids, or aunts and uncles knew. Being deep undercover meant living that life. He couldn't take a chance that some suspicious drug lord would have one of his lackeys start asking around. All he needed was for one unsuspecting friend, relative, or neighbor to say, *Oh yeah, I hear he's a cop,* and he'd be more than undercover. He'd be six feet under, driving the big brass Buick.

When people asked, he told them he was in the import/export business. His immediate family knew to say the same thing. Drug dealers assumed it was a cover for importing and exporting drugs. Neighbors thought he made money buying trinkets in Mexico and selling them at inflated prices around the U.S. The cover story gave him an occupation and went a long way toward explaining his odd hours.

He retrieved his department-issued 9mm Glock from the lockbox in his dimly lit, cramped hallway. Normally when he went out on a job, he left all potential signs of being a cop at home. Tonight wasn't a normal night.

He shoved the Glock in the holster underneath his finely tooled leather jacket. Soft as butter. Expensive as hell. More evidence for a wary thug that he was successful at what he did. Savvy drug dealers didn't do business with losers.

He went out into the late October night. The air cooled his overheated skin. For a second it felt like he could breathe. At least a little. He leaped into his black Range Rover—another piece of his cover—buzzed down the window, and started to drive.

He had been back on active duty for a week, following nearly a month on leave after Henry was shot. Ben had worked tirelessly—some said obsessively—to find any clue to his partner's killer. He hadn't found anything. Until yesterday. He had gotten the name of a cocky dealer who might have seen something. But he wasn't talking to police.

Ben had found out where the guy was going to be at one in the morning. Benny the Slash planned to pay him an unexpected visit. The small building in south El Paso had already been bugged, and backup was staking the place out. All Ben had to do was get the guy to start talking. That required trust. Ben intended to get it.

The El Paso streets were deserted, the shops dark, the overreaching sky as black as velvet. The perfect order of streetlamps ran up the median and the flashing traffic signals blinked red and yellow like a string of Christmas lights on a mantel.

He pulled onto I-10 at the Mesa Street ramp, heading for downtown. If he hadn't given up smoking a year ago, he would have shoved a Marlboro in his mouth and sucked hard. Instead he found a stick of gum and muttered about a man needing a few vices in his life.

Without so much as a single car or traffic signal to slow him down now, Ben sped along fast, too fast, one hand loose on the wheel, his elbow hooked over the open window. He blew past the University of Texas at El Paso on his left, carved into the rugged Franklin Mountains. Juárez was close on his right, so close that he could make out the darkened windows of sleepy Mexican homes on unpaved dirt roads. A little farther on, he saw the closed, boxy Mexican version of Wal-Mart, multicolored and flamboyant. During the day, loud mariachi music blared from 1960s-era speakers.

The only thing that stood between Texas and Mexico at this juncture was a thin strip of the Rio Grande that was frequently dry given all the dams that clogged the water flow miles upstream in New Mexico and Colorado. But unguarded borders weren't his problem. Henry's killer was.

In minutes, Ben pulled off the freeway at the downtown exit, turning right with a minimum of brake. He didn't slow down appreciably until he got past city hall and the modern, roller-coaster-looking façade of the civic center. Once he was making his way along Santa Fe Street, his heart eased in tandem with the speedometer. His mind shifted into that place where his senses took over. He was looking. Sensing. Ready to pounce.

There were very few streetlamps this far south, and he crawled along the dark, ominous streets by the border-crossing bridge like a hooker in the night, looking for action.

He found it soon enough.

Ben saw the guy he was looking for walking down a side street, alone. No posse, no gang members. Which was exactly how Ben intended it.

A sizzle of satisfaction raced along Ben's nerve endings.

The low-life dealer acted cool, a hitch in his step as if

he were playing a role in an MTV video. But this was no video. This was real, and Ben would bet that beneath the baggy jacket the man carried a gun, no doubt sleek, powerful, deadly. And Mr. Music Video wouldn't hesitate to use it. Just as a dealer hadn't hesitated in killing an undercover cop and leaving him to die in an alleyway not far from there. The threat had been clear:

Don't mess with us or we'll mess with you.

The question was, who had the threat been intended for? Had someone gotten wise to Henry's cover? Or had Henry encroached on someone else's territory?

Ben intended to find out.

He slowed the Rover even more. His target wore low-slung jeans, oversized workout shoes, and a long chain attached to a side belt loop, swooping down then up, ending in a front pocket.

Turning off his lights, Ben slid to the curb at the corner. He flipped open his cell phone and dialed.

"I'm going in," he said.

"Be careful, Slash."

Careful. He smiled wryly at that, but didn't respond.

He was out of the vehicle with barely a sound, walking silently, pursuing. Adrenaline and purpose coursed through him like a welcomed friend. This was where he needed to be. This was where he'd find relief from the nightmares. Which was why he volunteered for this assignment—had argued to get it.

When the target stopped in front of a small, abandoned adobe building, he quickly looked from side to side, then entered. Ben stood in the shadows and waited a handful of seconds before he followed. He didn't feel an ounce of fear. Somewhere in the recesses of his mind, he knew that was a bad thing. No sane cop went into this kind of situation without a healthy dose of concern. The kind that kept all senses firing. The kind that helped a man avoid mistakes. But then again, Ben wasn't thinking about mistakes.

When he entered, his target had just lit a small lamp, giving Ben the advantage.

The guy looked up, startled. "Who the fuck are you?" he demanded as he backed up on the dirt floor in a scuffle of shoes.

Ben instantly raised his hands in a gesture of nonthreat, feeling the pull of his holster and Glock against his shoulder. "Don't get jumpy on me, Nando," he said with calm assurance. "I'm just here to do a little business."

The guy's eyes darted around the room, his cool swagger suffering. "I don't know you, *puto*. I don't do business with motherfuckers I don't know. Get the hell outta here."

Ben feigned surprise. "You mean to tell me you don't do business with motherfuckers who have plenty of high-quality product that needs to be moved? When I said I wanted to do business, I meant I wanted to do big business." A slow, menacing smile of utter confidence slid across his lips. "And I can promise you, your profit will be a whole hell of a lot better than what you're getting with Morales."

Morales was connected to a Colombian drug cartel and controlled almost every ounce of drugs that went in or out of West Texas. Nothing happened without Carlos Morales's say-so or approval. But recently the man had gotten greedy, putting the squeeze on everyone until the word on the street was that only Morales was making money. In any business, legal or not, it had to be a lucrative deal for everyone involved. Carlos had made the mistake of forgetting that fact.

Then again, most drug dealers—big or small—couldn't spell Business Management 101, much less know anything about it.

Unfortunately, despite the guy's mistakes, neither the El Paso Police Department's drug task force, the DEA, nor the FBI had been able to get the goods on the elusive Morales. But they would. For now, Ben would concentrate on a punk who very likely knew something about a murder.

"Whaddya mean about better profit?" the guy wanted to know.

Interested already. Ben almost smiled.

"I mean that Morales can't be the only *pendejo* to make money in this town. The rest of us have bills to pay, no?"

The guy snorted in agreement.

"So you and me, let's do a deal." Ben used both hands to gesture to himself, then to the guy. He waited a beat, then walked farther into the empty front room, his peripheral vision taking in everything from the darkened archway leading into a tiny kitchen, to a murky window with a single pane cleaned.

The windowpane, a sign of his backup, registered in his mind, but just barely.

Ben focused. "We do a deal once," he offered, "then we see. If it works out for everyone, we're in business. I supply you with the product. You pay me fifty percent of street value. Then you sell it for whatever you want. If you don't like how it goes, no hard feelings and you continue dealing for Morales. What do you say?"

Ben could all but see the wheels in the guy's brain

spinning as he attempted to understand the potential, but also tried to figure out the possible ramifications.

"How much you talkin' about, man?"

The lowlife was trying to decide if he wanted to do business. But it was looking good. What better way to gain trust than through the promise of cold hard cash? And if trust didn't win the day and gain information, Ben knew he just had to get his target to do the deal, and get it on tape, then he'd have himself a dealer. A perp caught red-handed frequently spilled information like a gush of water from a spigot.

One way or another, he would get what he wanted.

"I'm talking sixty to one hundred kilos," Ben said.

A scoff. "Ah, man, what's so great about that?"

"Per week."

The guy's eyes went wide for half a second. "A fucking week?"

"Exactly. I'm telling you, I mean business. That is, if you can move high-quality cocaine that fast."

The guy relaxed a bit, greed eating away at caution. He snorted. "Me, I got the best channels of distribution in town. High schools, fucking health clubs."

Fury shot through Ben. It was all he could do not to slam this scum up against the wall. But he had to be patient.

"I'll need a sample," Nando said.

Expecting this, Ben coolly pulled out a little bag of white powder. Nando pulled out a small vial and quickly tested the product. After a second, he held the glass up to the light, then whistled and nodded his head, his dark eyes gleaming.

"So, do you want to do the deal?" Ben asked.

Nando walked over to a small cubbyhole and pulled

out a scale that had been hidden away. Like a clerk in a candy store, he weighed the bag before he smiled, then counted out several hundred-dollar bills. "Fifty percent of street value. You've got yourself a mover, man."

Bingo.

"So, tell me," Ben said, counting the money to buy some time, "what have you heard about the murder of that guy last month in the Lejos alleyway?"

The dealer stiffened. "What're you asking about that for, man? Nobody wants to talk about that." His breathing grew agitated. "It was stupid." His eyes narrowed.

But before Ben could respond, a noise at the front door startled this guy.

Fuck.

Ben pivoted just in time to see another man enter. The same baggy clothes, the same bad-ass grin they must teach at drug dealer school. But his grin fled the second he saw Ben.

"Fucking A, Nando, what are you doing?" the new guy wanted to know. "Who the hell is this?"

"He's cool, man." But the question had shaken some sense into Nando that greed had pushed back. "We're doing a deal," he added, but his brow furrowed suspiciously as he looked at Ben. "Why the fuck you askin' about that guy who was offed in the alley?"

Ben could all but see the moment that Nando realized he had been pulled in too easily.

The new arrival cursed, then didn't hang around for more. He turned on his heel and fled. Ben stood between Nando and the door. The dealer swore, then bolted farther into the house. Ben hurtled after him running through the dark like a man possessed, his heart pounding in time with his footsteps. He could hear the guy running ahead of him until a back door opened then banged closed. Ben flew outside, ending up in a backyard surrounded by high walls. Nando wheeled around, looking frantic, furious, and scared, before he ripped a gun out of his jacket.

Ben stopped on a dime, his Glock extended. "Don't make things worse," he said with deadly calm. "Just put the gun down, Nando."

"No way!" The dealer trembled, his eyes wide. "Get outta my face."

Not so cool now.

Amazing how staring down the wrong side of a gun barrel made the whole world look a little different.

"Tell me what you know about the murder, Nando."

"I'm not telling you nothing! I'm not afraid of you!" the guy spat, though his voice cracked and his eyes were bloodshot from pressure. "You can't do nothing to me." He gave a brave burst of laughter. "No, man, you can't touch me. But I'm going to fucking kill you, man. You don't mess with Nando Ramirez—you understand, *puto?* Don't mess with me!"

All of a sudden, everything hit Ben. The cold air. The sleepless nights. Exhaustion slid through him like single malt scotch flooding his veins. He felt overwhelmed by the smell of the rotting backyard in a world riddled with drug dealers who had more power than the police. Drug dealers who would shoot a man in the back of the head like the pack of cowards they were.

Suddenly he felt spent and crazy. And he took a step closer. "Put the gun down."

The guy's eyes went wild. "No!" His head jerked from side to side, his panting breath so loud it echoed against the crumbling walls. Nando was either trying to find some miracle escape route or he wanted to see if he was really alone.

"I'm putting mine down, see?" Ben lowered his firearm to his side and took another step closer. "All I want to do is talk."

"Man, stop!" the guy screeched. "I'll shoot, I swear."

"Come on, Nando. Put the gun down." Then another step.

The guy's hand shook more with each step Ben took.

"We'll talk. That's all. You help me. I'll help you. We're going to make big money together, remember? What do you say?"

Ben could tell the second the dealer was going to lower the gun, the inevitability of failure flashing in his eyes. The inability to actually follow through with his brazen taunts.

But then everything went wrong.

A noise sounded at the doorway. Hell.

"Drop the gun!" a voice shouted.

Nando was about eight paces away, so close that Ben could see panic rage out of control in his dark eyes. Nando was scared and pissed off as he reaffirmed his grip on the gun and his finger curled on the trigger. He was going to shoot.

The world went into slow motion. Ben tried to get his own gun up as he lurched to the side. But it was too late. The sound of a gunshot echoed in his ears like multiple shots, then the sensation of being hit.

Ben staggered back until he banged against the wall, everything around him looking like a distorted dream. Nando stood in shock. But the surprise gave way to a sunburst of red spreading over his chest.

The shooter had been shot, too.

Ben tried to get his brain to work. He was barely aware of the voices, of Nando crumpling to the ground.

Looking down, Ben didn't see anything other than a rip in his jeans, barely visible in the dim light. But he felt the blood running down his thigh. He held himself propped up against the wall with sheer strength of will as the small backyard filled with cops.

"Hell, Slash, what were you doing lowering your gun like that? Trying to get yourself killed?" Someone snorted. "You're damn lucky we got in as fast as we did."

If they hadn't burst in and scared the crap out of Nando, Ben wouldn't have been shot. But he couldn't get his mouth to form the words.

His brain finally put names to the distorted faces that swam in front of him. Crayton and Beal.

"You and Henry and your hotdogging. It's crazy, I tell you," Crayton said as Beal leaned over the downed shooter.

"He's dead," the cop reported. The short, redheaded plug of a man looked back at Ben. "What the hell were you thinking? Were you trying to eat a bullet?"

The words had a strange wobbly sound to them, and Ben had to work to make them out. Then finally, slowly, his legs gave way, and he slid down along the wall.

"Jesus," Crayton called out. "Slash is down. He's been hit."

That's the last Ben heard before the world went black.

To: Chloe Sinclair <chloe@ktextv.com>
    Katherine Bloom <katherine@ktextv.com>
From: Julia Boudreaux <julia@ktextv.com>
Subject: re: cancel

What do you mean you're canceling your honeymoon?! Chloe, you can't cancel. Kate, tell her she can't cancel. Ben is going to be fine. You told me yourself that he checks out of the hospital tomorrow.

xo, j

p.s. How does any respectable grown man get shot anyway?

To: Julia Boudreaux <julia@ktextv.com
    Katherine Bloom <katherine@ktextv.com>
From: Chloe Sinclair <chloe@ktextv.com>
Subject: Concern

Checks out, yes. But he's still recovering. I still can't believe he was shot! Thank God it's only a flesh wound to the thigh. Had it hit him at a different angle, he would be dead. On top of that, he's in between apartments. So he's going to stay with us until he's 100 percent.

Chloe

p.s. As I understand it, Ben was in south El Paso and got caught in some sort of drive-by shooting. In all the mayhem, I never got a clear answer about it, but I think he was coming out of a bar.

Chloe Sinclair
Award-winning KTEX TV

To: Chloe Sinclair <chloe@ktextv.com>
    Julia Boudreaux <julia@ktextv.com>
From: Katherine Bloom <katherine@ktextv.com>
Subject: re: Concern

Chloe, Ben can stay in the guest cottage while you're gone. Jesse and I are in town all month. He'll be fine.

Kate

Katherine C. Bloom
News Anchor, KTEX TV, West Texas

To: Katherine Bloom <katherine@ktextv.com>
    Julia Boudreaux <julia@ktextv.com>
From: Chloe Sinclair <chloe@ktextv.com>
Subject: Sweet but . . .

That's really great of you, Kate, but Sterling doesn't want his brother having to fend for himself this soon out of the hospital, or be alone, for that matter . . . especially while we're off honeymooning.

C

To: Chloe Sinclair <chloe@ktextv.com>
    Katherine Bloom <katherine@ktextv.com>
From: Julia Boudreaux <julia@ktextv.com>
Subject: This is crazy

If Ben can't be alone, he can stay with me. Missing your honeymoon is insane. You need that time, just you and Sterling, to really get to know each other. And I wouldn't say that if you hadn't already told me that Ben was going to be fine.

Go, enjoy, don't worry. I'll deal with Ben.

xo, j

p.s. I should have known that *Ben* and *respectable* don't belong in the same sentence. And you know, now that I think about it, no one has ever told me what he does.

To: Julia Boudreaux <julia@ktextv.com>
    Katherine Bloom <katherine@ktextv.com>
From: Chloe Sinclair <chloe@ktextv.com>
Subject: Worry

Jules, you know I love you, but we both know that you and Ben
don't get along. I live in constant dread that major fireworks are
going to explode between you two—and not the good kind. I'm
afraid that without anyone around to run interference, and him in
a weakened state, you just might finish him off with . . . well . . .
a verbal slaying.

Your adoring best friend,
C

p.s. Sterling won't talk about Ben much. But while his family was
at the hospital, I asked their mother about him. She said Ben is
some sort of sweet, loving import/export wonder guy. Which
could explain why he was in a bar by the border.

To: Chloe Sinclair <chloe@ktextv.com>
    Katherine Bloom <katherine@ktextv.com>
From: Julia Boudreaux <julia@ktextv.com>
Subject: Verbal slayings

Funny, C. I think we both know that, even shot, Ben Prescott
is no weak daisy—which clearly must have been his *only*
qualification to be the bodyguard for *The Catch* last month
since it turns out he's some import/export guy! I can't believe
we had a guy who sells tchotchkes in charge of protecting us
during the taping! What was he going to do if some criminal
broke onto the set? Throw miniature brass decorative objects
at him? <g>

As to verbal slayings, if anyone is in danger of them, it's *moi*. But
I can handle him. Go on your honeymoon and have plenty of
wonderful newlywed sex. Then you can return and take care of

Ben to your heart's content. I promise not to kill him while you're gone. Girl Scout's honor.

xo, j

p.s. Ben? Sweet? Proof that a mother's love is blind.

chapter two

There were some men a smart girl just knew to steer clear of. Ben Prescott was one of them.

Julia had met him a month ago. He was Chloe's new brother-in-law, and Chloe wasn't lying when she said that Julia and Ben hadn't gotten along since the day they met. Which made Julia wonder about herself, since she had knowingly invited the hard-chiseled, narrow-hipped, smooth-talkin' bad boy to stay with her.

Sitting in her father's study, attempting to work, Julia was barely aware of the doorbell when it rang. It didn't occur to her to get up and answer. When it rang a second time, she called out, "Zelda, sugar, can you get the door?"

But the minute the words were out of her mouth, she remembered. Three days ago she'd had to let the last of the Boudreaux staff go. And to make it worse, she'd had to say good-bye to the one person who had held on the longest, had remained the truest, had been completely devoted by taking pay cut after pay cut. No one would have believed how much the housekeeper had meant to Julia. But given Philippe Boudreaux's revolving door policy regarding women, girlfriends, and dates since Julia's mother had died nearly two decades ago, Zelda had been like a sweet, wonderful great-aunt of constancy.

But now Zelda was gone, yet another of the many changes that had occurred in Julia's life since her father's death.

She refused to think about the number of relatives she possessed—none—or the fact that her pseudo-family of Kate and Chloe was marrying off faster than she could buy wedding gifts. She pushed up from the broad sprawling desk with its cavernous leg area where she used to curl up and sleep while she waited for her father to come home when she was a child.

Memories—the kind that filled the mind and made the heart twist and eyes burn. She missed her father, every single day. But just as she had said about Ben Prescott, she was no weak daisy either, and she wasn't about to let this setback in her life slow her down—much less ruin her.

Taking a deep breath, she dashed away the threat of tears. She took comfort in the knowledge that after selling KTEX TV, the house in the mountains, her father's assorted antique cars, all of his stocks and bonds, plus most of her jewelry, she'd been able to pay off her father's debt and had enough left over for one, maybe two months' worth of bills. As much as she hated the thought, she knew she'd have to sell the house. But every Realtor she spoke with told her that putting a house on the market just before the holidays was a surefire way to announce desperation. And desperation meant lower offers. If she could hold out for a few more months, make it into spring, she was guaranteed a better price.

So she would wait. Which meant she had to find a way to make a living—and that meant she needed to prove she could create and produce content for KTEX.

She strode to the front door, wearing her favorite white wrap-around blouse and bright green leopard print jeans. Her heels were high, her toenails painted hot pink. A reminder of her once pampered rich girl's life. No more $500 pants for her.

Cocking her head, she waited a second as the thought sunk in.

"Nope," she said to herself, "still doesn't bother me."

Which was odd, since she thought she'd miss the money, miss owning the station. Miss her old life. But all she missed was her father.

She had left her long dark hair loose, hanging straight nearly to the small of her back. One day she'd have to cut it. She couldn't wear her hair long forever. But at twenty-seven, she wasn't yet ready to cut away her youth.

The doorbell rang a third time just as she pulled open the front door. Chloe and Sterling stood on the front steps. Sterling's strong jaw ticked with impatience, and Chloe halted mid-search as she rummaged in her purse for a key. But it was Ben, as always, who commanded Julia's attention.

He leaned against the redbrick half wall that lined the three steps that led to the front door, looking like he didn't have a care in the world. He also looked about as happy at this turn of events as she was.

His heated gaze slid over her, one dark brow rising in quiet assessment when he got a good look at her pants. As much as the man didn't like her, he looked like he wouldn't mind stripping the Escada leopard jeans off of her and slamming hard and deep.

A tingle of sensation raced through her at the thought. It had been way too long since she'd had sex.

"I thought you forgot we were coming," Chloe said, forcing a smile.

"Heavens, no, sugar. Just forgot I no longer had anyone to answer the door," she answered with typical candor.

Sterling appeared a tad uncomfortable about that, since he was the one who had bought the station from her. But Julia knew he had given her more than a fair price for KTEX, and he had offered her a job to boot. He might be a cutthroat corporate raider, but when it came to Chloe, he turned into a knight in shining armor. Now Julia just needed to prove to everyone and herself that she deserved what had been offered. A job.

"Come in," she said, stepping aside.

Sterling reached down to pick up a thick canvas duffle bag.

"I can do that, Sterling," Ben stated through gritted teeth.

"Damn it, Ben, the doctor said you can't lift anything. That is, unless you want to end up back in the hospital."

That shut the grumbler up.

Sterling and Chloe headed inside. Ben pushed away from the low wall and started to follow.

"I'm happy you're here," she said, trying to mean it.

There went that dark brow again, rising, the gesture appearing all the more sinister given the thin scar that slashed the brow in half. More than once since she'd met him, she had wondered how he hadn't lost an eye.

She pulled a beauty-queen smile for him as he strode past her, his gait stiff, making her wonder how high up on the thigh he'd been hit. Lost in thoughts of thighs more than wounds, she stood there staring out into the front yard, not moving. She heard him grunt when he got inside, showing just how much of a rugged, unmannered heathen he truly was. She bet he was great in bed.

Damn.

She shook the image from her head and stared to turn away, but a utility truck parked across the street caught her attention. For a second she thought the driver was holding a camera.

"Yes, I can imagine how happy you are to see me," Ben said.

His voice was so close that she whirled around. He was right behind her.

"Oh," she squeaked.

She, Julia Boudreaux, tormentor of all deliciously bad men, squeaked. She couldn't believe it. She couldn't believe how Ben Prescott could turn her into someone she was not—a squeaking schoolgirl. And she wasn't, she told herself firmly. She ate men like him for breakfast, then spit them out in time for dinner.

But what really unsettled her was how he looked now that she was standing so close. Beneath the icy exterior was a man who was trying very hard to act like he wasn't hurt. Her heart leaped with unaccustomed worry. If he really wasn't okay, maybe she'd been a little hasty in offering him a place to stay. She didn't know the first thing about taking care of anyone, much less a man who had been shot.

Worse news, however, was something else she noticed. He smelled like a hot, sexy man. And she should know. She was an expert on hot, sexy men. But this was a specimen that her internal radar warned her against. Letting her guard down around this man spelled nothing but dark storms and turbulent seas. With her father's sudden death, and now her life turned upside down, she was managing, yes, but the last thing she needed was more bad weather.

"Do I make you nervous, cupcake?" he asked.

Cupcake, she mouthed silently with an incredulous shake of her head.

The corner of his mouth crooked up in amusement.

"Nervous? Me?" she asked innocently. She bit her lip and looked at him through lowered lashes. "Not at all. Though I wonder if I make you nervous . . . beefcake."

That wiped the grin off his too handsome face.

There, she felt better already. She had regained her footing.

"Shall we go inside?" she asked.

She didn't wait for an answer. She took one last glance across the street and found the utility man out of his truck and hard at work with tools and wires, relieving her that it wasn't anything weird after all. Smiling, she swept past Ben like a queen at court. Or at least she tried. He caught her arm, grimacing when she jarred him, though he quickly pulled his features into a hard, implacable mask. God forbid this caveman show an ounce of pain.

"Just so we understand each other," he began, "I have no interest in staying with you, but I'm not going to be responsible for Sterling and Chloe canceling their honeymoon."

"Oh, darn." She pouted prettily. "I'm heartbroken. I thought you were about to rip off that leather jacket to reveal a tuxedo, whip out a bouquet of wild pink roses, and then propose." She stamped her foot. "Damn."

"Funny."

"Do you think?"

For reasons she couldn't imagine, his eyes suddenly sparked with humor. "What I think is that you're the only woman I know who'd rather have wild pink roses than the standard red."

"I'm anything but standard, beefcake, which you should know by now."

She flipped her hair over her shoulder, then leaned close and whispered, "If you don't want to play Wedding Proposal, maybe you'd rather play doctor. Remember that little game we played a few weeks back? If you want, I can give you another exam."

She expected him to flinch, maybe even blush. Instead he tipped his head back and laughed. The sound was deep and rich and infectious, and she might have laughed along with him if she hadn't been so miffed that he was the only man she knew who never did anything that she expected.

Swallowing back annoyance, she headed toward the grand living room where Sterling and Chloe waited, just beyond the wall of stained glass.

"Where should I put this?" Sterling asked, hefting Ben's bag.

"I have a guest room ready. The one down the hall with the door open. Thanks."

Sterling heaved the duffle over his shoulder as if it didn't weigh more than a feather and walked to the east wing of the house.

Julia turned to Chloe. "I'm so excited about your trip. I can't wait to hear all about it when you get back."

"I'll keep in touch while we're gone."

"No keeping in touch! This is supposed to be just the two of you. Ben and I will be fine."

"Yeah, don't worry about us," Ben stated, though his voice had softened into a gruff kindness for his new sister-in-law. "You and Sterling need the time away."

"I'm not worried about you two—"

Julia and Ben snorted in unison.

"—it's the new station manager I'm a little worried about."

"What's wrong with him?" Julia instantly wanted to know.

"Nothing, I'm sure. Sterling knows him, and thinks the world of him. But, well, KTEX has been my baby for so long . . ."

"And it's hard to let go," Julia finished for her. "Not to worry, we both love KTEX. Between Kate and me, we'll keep an eye on him. You need to worry about making *new* babies."

Chloe flashed red. "Julia!"

"Oh, don't go all prude-girl on me, Miss I-better-seduce-Sterling-so-he'll-lose-interest-in-me."

The embarrassment on Chloe's face brightened even more. Ben actually chuckled.

"I've heard some pretty flimsy excuses in my day, but that one takes the cake." Julia laughed. "First Kate going all sexy on us, then you. Thank God I don't have to turn into the complete opposite of who I am. I'm already sexy, sugar."

"Julia!"

Ben snorted again.

Julia smiled and winked.

Sterling reappeared. "Julia, I appreciate your doing this. I know my brother won't be any trouble."

"I'm standing right here," Ben stated from where he leaned one shoulder against the wall.

He was doing a lot of leaning, Julia noticed, looking ultracool, like a living James Dean. And not the sausage guy.

"I know you're there, Ben, and I know you'll be the perfect gentleman."

This time it was Ben's strong jaw that ticked. Though when he spoke, he plastered a smile on his face. "Me, cause problems for the lovely Julia?"

Sterling sighed. "Maybe we shouldn't—"

Julia leaped over to Ben and hooked her arm through his with exaggerated enthusiasm. "Look at us," she chimed.

Ben managed a grimace that passed for agreement.

"Like two peas in a pod," she drawled, "as happy as can be." Julia smiled at him like she'd found the Holy Grail.

"All right, all right," the older Prescott muttered. "We're going. But I expect you to keep your promise, Ben."

The younger Prescott scowled.

"Just stay here until the end of the month," Sterling persisted. "Your apartment won't be ready until the first, and this way I don't have to worry about you."

Ben's jaw cemented. "I'm not your kid brother anymore, Sterling."

Sterling actually smiled at that. "Sure you are. You'll always be my kid brother. Consider this a wedding gift for Chloe and me."

"I already gave you china," Ben grumbled.

Sterling's smile widened. "I'd rather have your word that you'll stay here until we get back."

"Hell."

Sterling took that for agreement, and he reached out

and shook Ben's hand. "Thanks," Julia heard Sterling say softly.

Julia and Chloe hugged.

"Are you sure this is okay?" Chloe whispered.

"Absolutely. Don't you worry about a thing. Ben and I are going to be fine. Great. Better than great."

She hoped.

Chloe rolled her eyes, then added with a squeeze, "I love you."

"I love you, too. Now get out of here and go have an umbrella drink for me."

The door closed, leaving behind a startled silence. Ben and Julia stared at the suddenly empty entry hall.

"Well," Julia said.

"Yep," Ben added. Then he nodded. "I'll go and . . . unpack."

He really didn't seem like the go-to-his-room-and-unpack sort of guy. But the less time they spent around each other, the better.

"Great, I'll go to the kitchen and . . . do something."

She turned and headed away. She could feel his eyes on her back, the cool assessment. But she wasn't about to be intimidated. She walked away with the provocative swish of a *Playboy* bunny, certain she was turning his manly control to putty.

All she got for her efforts was a deep rumble of laughter that didn't stop ringing in her ears, even after he had disappeared into the east wing of the house.

Determined to concentrate on work, Julia poured herself a Coke, then returned to her new office. Her goal was to have a television show of some sort developed by the time Chloe and Sterling returned in a month.

She was proud of the way she'd handled the sale of KTEX and paid off her father's debts. She had done it, and done it well. She could create a show, too. Surely.

A shiver of concern raced down her spine. What kind of new, fresh, interesting show could she create? It seemed like everything was done to death. The more she tried to think of something new, fresh, and different, her brain locked down a little more. By the time she finished her soda, she had gotten no further along than scribbling a bunch of doodles on her notepad. She felt bored and antsy, and was dying to get out of there.

She thought of a million things that needed to be done around the house. She even gave a thought to doing some laundry. But procrastination didn't accomplish anything.

Though surely she should check on Ben, she reasoned. That was it! What kind of a hostess was she if she didn't check on her guest? A wounded guest at that.

She bolted out of the study with its book-lined walls and fine rugs. She fled the west wing, leaving behind the living room, dining room, kitchen, utility area, and three-car garage before she came into the high-ceiling entryway of marble and glass. A wall of stained glass separated the entry from the largest room in the house. Most of the time it was set up as another living room. But the furniture could be moved out, the carpets rolled up to reveal a glistening hardwood floor, and suddenly they had a ballroom.

The house was U-shaped, the foyer and ballroom forming the base of the U. On the other side of the entrance stood the long hall that lead back to the many bedrooms and an informal den. Heading down the carpeted hall, she found the guest room she had intended for Ben to use empty. Instead Sterling had put his brother in the room that connected to hers. The setup had been intended as a minisuite of sorts, two connected rooms that shared a bath. Definitely not the place she wanted Ben Prescott. But clearly Sterling wanted her to be close by the patient.

She felt a poignant tug at the thought that two brothers could have such a caring bond.

But the thought had barely flitted through her head when she tripped to a halt just outside the guest room doorway. She could see Ben standing next to the bed, using ironclad control to get his jacket off, then his shirt. The sight of his bare chest made her breath snag in her throat.

He was beautiful, like a statue, finely carved of smooth, bronzed skin over muscle. His shoulders were wide, his waist trim and washboard hard. Even after a week in the hospital, he was still amazing.

Gingerly, he lowered himself to sit on the edge of the bed as he tried to work off his pants. The grimace of pain brought her out of her reverie. Guilt pushed at sexual awareness.

Without a word or a knock, she opened the door wide like a grand dame entering stage right. "Why didn't you tell me you needed help?"

He jerked his head up. "Because I don't need any," he bit out. What little niceness he had shown earlier was gone completely. "Just get out."

"That tone might send some weak-spined individuals running for the hills, but you forget who you're talking to."

He actually groaned at this and hung his head. She had seen his brother do that a time or two when Chloe had done something particularly annoying.

"That's right. I'm Julia Boudreaux, a woman used to getting what she wants."

She went for his belt buckle.

He grabbed her hand.

His strength was solid but surprisingly gentle, considering he clearly didn't want her touching him.

"You're good at that, aren't you, cupcake?"

If he meant to embarrass her, he had the wrong girl.

"As a matter of fact, I am. And I will refrain from calling you beefcake again since it makes me cringe to think the word, much less say it. Now get your hands out of the way. You don't have anything I haven't seen before."

Though that wasn't altogether true, since she really had felt an astounding . . . piece of steel . . . in his 501s the day she had done her best to shock him when she pretended to play doctor. But she wasn't about to tell him that. She could just see the strut of arrogance that would cause.

His eyes narrowed and she was almost certain he growled.

"I can do it," he repeated.

She ignored him. "Let's start with your boots. We'll work up to the belt."

After a second, it was like he didn't have the energy left to fight, and he fell back on the mattress, his boots still planted on the floor. She grabbed first one, tugged, ughed, then finally had to turn around and straddle his leg in order to remove it.

"Success!" she yelped, lurching forward in her stilettos when the boot came loose.

When she finally had both boots lined up against the wall, she was almost certain his face had broken out in a sweat.

Hmmm. Yet another bad sign. Nursing really didn't figure into her skill set.

"Let me get your jeans off."

"I can do the rest."

"Are you insane?"

He muttered, "I'll sleep in my pants."

She stepped back and smiled at him. "Isn't that sweet. Our hunky bad boy is shy."

"I'll show you shy."

It happened so fast that she barely had time to register what he was doing. By the time she had, she was lying flat on her back, Ben on top of her. She barely noticed his grimace of pain for the feel of him pressed against her.

"Oh," she managed over the rapid beat of her heart.

She couldn't begin to explain what this man did to her. His body had an unerring ability to undo her.

He, on the other hand, was an entirely different story.

But right that second she wasn't thinking about personalities. She felt the hard press against her thigh, and desire slid through her, making a very convincing case that there were times when personalities could or should be ignored. Just looking at Ben Prescott, she'd bet the house he could make her purr like a kitten. And maybe, she reasoned, having a tiny little taste of what he had to offer wouldn't be so bad. . . .

Her teeth clenched. Absolutely not.

She cut desire off like she'd taken scissors to her Neiman Marcus credit card. She was supposed to be helping him, giving him a place to stay until his brother returned. She was not supposed to seduce him, then inevitably break his heart. And if she gave in to the all-too-tempting orgasm train that beckoned in his eyes, that's what would happen. Because that's what she did. She broke men's hearts. Always.

Chloe would kill her if she broke so much as a hair on this man's head.

So she'd leave him alone.

"Okay," she said, trying to ignore his body pressing seductively against hers. "You win. You've proven that you are a manly man. Now let me up so I can take off your pants."

"Promises, promises," he muttered.

But he rolled away and couldn't hold back a groan.

What energy he had left deserted him. In seconds, she was standing, then seconds after that she had the soft 501 Levi's tugged down around his ankles. The hard-on that had pressed against her seconds before was gone, though he was still impressive. But that wasn't what caught her eye.

A large white bandage butted up against his white Jockey shorts. From the looks of it, he'd nearly been shot in the groin.

"Oh, my stars," she breathed.

He snorted, but didn't say a word. He managed to get himself farther onto the bed, his muscles rippling with effort, the lines of his face strained, and finally settled back. He was sound asleep as soon as his head dented the feather pillow.   ·

She could hardly believe it. He really was asleep. And remarkable. And wounded.

"That has got to hurt," she whispered. "Why didn't you tell me?"

She waited a second, but didn't get a reply.

Carefully, she tugged the French-milled sheets and flannel blankets up over his shoulders. She told herself to leave the room, to leave him in peace. And she would, really. Just as soon as she gently brushed away the stray locks of dark brown hair that had fallen on his forehead.

Back in her study, Julia sat down, crossed her legs, and tapped the end of a pencil against her cheek. She decided she would call a truce with Ben. She was going to be a gracious hostess. No more thinking about hard steel weaponry and the orgasm train. By the time he left the house, maybe they'd even be friends.

"Friends," she said out loud. "Friends with a man," she added, surprised at the newness of such a thought.

But she liked the sound of it. She could be his friend. They could coexist in this space without thoughts of sex, beds, dating, or any of the other complicated issues she had no interest in delving into with this man. To make the prospect even more appealing, when Chloe returned from Nevis, she would be thrilled that Julia had been nothing but sweet and was getting along with her new brother-in-law. It was the least Julia could do for her best friend.

Confident in her new plan, she turned her attention to the computer screen just as the phone rang.

"Hello?"

"Is Ben there?"

A woman's voice, sounding pathetically hopeful. Not to mention, how did a woman know that Ben was there?

"He's asleep right now. Can I take a message?"

"Oh."

The disappointment was palpable.

"No, that's okay. I'll call back. Do you know when he'll be awake so I can talk to him then?"

"Is there some sort of an emergency that I can help you with?"

"Emergency? No." The woman sighed. "I just wanted to see Ben. Everyone's talking about him getting shot. A friend of his told me he was staying with you. Do you think it would be all right if I came over to see him?"

The woman sounded breathless. Were women really this desperate?

"That's a question for Ben. If you'd like to leave your name and number, I'll have him get back to you."

The woman did as asked. "Please ask him to call."

Julia hung up, only to have the phone ring again. And again. Over the course of twenty minutes, she took a slew of adoring phone messages for Ben, and she didn't get a bit of work done. After the last woman begged her to wake Ben, Julia politely declined, then took the phone off the hook.

She had to focus, not play secretary for the derelict down the hall. No, not derelict, she reminded herself quickly. He was her new friend. Yes, friend.

Feeling pleased, she Googled reality shows, pouring over each in hopes of an idea hitting her.

There was *The Bachelor. The Bachelorette. Joe Millionaire. My Big Fat Obnoxious Fiancé.* Hello? What were these people thinking? But she could guess. The producers must have been in the exact same position she was in right then. She, like they, needed something new and different. The difference between them and her was going to be that when she actually came up with something, it *would* be fabulous.

She continued on to *American Idol, Survivor One Zillion.* Then she saw a whole slew of makeover shows.

She gasped at the thought. She loved makeover shows.

In fact, who didn't love makeover shows? She could go out and find women to make over.

She grimaced. That wouldn't be fresh or new or anything that would knock Sterling's socks off when he returned.

That's when it hit her. She should make herself over.

The thought sent shock waves through her, utterly horrifying shock waves. But riding on the waves like a California surfer was intrigue.

"Make over me?" she wondered aloud.

The truth was, this business of her whole life turning upside down had thrown her. Her world had changed so drastically that she hardly recognized it. So why shouldn't she change as well?

She went very still. When she leaned forward, she caught a glimpse of cleavage revealed by her blouse. She had been a bad girl for so long it was hard to imagine not showing a good bit of her figure. What would she do without her tight pants and short skirts?

She glanced down at her four-inch stiletto heels and grimaced with very real pain at the thought of doing without her shoes.

But that was what she needed to do, she realized with a start. Start over, start fresh, make herself over into the new, improved Julia Boudreaux.

A shiver of excitement raced through her, because truth to tell, life as a femme fatale was exhausting. The hair, the clothes, the makeup. The shopping was enough to wear a weaker woman down. Keeping up with the trends was a nightmare. You had to know what was hot, what was not. God forbid a girl get caught carrying last year's Prada bag.

There were people who thought Texans were only

concerned with horses, *Hee Haw,* and bales of hay. But they were wrong. If she ranked style-conscious states in order, New York would win hands down—all those rich East Side matrons and runway models. California would easily come in second—all those movie actors and wannabe starlets. But Texas would place a respectable third. Heavens, Neiman Marcus was founded in Dallas, Texas.

But the hardest part of being a bad girl was dating so many delicious men. People thought it would be nothing but nonstop fun and excitement. It wasn't. It was exhausting. Keeping their names straight, making sure she didn't run into one date after she had just left another. Sometimes there just weren't enough days in the week.

She remembered Ben's crack about her being good at taking off men's pants. She hadn't wanted to admit how the remark had actually hit its mark. It had hurt, which surprised her. For some reason the thought of this man thinking she was easy didn't sit well.

Granted, she liked sex. She wasn't afraid to admit that. But she didn't sleep with men in hopes of getting them to like her, or in hopes of finding some elusive comfort, either. She had sex because she enjoyed it. End of story.

On top of that, the fact was she didn't sleep around nearly as much as people assumed. She was no celibate, but she was not a one-night-stand sort of woman.

Regardless, she was ready to start fresh, make herself over. She felt a startling need to become a picture of respectability. She would be a bad girl gone good!

Purpose pumped through her veins. For the first time in months she felt excited, with a sense of purpose. She loved the idea of starting over, loved the thought of being given a clean slate.

For a second, she considered making her transformation into a show. Certainly she could document the process. Though she couldn't imagine turning her own situation into a television program. Not only did it feel self-serving—*Look at me, world, I'm cleaning up my act*—but she had never been one to share her private feelings. She had always been the party girl without a care in the world. She wasn't going to start showing the new her for ratings.

Nope, her transformation was for herself only. But for a show, she would turn her eye to makeovers for other people. Though the question still plagued her. Who?

She thought about making over maids into wealthy matrons, paupers into princesses.

Nothing felt right.

She surfed the Internet some more until she hit *Queer Eye for the Straight Guy*. The show had taken America by storm. Gay guys with a sense of style, taking slobs and nerds and turning them into suave fashion plates.

Her heart began beating hard as an idea started to develop.

She was going to make over herself, no question. And she was doing it because she wanted to start over. But there was another piece to her transformation, she realized, that needed to happen. She was changing her life— out with the old, in with the new—because she was tired of being wild. She was tired of bad boys.

She sat up straighter in her chair.

She was sick of passionate hunks. She didn't think she could stand to see a single other rugged cowboy. And what woman wasn't tired of having to deal with such insensitive guys?

Julia stood up and started to pace, her stiletto heels sinking into the thick Aubusson rug.

What woman wouldn't want to find a man with the looks and confidence of a bad boy and combine it with the sweet sensitivity of a moon-eyed nerd? What if that guy existed? Or better yet, what if someone created that man?

Her head spun. Her breath grew shallow at the realization that this was the sort of makeover show she could do. She would create her own version of *Queer Eye for the Straight Guy*. She would take bad boys and turn them into sweet, sensitive guys. She'd be like the professor in *My Fair Lady*. A modern-day Henry Higgins for men.

It had big, huge, amazing hit written all over it!

She would be able to prove to herself that she deserved the job at KTEX. And she would make Chloe proud. She'd show Sterling that he hadn't bet on a bad horse. She was going to create a winner yet!

She raced back to the desk. She pulled out a slip of paper and started a list. She would still make herself over—she'd turn herself into a responsible woman. But for her show she would find a man to make over. She would tape the whole process, then edit it together as a television hit.

There were tons of details that had to be figured out. But those could wait. The first thing she had to do was find a bad boy she could turn into a sensitive guy.

To: Julia Boudreaux <julia@ktextv.com>
From: Katherine Bloom <katherine@ktextv.com>
Subject: Dead or alive

Is Ben still alive? Or have you finished him off? Just checking . . .

Your devoted best friend,
Kate

Katherine C. Bloom
News Anchor, KTEX TV, West Texas

To: Katherine Bloom <katherine@ktextv.com>
From: Julia Boudreaux <julia@ktextv.com>
Subject: Insulted

Sniff. What kind of a woman do you think I am? A black widow
spider? Though, in truth, the image has always held some
appeal. But no, he's alive and kicking, or at least he's alive, and
doing as well as a wounded man can, I suppose.

But enough about the wounded bear in the east wing of my little old house. Do you want to go to Bobby's Place for a little evening refreshment?

xo, j

To: Julia Boudreaux <julia@ktextv.com>
From: Katherine Bloom <katherine@ktextv.com>
Subject: Sorry

Can't. I have plans with Jesse. We're going to the movies. Do you want to come along? It's been ages since we've done something together.

Though now that I think about it, tonight is Girls' Night at Bobby's. You've never had a problem going by yourself before. What gives?

K

To: Katherine Bloom <katherine@ktextv.com>
From: Julia Boudreaux <julia@ktextv.com>
Subject: re: Sorry

Nothing gives. It's just that I realized that going to a bar by myself is not on my new agenda. I'm turning over a new leaf. Just tea, crumpets, and sensible clothes for me. Hmmm . . . Which means, I suppose, I shouldn't go to Bobby's Place *at all*. Errr.

Being sweet and good is going to be harder than I thought.

xo, j

To: Julia Boudreaux <julia@ktextv.com>
From: Katherine Bloom <katherine@ktextv.com>
Subject: Huh???

What is this about turning over a new leaf?!!!

Please advise,
K

To: Katherine Bloom <katherine@ktextv.com>
From: Julia Boudreaux <julia@ktextv.com>
Subject: Drumroll please

I'm making myself over. Before you know it, I will be the new Julia Boudreaux, a sweet, proper, and ultraresponsible southern belle from West Texas.

xo, Julia

p.s. Can I borrow some clothes?

To: Julia Boudreaux <julia@ktextv.com>
From: Katherine Bloom <katherine@ktextv.com>
Subject: Oh, dear

This sounds like trouble. . . .

chapter three

Ben woke to the smell of cinnamon and baked goods. It felt like he was floating on a cloud of childhood and the past. No worries, no troubles. Nothing was wrong.

Until he moved.

Heat shot down his leg and up through his groin. Fuck. And not the good kind.

The sharp bite of pain cleared his head of sleep, and after a second he realized where he was. At Julia's, with a gunshot wound to his upper thigh.

His mood blackened instantly. He still couldn't believe he'd been shot.

Ben Prescott had been a legend in the police academy—number one in his class. He was better than good; he was the one who had set the standards for everyone who came after him. His marksmanship was outstanding and his reflexes were phenomenal. He had the unteachable quality of being hyperaware of everything going on around him, giving him the ability to react quickly and fluidly as a situation unfolded.

But a week ago, emotion had gotten in the way. Emotion had made him careless—had affected his concentration. Emotion made a man vulnerable. And in his line of work he couldn't afford to be weak.

He had been careless following the perp farther into the building and lowering his guard. Hell, he thought, plowing his hands through his hair. He deserved to get shot.

With effort, Ben pushed out of bed. Everything from grimacing to putting his feet on the floor took effort. But he didn't want anyone, including Sterling, to know that. If the older Prescott had learned the truth, he never would have left for his honeymoon. As Ben said to Julia, he wasn't going to be responsible for throwing a wrench into the first true happiness Sterling had ever known.

So Ben had kept quiet because of his brother, but also because he didn't want anyone else in his family staying any longer than they already had. Getting his mother, grandmother, and sister to return to St. Louis had been like pulling teeth. His family might be short on giving hugs and sending Valentine's Day cards, but he knew they cared a great deal in their own bossy, domineering way.

He wasn't much different when he went after something he wanted. When he had announced that he was going to be a cop instead of joining Prescott Media, his family had objected—strenuously. He knew they cared. He knew it was all about them being worried. But no amount of cajoling, begging, or even threatening had changed his mind. Not back then, and not this time when they had tried to get him to return to St. Louis after he had woken up in the emergency room.

But he kept his mouth shut because he knew they meant well. And he would put up with whatever Julia Boudreaux had to dish out. Besides, he thought with a wry chuckle, he hadn't become a cop because he liked playing it safe.

But his grin turned to a groan at the thought of her. He'd never met a woman more in control of herself and her surroundings than Julia. If she wanted something, she went after it. And based on everything he had seen while staying in her house as a bodyguard of sorts while they were taping *The Catch and His Dozen Texas Roses,* she got what she went after.

She really was a piece of work—sexy as hell, no question, but still a piece of work. Her short tight skirts never failed to give him the sort of hard-on that demanded instant release. But for reasons he wasn't interested in examining, he'd had little interest in release with any woman other than her since he met the raven-haired bombshell. Though he'd take cold showers until hell froze over before he got tangled up with her. Julia Boudreaux was nothing but a sexy heartbreak in heels, and he swore he'd steer clear of her.

After a grimace and a good deal of effort, he managed to get his jeans on and shove his arms through the sleeves of his shirt. With sweat breaking out on his forehead, he decided his boots were a no-go. Hobbling into the bathroom, he took a leak, thought about a shower and shave, then decided a splash of water to his face and a quick brush of his teeth would take all the energy he had to spare. Maybe after he'd had his fill of whatever breakfast fare was going on in the kitchen, he'd rethink the shower.

Feeling like he hadn't eaten in a month, he went in

search of whatever it was that smelled so damn good. The thought of food and sitting in Julia's kitchen took his mind off his throbbing thigh. The first time he saw her kitchen, he had liked it. The room was warm, a mixture of class and comfort. He had lived out of corner kitchens with hot plates for stoves for a long while now. After a lifetime of servants and impersonal stainless steel kitchens with the latest of everything, Ben had actually liked the simplicity of a grungy sink and single hot plate.

But since the first day he had walked into Julia's kitchen, he had felt at home. He had expected her to be all about cold marble countertops and fawning servants. But even when she'd had servants, more often than not he could find Julia in her skimpy outfits at the stove making a pot of tea, or baking cookies for the slew of women she'd housed for *The Catch*.

Today, whatever comfort he thought he would find in the kitchen vanished when he finally got there. He could hardly believe his eyes. None other than Betty fucking Crocker stood at the oven, complete with a knee-length poofy dress, an apron lined with white ruffles, and the kind of low-heeled, nondescript shoes worn by Sunday school teachers. This picture had nothing to do with the tight-skirted, high-heeled Julia he had come to know, if not love. She even wore her dark hair pulled back in a ponytail.

"Who the hell are you and what have you done with the wild woman I've come to know and dislike?" he asked as he entered.

Julia whirled around, her skirts swirling like a ballerina's, those violet eyes wide, her fluffy oven-mitted hand holding a pan of freshly baked cinnamon rolls.

"Good morning!" she chirped with a sunshiny smile. "How are you today?"

She set the pan down, smoothed her apron, and gestured for him to sit. "I hope you're hungry. I've prepared a feast."

He couldn't speak. Generally when he said things about disliking her, she had a ready comeback that was as tart as it was stinging. This Julia only smiled. He was sorely disappointed.

As she herded him to the table, he noted that despite the fact that the top of her head barely came to his shoulder, she wasn't the least bit intimidated by his size.

He sat down, the sound of her sensible heels on the tile floor grating against his pounding head. In seconds he had a plate of scrambled eggs with melted cheddar cheese sitting in front of him. There was bacon and hash browns, and damn if the rolls weren't dripping with a creamy butter icing. His stomach grumbled.

"See," she practically sang, "you are hungry! And every growing boy needs his strength."

"I am not a growing boy, Betty. If you'd like me to prove it, I'd be happy to oblige."

He reached for her, but she leaped away, then waggled her finger at him. "Tut-tut, no manhandling the matron."

"Matron, my ass—"

"Really, your language is abominable."

"*Abominable?* What the hell happened to you?"

She laughed and twirled away, her skirt ruffling again. Returning to the counter, she started icing the second batch of rolls.

"What do you mean, what happened to me?" she asked primly.

"You're . . . different. You've dressed up like some

sort of caricature of 1950s respectability. I thought Halloween was over."

She was still as beautiful as before. He didn't think Julia Boudreaux could be anything but a knockout. But overnight, she had gone from hot and sexy to simply sweet. And he didn't like it one bit. As much as he didn't like the old Julia, he wanted that one back. This new version made him feel off balance.

Julia's brow furrowed as she stared at the rolls. "Even if I did overdo it a little with the outfit, I *am* different."

Without taking a bite, he got up from the table despite the pain, then walked over to her. She didn't realize he was there until he stood a few paces behind her and she turned.

She didn't squeak or get some innocent schoolgirl look. Her violet eyes flashed with awareness, her full, sensual lips parting. Ridiculously, he felt better that the wild woman wasn't gone completely.

"What are you doing?" she asked.

"Getting a closer look to see what's going on inside that head of yours."

"Going on? Nothing. But if you really want to know, this is the first day of the brand-new me."

"What the fuc—"

"My life has changed irrevocably, and I've decided to change with it. From now on, I'm a good girl."

He couldn't find the words. He only knew he felt a childish need to prove that she could no more be good than he could.

He took a step closer. But she laughed and slipped away since he couldn't move all that fast.

"Tsk-tsk, Mr. Prescott."

"Tut-tut? Tsk-tsk? Have you lost your mind?"

She laughed again—this time it was her old, deep, throaty laugh, the sound at odds with her frilly dress. "If you're not up to eating in the kitchen, then I'll bring you a tray in bed," she offered.

He allowed his gaze to slide over her slowly, taking in the full breasts and slim waist, then lower to what he knew was underneath all that damned material. "I like the thought of eating, cupcake, and being in bed. Though I'm not interested in any sweet rolls."

Heat flared in her eyes, which she quickly banked, like throwing ice water on the fire. She really was going to do her best to tame the wild girl.

"If you're not interested in sweets, then how about some bacon," she countered, handing him a strip.

Chuckling, he took it and consumed it in two bites. She watched him chew, her breath slowing as he swallowed. But quickly, she shook her head, muttered something he couldn't make out, and returned her attention to the pan of baked goods. She picked up the bowl of creamy white icing. Though when she started to spread it on, he would have sworn her hand trembled.

He came up behind her and he felt her body tense.

"What are you doing?" she asked, her hand going still in midswipe of the icing.

He stepped even closer, capturing her against the counter, planting his arms on either side of her so she couldn't get away.

"Ben, this isn't funny."

She said the words tightly, her ire starting to show through the Betty Crocker façade.

"FYI, good girls are all about being sweet and kind. In fact, I don't think they ever get mad," he teased.

"Only because they don't have to deal with men like you," she stated through gritted teeth.

He barked his laughter. "Face it, Julia, you're anything but a good girl. Clothes don't change a woman. In fact, I'd bet money that dress isn't even yours."

"It is so."

He made a sound of disbelief. "When have you ever dressed like that?"

Julia decided not to answer on the grounds of not wanting to incriminate herself, or prove his point—sort of. The dress *was* hers, but it *had* been a costume she had worn when she went as June Cleaver to the annual Halloween party they held at the country club.

During the weeks leading up to the event, she had heard about the bets that had been placed regarding the costume she would wear. *Playboy* bunny. Sex kitten.

Miffed that she would be so stereotyped, she showed up as America's prim and proper mom. Who knew she'd ever wear the dress again? But at least until she got some new clothes or borrowed a few from Kate, she'd wear whatever she could find that wasn't tight, low-cut, or screaming with leopard spots. Not that she thought clothes made the man—or woman. But she figured she needed all the help she could get to help her makeover sink into her mind. The clothes were just the starting point . . . to be closely followed by no more sex with bad boys.

But she wasn't about to share any of that with Ben Prescott.

She drummed up a smile, even if it was forced. This guy was making it difficult to keep her vow to be kind, sweet, and responsible—not to mention to keep her vow to become his friend.

He only moved closer, crowding her space. She gave him a quick glance over her shoulder. His gaze was hard, hot, and hungry, and it had nothing to do with the food she'd spent the morning preparing. She could feel the heat of him melting away her hard-earned resistance. He smelled like toothpaste and a warm bed. Nice. Too nice.

Then he stepped closer until she could feel his body pressing against the small of her back. Warm and tight, and no question about it, that piece of weaponry he carried around in his 501s was impressive.

She closed her eyes and imagined, but just for a second. "Look, you've got an amazing body," she admitted. "And it's easy to guess that sex between us would be great. But it's not going to happen."

Ben went still, then he burst out laughing.

"Errr," she muttered, focusing on the cinnamon rolls with determination. "I didn't mean that—"

"Really?" he asked, his voice a sexy rumble.

"I mean, I didn't mean to be so . . ."

"Direct?" he provided. "That's one of the fascinating things about you. Thoughts go in your head and out your mouth without much in the way of editing in between. You aren't afraid to say what you mean. It's . . . rare. And interesting."

She sighed. "I'm not trying to be rare or interesting. I just want to be good. And it seems like you could be a little more accommodating to the new me."

He leaned down and came close to her ear. "Being good is no fun."

"How would you know?"

He laughed again. "That's one for Julia." He marked the air with his forefinger, scoring the point, then stepped back.

Julia whirled around to get free, intent on outlining the ground rules she realized they were going to need in order to coexist under the same roof. But the minute they were face-to-face, the sight of him hit her like a thunderbolt. His morning growth of beard, his disheveled hair that he hadn't bothered to brush but simply raked back with his hands. The cambric shirt that hung unbuttoned, showing the ripple of hard chest and washboard flat abdomen. The trail of soft dark hair that disappeared beneath the jeans that rode low on his hips, the top button undone revealing a tiny V of white skin that hadn't seen the intense West Texas sun.

The phone rang, but she couldn't seem to move.

"Are you going to get that?" he asked, his voice rumbling along her senses.

"Why bother?" she breathed. "It'll just be another in the long line of pathetically adoring women who are dying for a scrap of your attention."

"What?"

"Your female admirers. They've been calling all night while you were asleep. In bed."

Her mind started to churn as she thought of him in his bedroom. She had peeked in on her way to the kitchen that morning to make sure he was all right. Despite the clothes that had been strewn about in less than twenty-four hours all she could think about was that he looked hot and sexy as he laid there sound asleep. But now she remembered the mess of clothes.

She sucked in a slow, excited breath, and Ben looked at her in confusion.

"What is it?" he asked.

"You're bad," she said, exhaling sharply. "Bad with a capital B. A caveman! A Neanderthal!"

"Hey," he grumbled and pushed away. He returned to the table and started to eat.

"Oh, my gosh! This is great!"

He got a weird look on his face, then scooped up a bite of eggs. "What are you talking about?"

She clasped her hands together. "You're better than great! You even talk with food in your mouth!"

He glowered at her, clamped his lips together, and finished chewing. Still, he was perfect. How hadn't she thought of him last night?

He swallowed. "Will you tell me what the hell you're talking about?"

She rushed over to him. "My new TV hit! I'm going to put together a makeover show. But I'm not going to make over women like most people do. I'm going to make over men!"

"Men makeovers?" He looked at her like she was crazy and took a bite of bacon.

"Exactly! Sort of like that show *Queer Eye for the Straight Guy.* Only mine will be even more fun. I'm calling it: *Turn That Primal Guy into a Sweetie Pie!*"

He blew out the bacon.

"And I want you to be my first Primal Guy!"

Now he started to choke, on shock, no doubt. Quickly, she banged him on the back until he reached around and stopped her.

"Are you crazy?" he demanded. "I'm no primal guy."

"What do you mean? You're like a live-in science project of primal. A lab experiment. A petri dish of writhing, muscle-pounding, testosterone-filled primordial man."

She could tell he didn't know if he should be insulted or flattered.

"You're as primal as they come! And with me at the

helm, I know I can change you from the baddest of bad boys to the sweetest of sweetie pies. Say you'll do it."

His mouth fell open. Insulted or flattered, he'd had enough.

"You can forget it. I'm not some . . . some . . . lab experiment."

Okay, so he was insulted. She should have expected that. What man ever recognized himself for who he really was? How many men out there were clueless as to why their wives and girlfriends got angry with them? How many stared in dumbfounded amazement when their date threw a glass of chardonnay in their face?

This was so perfect. *Ben* was so perfect. She was going to change him. She was going to do the slew of women who had been calling all night a huge favor—and entertain a television audience in the process. The ratings would be through the roof.

"I'm going to transform you!"

He pushed up from the table and glared at her. "I'm not interested in being transformed. You got that, cupcake?"

She tsked. "Lesson One, really. Calling a woman cupcake is so unappealing. Let's lose that, okay?"

For a second she thought he might call her something far worse than cupcake, but he held back. Instead he turned on his heel, grimaced at what had to be pain from the quick movement, then strode out of the kitchen without looking back.

That might not have gone perfectly, she admitted. But she wasn't about to give up. Not by a long shot. She had a primal guy right under her nose. She wasn't about to let him go.

chapter four

A petri dish of testosterone.

Hell. Who did she think she was dealing with? Ben grumbled to himself as he left the kitchen. He wasn't some moron who would ever be on television. He wasn't interested in fifteen minutes of fame. He didn't want fame at all. Not to mention that appearing on some idiotic reality show wouldn't do a lot for his under-cover work.

Since he told very few people that he was a cop, it made it a real pain in the ass trying to explain what he did when he dated a woman more than once. The import/export business was the best he had come up with. But the odd hours were hell on the dating life.

For now, it was easier not to get involved in anything long term. He enjoyed women, but he had no interest in getting close to any of them.

He hadn't taken more than a few aching steps when the doorbell rang. This time Julia didn't forget to answer. She passed him in the hall—giving him a quick glance like a predator sizing up its prey—before her low heels clicked on the entry hall floor.

As soon as she pulled open the door, he heard a familiar voice. Seconds later he saw one of his oldest friends from the force. They'd started in the undercover vice unit at the same time.

"Look what the cat dragged in," Ben said, standing straight and strong, making sure he didn't let on to the ache in his leg.

Jake "Tag" Taggart whistled. "I wouldn't be calling names if I were you. You look awful. Though nothing new there," the man laughed.

It had always been a running joke between them—the fact that women flocked to Ben when it was Tag who was constantly in search of a date. He was an incorrigible flirt. And while he was never short on dates, they didn't clamor after him like they did Ben.

"Yep," Tag teased his friend, "even shot, my main man Benny the Slash looks pretty much the same. Like hell."

Julia stood off to the side, and when her eyes met Ben's, she mouthed, *Benny the Slash?*

He wasn't about to tell her that it was his undercover nickname. She didn't know he was a cop, much less an undercover, as they said on the force.

He pointed to his eyebrow. "A few friends started calling me that because of the scar."

He had seen her look at it earlier, and he could see now that she thought the story made sense. She believed it. That was the thing about undercover work. A cop had to make the cover seem real—every piece of it—otherwise he was dead.

"What brings you this way?" Ben asked.

"Mmmm, something smells good," Jake said without remorse. He looked at Julia. "I'd love a cup of coffee."

"Hasn't anyone taught you manners, Tag?" Ben asked.

"I might say the same to you, Slash. You haven't even introduced me to the pretty lady."

Julia chuckled and stepped forward. "I was talking to Ben about things like manners." She extended her hand. "I'm Julia Boudreaux."

"Jake Taggart, and the pleasure is all mine."

Tag started to lean over and kiss her palm, but Ben shoved him back toward the kitchen. "Julia, you've got some coffee for this guy, right?"

Not only did she serve up coffee, but as soon as she had both men in the kitchen sitting at the table, she set a new plate of eggs, bacon, hash browns, and sweet rolls in front of each of them.

As soon as she had freshened Ben's cup of coffee like a waitress, she headed for the door. "I'll leave you two to talk."

Ben watched her go. So did Tag.

"Mmmm, mmmm," Tag said. "That is one mighty fine piece of—"

"Put a clamp on it, Tag. Keep your mind where it belongs."

Taggart swiveled in his chair. "Is it possible that the ever elusive Ben Prescott has got it bad for the prim fluff-cake?"

How to explain? She wasn't prim. She wasn't a fluff-cake, either. He didn't even like her. But he really didn't like seeing his friend ogle her, either. Words failed him.

"Why are you here?" he asked instead. "And I take it you're *my friend* telling every skirt in town where they can find me."

Tag smiled. "Had I known you were staying with one fine lady, I might have done things differently. You should have given me more than the phone number here."

Ben had given him the phone number and address because he needed Tag to bring him a new cell phone after his had been crushed in the confusion when he had been shot. Plus, he had wanted Tag to bring over his Range Rover. He wasn't allowed to drive yet, but he didn't like the idea of being stranded without transportation. He might have made a promise to Sterling to hang out here, but he sure as hell wasn't going to be without a car.

On cue, Tag extended the new phone and Ben's keys.

"Thanks," he said, meaning it.

The two men had been through a lot together. The fact that Tag had become the squad lieutenant over all detectives hadn't come between them. When the brass had asked Ben to submit his name for promotion, he had declined. He had always wanted to be in the trenches. But that didn't mean he didn't understand his friend's desire for a more stable life. He was happy as hell for the guy.

Ben and Tag settled into a comfortable silence as they dug into their meals, both eating with the gusto of men who weren't worried about putting on pounds. Only minutes later they were done, sitting back and sighing their pleasure.

"She can cook," Tag said.

"Yeah." Ben tossed his napkin on the table. "So, how's it going?"

The smiling man grew serious. "A better question is, how's it going with you? Really."

Ben stretched out his leg as nonchalantly as possible. "I'm fine, Tag."

"You don't look so good. I worry."

"Don't. It was a flesh wound. No serious damage."

Tag studied him for a bit, then sighed. "I read the report."

"And?"

"I heard what happened in that backyard. The guy could have killed you. You shouldn't have gone after him."

Ben still remembered the feeling of standing there, of the craziness that had consumed him, pushing him on, making him push to the edge. But it had nearly worked, and it would have if he'd been able to get the gun that Nando had started to lower. Then he would have gotten answers, too.

"I know Henry's death hit you hard. Losing your partner takes its toll. But you're a damn fine cop. One of the best. Don't let this ruin you. Don't let the force lose another man."

"I appreciate it, really. But I'm fine."

"The chief isn't so sure. He wants you to see Halderman."

"The shrink?"

Tag shrugged. "I wanted to give you a heads-up. So if you don't want to spend a month with the guy, you'd better get your act together."

Ben grumbled, then took another sip of his coffee. When he set the cup down, he asked, "Have you learned anything new about Henry? Did they find the punk who ran out of the building?"

"No, we didn't find the guy. But the report is in. The night Henry was killed, there was no planned operation going down."

Realistically, if there had been one, Ben would have

known. They were partners, after all. But he had held out hope that Henry had caught a last-minute assignment Ben hadn't heard about. Tag just nixed that possibility.

Ben didn't want to think about what that meant. Henry had been working on his own—working without boundaries.

"How did he know the deal was going down?" Ben asked.

"We think he was finding dealers on the Internet, if you can believe it."

"Why do you think that?"

"In the probe, Regar mentioned it. Said Henry had gone computer savvy and had told him he found his latest deal on a Web site, of all places. These dealers get more inventive by the day."

"Has anyone checked into it?"

"Yeah. Haven't found anything, though. I don't get this computer stuff, but the whiz kid down at the station took a look and said there was nothing on Henry's computer to give us any leads." Tag stuffed his hands in his pockets. "I was thinking that while you're laid up, you could do some surfing, see if you can find whatever it was Henry found."

"I'll need a computer."

Tag smiled. "I thought you might say that. It's in the Rover. I'll bring it in before I go."

Not long after that, Ben walked his longtime friend out to the SUV, refusing to show the pain he was in, retrieved the computer, then watched Tag get into an unmarked car whose driver had clearly followed him there. As soon as Tag was gone, Ben felt the last of his energy drain away.

With effort, he headed back to the guest room and booted up the laptop.

Julia worked through the morning, writing extensive notes on what she thought her show should entail. Making over bad boys was inspired. Which reminded her of Ben.

She hadn't heard a peep out of him since his friend left, and that had been hours ago.

The man called Tag had a dangerous look to him, and yet again Julia wondered what Ben did for a living. The import/export business? Other than his brief stint as a bodyguard of sorts for Chloe's television show, she hadn't seen him work at all. Not that he could get much done with a bullet wound to the thigh. But somehow the import/export business thing didn't seem right. Though maybe she was wrong and the business provided him with the sort of income that allowed for a sixty-thousand-dollar Range Rover and a leather jacket that hadn't come cheap. Then there was the possibility that Ben lived off his brother's largess.

But what Ben did or didn't do wasn't her concern. Feeding him was.

After making a quick lunch and putting it on a tray, she headed to Ben's room. A computer sat out on the desk, but he wasn't to be seen. She paused, wondered where he could be, and that's when she heard the rustling in the bathroom.

Oh, dear.

His door was open, and with a grimace, she took a step farther inside the room. She considered leaving the lunch and giving him his privacy. But when she leaned over and set down the tray on the desk, she caught sight of his reflection in the bathroom mirror. He stood at her marble sink counter, his blue cambric shirt unbuttoned and wrinkled, his jeans gone, the front of his Jockey briefs white against his skin. She could make out a hint of his strong thighs, and a hint of the dark hair that disappeared underneath an oversized white bandage. A tremor ran through her. Uneasiness mixing with a very hot longing.

But it was his face that finally demanded her attention. He still hadn't shaved, and the stubble on his strong, square jaw was black as night, making him look like a disreputably handsome movie star. Though it wasn't his matinee idol looks that caused concern. Ben was flushed with sweat, and he groaned with strain as he struggled to change the bandage on his thigh. Then he collapsed with fatigue onto the top of the closed toilet.

She saw something in him that she never would have guessed possible in this man. A tremendous weariness that appeared both physical and mental. This was beyond being unwilling to show that he was in pain, as she had concluded yesterday. Seeing him now when he thought he was alone, when he let his defenses down, she understood he needed more help than he was letting on. Ben Prescott was holding on, fighting to put up a brave front.

"Looks like I'm going to have to play nurse after all," she said quietly to herself.

There had never been a man in a bedroom who had intimidated her before. But a wounded bear in a bedroom gave her pause. She only hoped that she really didn't kill him as Chloe had feared.

Julia took a deep, fortifying breath. No one had to tell her Ben Prescott wasn't going to like her help one bit.

But she wasn't about to let this prideful lout get worse on her watch. Especially when she needed him at 100 percent so she could feature him on her show. It never occurred to her that she couldn't get him to say yes eventually.

Marching to the bathroom, she knocked on the door frame.

She saw him flinch in the mirror, before their eyes caught and held in the silvered glass.

"Go away," he ordered.

She pushed the door open the rest of the way. "You keep forgetting that I don't scare easily."

"You should. I'm not some oversized pup dog that you can wrap around your little finger. I can do things to you that would make you weep."

She looked at him through lowered lashes. "Promise?"

Ben grumbled. "Have you ever been intimidated in your life?"

About five seconds ago at the thought of having to play Nurse Nancy to a wounded bear. But she kept that to herself.

"Can't think of a time. Now let me help you up." She grabbed his arm and he only half resisted. "You need to get in bed and I'll change the bandage."

"You are not going to change anything."

"Yeah, yeah, save it for one of those fluttering butterflies who've been calling you. They might be impressed."

He grumbled the whole way, but there was no question she was bearing a good bit of his significant weight.

"I'll change the bandage, then you need to eat."

That, he didn't protest.

She got him to the mattress, where he dropped down with a groan of pain and a sigh of relief.

"Maybe eat first," he said, like he couldn't afford the energy of a complete sentence.

"Sure."

He managed to get himself positioned against the backboard of the bed, before Julia set the tray over his lap. He didn't say a word for the entire first half of the sandwich, almost like he didn't take a breath. At the halfway mark he leaned his head back while he finished chewing, groaned, this time in some kind of pleasure, then swallowed. You'd think she hadn't fed him six hours earlier.

Julia stared at him in dumbfounded amazement. Growing up as an only child, and with her two best friends not having any brothers, other than her father, Julia hadn't been around all that many men in her life—at least not on a day to day basis. She went out with them, had stayed over more than once, but always left before breakfast. She wasn't one to get too involved in a man's life.

This—Ben eating—was all too . . . intimate. And the strength that seeped through him as the food began to sink in was disquieting. She liked him better weak and vulnerable. And now she was supposed to help change the bandage on his thigh.

She silently scoffed at her own weak-spined thoughts, could hardly believe she'd had them. He was a man like any other.

"I'm impressed, cupcake."

She jerked her mind into focus and raised her chin. "Impressed?" she asked with the utmost professionalism.

Ben moaned his disappointment. "That cupcake remark was supposed to get you all in a twist."

"You're *trying* to make me crazy?"

"Just trying to get rid of that look of horror you've got pulled across your face. Can't say I've seen that particular expression when a woman was staring at my private parts." He chuckled.

"Amusing. I was thinking about the bandage."

"I guess that's some consolation," he teased.

"Are you done eating?" she asked when he took the last bite, sighed with contentment, and relaxed into the pillows.

"Mmm, mmm, that was mighty fine. And yes, I'm done."

She whisked the tray away. "I'll be back in a minute."

"No hurry."

In the kitchen, she quickly set the lunch dishes aside, then returned to his room. While she was surprised to find him sound asleep, she was thankful, too, since it would no doubt be easier to change the bandage without him staring at her. Studying her. Accidentally brushing his arm against hers.

Retrieving the tape, gauze, hydrogen peroxide, and warm water compresses he had in the bathroom, she sat down gingerly on the side of the mattress. He murmured and burrowed deeper, but didn't wake.

With the tray gone and the man sleeping, she couldn't stop herself from looking at him. He really was handsome and extremely well built. His tanned chest had just the right amount of dark hair on it that disappeared beneath the waistband of his briefs. Despite the bandage, he was an incredible specimen of man.

Forgetting herself, not to mention forgetting her new determination to be a good girl, she reached out and touched the line of hair on his chest. The softness filled her senses. His skin was like lightly browned butter, smooth and perfect. And she traced the line of hair with a single fingernail. Lower, then lower.

Until she noticed the distinctive bulge in his Jockey shorts.

Her gaze flew up, only to find that Mr. Sleeping Beauty was no longer asleep.

She tried to make light of the situation. "I guess in this fairy tale, it doesn't take a kiss to wake someone up."

He grabbed her wrist with surprising quickness.

Not a good sign.

"Unless you plan to do something about that," he said with a menacing grin as he nodded toward his shorts, "I'd suggest you get the hell out of here."

She jerked away and leaped up, the bandage forgotten. "I'm going," she said, and she would have sworn she felt a blush on her cheeks. It took a second before she realized what a good sign this was. Her. Blushing.

Progress!

It was easier to think about that than face the fact that she really, really wanted to finish what she had started. Her fingers itched to go lower.

With a smile plastered on her face, she bolted from the room and headed for the safety of the kitchen. There she'd find something long, decadent, and delicious to satisfy this crazy desire.

She hoped like Hades she had some éclairs left.

Ben, love! Just checking in to see how you are making out.
Even if Mother isn't the over-motherly type, she worries. As
do I. She's still not recovered from seeing you lying practically
dead in a hospital bed in the farthest reaches of Texas. Who
knew they really did have Wild West shoot-outs in . . . well, the
Wild West.

But enough about you. Have I told you about my new condo? It's
fabulous. Can you believe it, me on my own. As soon as you're
well, you've got to at least make a trip home to see it.

Let me know how you are. Really.

Love,
Diana

To: Ben Prescott <sc123@fastmail.com>
From: Vendela Prescott <vendela@prescottmedia.com>
Subject: No answer

Dear Ben,

I've called your apartment, but I keep getting a recording that says it's no longer a working number. Where are you? You can't keep disappearing on me.

Your loving mother

To: Vendela Prescott <vendela@prescottmedia.com>
    Diana Prescott <diana@prescottmedia.com>
From: Ben Prescott <sc123@fastmail.com>
Subject: re: No answer

I'm staying with a friend. I'm doing great. The wound is healing like a champ. So not to worry. If you need anything, you can reach me at 915-555-2463.

Also, glad to hear the condo worked out, Diana. I look forward to seeing it next time I'm home.

Ben

To: Rita Holquin <rita@yahgoo.com>
From: Ben Prescott <sc123@fastmail.com>
Subject: Computer

Dear Rita:

I hope you and the kids are doing okay. I appreciate you coming
by the hospital to visit. I want you to know that I meant what I
said when I told you I'd do whatever it took to find Henry's killer.
I don't have much yet, but I'm working on it. Also, do you know
where Henry kept that notebook computer he bought for home a
few months ago? Can I borrow it?

Please let me know if I can help in any other way.

Ben

chapter five

The doorbell rang at ten minutes after twelve the next day. Ben was in his room, and Julia answered the door after the first ring. Even more progress, she thought proudly.

She was disproportionately impressed with the accomplishment, but after yesterday's lapse, when she had touched Ben, she was looking for any sign that she really could change. If answering the doorbell was it, she'd take it.

A woman she had never seen before stood on the front step. Julia didn't know her, though she didn't look like Ben's type. For one thing, she appeared harried. On top of that she had a black case in her hand, wore a wool tweed suit, and had on glasses.

Julia mentally took in the very reserved attire. Nope, not Ben's type, she was willing to bet. She was probably a saleswoman.

"Hi," Julia said. "Can I help you?"

Not that she really could. With no money to spare,

she couldn't afford Mary Kay, Avon, or any other door-to-door vendor.

"Is Ben here?"

So she was wrong. He went for the harried type. Who knew?

"He is, but he's sleeping." Again. This fact probably needed to worry her, she thought.

"I'm Rita, Henry Holquin's wife—" The woman's eyes went wide, then all of a sudden they burned with tears.

Julia's own eyes went wide at the sight of the unexpected show of emotion.

"I mean," the woman corrected, "I'm Henry's widow."

Julia hadn't a clue who Henry was, but she knew that this woman was fragile and most probably recently widowed. She wondered if the dead Henry had anything to do with the shot Ben.

"Ben e-mailed me last night and asked if I could bring him this." Rita held up the black case.

"Oh. Well. Come in, please." Julia took the woman's hand and led her inside. Without asking, she led her to the kitchen and had her sitting at the table with a cup of tea in front of her in seconds. That, she knew how to do. "I'm so sorry to hear about your loss. Is it recent?"

"It happened a little over a month ago. Henry was Ben's . . ." The woman got an odd look on her face, then finished with "Ben's friend."

If that wasn't the weirdest response Julia had ever heard, she didn't know what it was.

"Sit here and drink your tea. I'll get Ben."

But she didn't have to. He walked into the kitchen. "Hello, Rita."

The tiny woman leaped up from the table and instantly was in Ben's arms. He held her, stroked her back as she cried. "I miss him, too," he said, his voice tight with emotion.

Julia felt uncomfortable watching such a scene—the tears and need freely spilling from the woman, the bone-deep caring she never would have guessed at coming from Ben.

He had arrived in the kitchen still not showered, though Julia could tell he had attempted to clean himself up. She could see the pain and the need to cover the pain lining his strong face.

When he led Rita back to the table, Julia thought the hitch in his step was getting worse. Despite that, standing there caring for tiny Rita, Ben appeared competent and strong—with a strength that was physical, yes, but a strength of character as well. Not that he had shown an ounce of it to her.

"I'll let you two talk," she said, turning abruptly and leaving the room.

Ben watched Julia go. Just thinking about the way she had touched him yesterday sent a bolt of desire riding through him.

He didn't know what was up with her—all this talk of being a good girl with her proper-ass clothes. But he had enough problems to deal with. He didn't need the extra aggravation of Julia Boudreaux giving him a hard-on every time he turned around.

Focusing, he looked back at Rita. She had lost weight and had dark circles under her eyes. Henry had always taken care of everything in his family's life, dominating his wife and children.

Rita worked, but only because a cop's pay didn't cover the looming expense of college for two kids. With Todd and Trisha in high school, Henry had started to worry that he wouldn't be able to afford their books, much less tuition. And Henry had wanted his kids to go to college.

"I brought the computer over on my lunch hour."

"I appreciate it, Rita. I'm not supposed to drive yet, otherwise I would have come for it."

"You doing okay?"

"Don't worry about me. Tell me how you're doing."

"Hanging in there."

"Are you sure?"

She started to cry again, silently, brokenly, and he placed his hand on her forearm. "What is it?"

"Everything. The kids." She cried into a tissue.

"What's up with the kids?" he persisted.

"Well," she sighed, "I caught Todd stealing money out of my purse, and Trisha took the car . . . and wrecked it."

"Wrecked it?" He came forward to the edge of his seat. "Is she okay?"

"Yes, she's fine."

"I didn't think Trisha was old enough to drive."

"She's not! She snuck the car out and was joyriding with her friends when she crashed it."

"She had others in the car? Is everyone okay?"

"Yes. It happened in the school parking lot and no one was going fast, but now with Henry gone, the kids do whatever they want. I don't know how to stop them."

Henry had always been the disciplinarian. Rita never had much of a backbone when it came to their son and daughter.

A knot started to form in Ben's belly. He could afford to send Henry's kids to college. He had a trust fund. On principle he had never touched it. But for Henry's children he would. That he could handle. But this, actually having to deal with kids who were being wild, took something that he didn't know how to give. And he didn't want to try.

But what he wanted didn't matter.

"Let me talk to them," he offered.

"Will you?"

"Sure." He hesitated. "Last time Henry and I talked about the kids, he still hadn't told them he was an undercover. Is that still true?"

She sighed. "Yes. He said he would, but"—her voice snagged in her throat—"he was afraid to risk it."

"Hell."

Most undercovers' families—wives, parents, kids—eventually learned what they did. Most knew early on that they were cops. Later, as the undercover thought it was appropriate, he or she would explain about the undercover status. But some cops, like him, felt it necessary to keep their two lives separate. Henry had been that way, not wanting his kids to know what he did. Kids could slip; kids could say something unintentionally, or even intentionally to make a point to another kid, that could threaten an undercover's life.

Henry had never been willing to take that chance.

Ben had to make sure he honored his partner's wishes. Which made it difficult to say anything specific to make two teens feel good about their father.

"When can Trish and Todd come over?" he asked.

Rita glanced down at his leg, which he held stiffly out in front of him. "How about after school next Friday? That gives you time to get back to . . . normal—or at least until you're doing better."

He should have thought of that. "I'm fine, really. But

I agree that we don't want to remind them of their dad getting shot. Next Friday it is."

The kitchen clock ticked on the counter. "I better get going if I'm going to make it back to the office in time."

"Thanks for bringing the computer by."

She gave him a quick hug, those tears springing up again, before she dashed out the door.

Ben didn't move. He sat at the table knowing that Rita was right not to let him see the kids yet. He felt like hell, inside and out. His leg hurt whenever he put weight on it, and Trisha and Todd didn't need to see that. But by next Friday he fully intended to feel better.

He started to open the computer, but decided against it. The last person he wanted to see it was Julia. Taking the case, he returned to the guest bedroom. At the desk, he moved his own computer away, along with stacks of papers where he had been taking notes. He still hadn't a clue where Henry could have been surfing in order to find drug dealers. But his partner's new laptop might hold some answers.

It didn't take more than a few tries to figure out Henry's password. Ben knew just about everything there was to know about his longtime partner. And like most computer novices, the man had used easily remembered information as the key to his private world. Easy for Henry to remember. Easy for anyone who had access to information about Henry to find and remember. In this day and age, just about anyone had access to just about any information.

Henry's password was his firstborn's middle name.

Ben was into Henry's computer on the second try and into his e-mail on the fourth try. But it was Henry's screen saver that made Ben suck in his breath.

It was a photograph of Henry and his family, all of them smiling as if they didn't have a care in the world. But their world had taken an abrupt shift when Henry walked into that alleyway.

Ben had seen the body, had arrived on the scene after the fact. His partner had been shot execution-style. Ben was going to find out who pulled the trigger.

He started in Henry's e-mail. Other than nearly two months' worth of spam, it was empty. Even the address book didn't have a single name inside.

Next he went to the hard drive and looked for cookies and temporary Internet files. Both were empty. Cleaned out. Either Henry had purged everything just before he was shot, or someone had planted spyware on the hard drive, giving them the ability to erase whatever that person didn't want traced.

He made a note to ask the police computer whiz to check it out.

After that, Ben searched through each of Henry's files. File after file, nothing looked promising. Running a hand over his weary eyes, he was just about to call it a day when he tried one last thing. Embedded deep in the maze of folders, he found a file called Cotton Candy. Inside there was a single e-mail from someone called the Lion. It said nothing remarkable, other than *Everything's set*. It was dated the morning of Henry's murder.

Ben felt hot all over as the all too familiar fury raced through him. Henry must have been set up. Walking into the alleyway had been like walking into a minefield.

Ben had no knowledge of any dealers going by the name the Lion. The world he and Henry worked in existed on code names and assumed identities. When Ben worked, he went by Benny the Slash. There would be

nothing unusual about someone calling himself the Lion.
Though Ben knew if this was the killer, the chances were
that this e-mail was set up on a Web-based account that
left no residual signs and couldn't be traced. Regardless,
he would check it out.

For a second, Ben leaned back in the chair. But wal-
lowing in anger didn't solve anything. He made another
note to search for a Web address for the Lion.

After examining the e-mail and the hard drive, Ben
moved on. He made a list of possible Web site types
where Henry might have found drug dealers.

Need money fast.

Classified selling sections.

Ben started by Googling *need extra cash*. The search
engine spat out 3,510,000 results, listing ten per page. It
would take the rest of his life to go through all of them.

Refining his search, he typed in *need extra cash message boards*. That significantly reduced his choices down
to 221,000 sites, but still too many to investigate.

Another search: *Need extra cash message boards El
Paso, Texas*. 5,290 hits.

Crap. But from there he started to surf. On site after
site, he scrolled through the list of chatting onliners, but
found nothing that leaped out at him. He decided the
only way to learn anything of use was to test the waters.

He posted a note: *Looking for an opportunity to
make easy money in El Paso*. Then a second: *Have car,
can work at night in El Paso area.*

Now he'd have to see what happened.

He heard sounds in the room next door.

Julia.

The woman could make a saint want to commit murder and happily face the consequences. It had been bad

enough when she was hot as hell and in your face about it. But now this determination to suppress who they both knew she really was drove him crazy. One minute sweet and innocent, the next the real Julia surging forth like a tiger bursting out of its cage.

He wondered why she felt the need to be what she thought was a new, improved Julia. When he walked into the kitchen earlier, she had been wearing woolen pants with pleats, a sweater, and shoes that looked a lot like loafers. Julia, in loafers. It was hard to imagine.

Shaking his head, all he could think was thank God she hadn't cut her hair. A man could get lost in that long mane of black lacquer sensuality.

Ben cursed when he felt his cock stir just at the thought of what he wanted to do with her.

He felt hot, consumed, and he lamented the fact that he couldn't get the woman out of his head.

Why are you running promo spots asking for rugged, insensitive hunks?

Kate

Katherine C. Bloom
News Anchor, KTEX TV, West Texas

Wass up? Are you wearing baggy jeans down to your knees with Adidas tennis shoes with no laces?

And yes, I'm looking for the most Neanderthalish men in West Texas. It's for the idea I came up with for a show. Unfortunately, while I have a true Cro-Magnon man living under my roof, I've decided he isn't the right guy for my plan.

xo, j

To: Julia Boudreaux <julia@ktextv.com>
From: Katherine Bloom <katherine@ktextv.com>
Subject: re: Excuse me?

No baggy jeans for *moi.* But I am doing a special segment on hip-hop in El Paso. Who knew how prevalent it is? I'll definitely bring in a new demographic with this show.

As to archaic men, I thought you were swearing off bad boys. What kind of show is it going to be?

K

To: Katherine Bloom <katherine@ktextv.com>
From: Julia Boudreaux <julia@ktextv.com>
Subject: Surprises

I *have* sworn off bad boys. As to the show, I'll fill you in once I get the pieces to fall in place. It's going to be great!

xo, j

chapter six

Julia quit her e-mail, then turned off the computer. She had the foolishly giddy thought that soon she'd have a signature line on her e-mail with a title. Producer. She just had to pull her new show idea together.

Putting up the promo piece on Kate's show would definitely draw plenty of men. But to make this truly work, she needed more than men. She had to have the products and services that would actually transform the man. Everything from a haircut to house furniture. And she needed all of it for free. The only form of payment the vendors would receive was publicity on the show. Which was why she had placed an ad in the newspaper classified section under Services Needed.

Based on the advertising success of both Kate's show and Chloe's show, Julia knew there were plenty of people out there who were more than willing to trade goods for publicity.

Every time she thought about taking some rugged, insensitive guy and turning him around and making him sweet, it sent a shiver of excitement down her spine.

She remembered Ben's reaction of stunned disbelief when she had told him the idea. Clearly, he hadn't been as impressed as she was. Which is why she finally decided Ben wasn't the man for *Primal Guy*. She didn't need a grumbling naysayer, no matter how good looking, ruining her show.

Until entries from guys who were actually interested in being made over started rolling in, she would concentrate on completing her own makeover. All she had to do was think the word *Ben* and all her determination to change fled out the door. And it wasn't the sex that she was missing—though just one look at that body of his and sex loomed large in her mind. It was being nice and sweet that was so unbelievably hard to maintain when she was around him.

But she could do this. And she could do more than change her clothing style, blush with embarrassment on occasion, and answer the door herself.

She studied her reflection in the mirror, then decided what she had to do.

Thirty minutes later, she stepped into the hairspray fumes and screaming blow-dryers of the Velvet Door Salon.

"Hello!" the stylist enthused. "Sit, sit."

Julia refused to worry. This was the right thing to do.

The woman pulled her hair from the ponytail holder. "Such beautiful hair. Are you sure you want to cut it?"

"Absolutely sure. It's time I cut away the past."

The woman's eyes went wide. "Yes! I know just what you mean. Like starting over."

"Exactly."

The hairdresser took her arm. "I am going to cut your hair and it will be just as beautiful as it is now. Only different."

"I was thinking of a blunt cut to my shoulders."

"Pah, so sensible."

"Sensible is exactly what I want."

"Okay," the woman said, looking doubtful. "If you're sure."

She wasn't, but she didn't say that. The stylist talked nonstop as she washed Julia's hair, then combed it out, making it possible to forget what was about to happen.

"How about if I cut it shorter, but maybe do something a little more fun than a blunt cut?" the woman asked.

"Thank you, but no. I want a conservative, pageboy type style," Julia stated with a nod.

And after little more than thirty minutes, Julia was staring at a woman she barely recognized. She refused to admit that she wanted to cry.

Who knew change could be so painful?

"It's not bad," the stylist cajoled.

Not bad?

Julia shuddered, then raised her chin. She was a lot of things, but she'd never been vain. Though perhaps that was because she had always taken her looks for granted.

"Thank you, it's perfect."

Then she had no choice but to return to Meadowlark Drive.

When she pulled up in the driveway, she couldn't help it. She pulled out the clips and bands she always carried with her and whipped what was left of her hair back into a bun. Not that she cared what Ben thought. It was more that she realized that she felt foolishly vulnerable without her hair.

She smiled, thinking of Samson with his hair. But she would be the opposite. Cutting away her hair would make her more powerful—taken more seriously than ever before.

Pulling around the side of the house to the three-car garage, she parked and walked in through the back door. The house was quiet.

For a second she stood in the kitchen, feeling the warm November sun beating through the wide windows. She had the distinct feeling of being alone. Her father had been gone much of the time when she was growing up, but this was different. This was permanent.

Dropping her keys and purse on the counter, she went to change. She headed across the house and down the carpeted hall. Ben's door was open and as much as she tried not to look, she couldn't help but notice the clothes that hung around the room like party decorations. The bed was unmade. She could see into the bathroom. Toilet seat was up. His towel was tossed into the sink. The place was a mess.

He, on the other hand, wasn't.

He was on the computer—as usual. She could tell he'd had a shower. Finally. His hair was clean but disheveled, as if he'd stepped out of the shower, raked the dark strands back with his hands, and called it a day. Clearly he wasn't the kind of guy who spent a lot of time with blow-dryers and hair gel.

Like a bad habit, yet again she inhaled sharply at the sight of him, at the contours of his chest rippling beneath his open shirt. She hated to admit that she was attracted to the brute force of Ben Prescott. The dark

eyes that sent a shiver of longing through her body, settling low, made her feel the need to press her legs together against the desire that always flared when he was
around.

Yes, she was honest and straightforward enough to
admit she was attracted to the man, but actually giving
in to that desire was another story. She didn't want brute
force.

She wanted a sensitive man. A man who brought
flowers and wore tuxedos. She was through with men
like Ben in their rugged leather jackets and jeans that
cupped the crotch. She wanted a man who wouldn't be
looking for the next good fuck the minute he'd had her
in bed. Not that any man had left her. They hadn't. She
always did the leaving. She was an expert at leaving.
And now she would become an expert at self-discipline.

When she finally glanced at his face, her eyes narrowed in embarrassment when she found him looking at
her.

"Do you want something, cupcake?"

The way he said the words made it sound like a se-
ductive invitation.

"No," she stated firmly. "Or, well, yes, but I don't
want *that*."

He chuckled, though in the back of her mind it started
to register that something was wrong.

"We need to talk," she said.

"Talk?"

"Like two mature adults."

"As opposed to two immature adults."

She shot him an impatient grimace. "As opposed to
one mature adult and one immature adult."

He laughed. "I assume you're implying I'm the latter."

She shrugged innocently.

He winked at her. "Shoot. What do you want, Ms. Mature?"

"It's best that we keep our distance from each other while you're here."

"Fine."

"Fine?!" Then she cringed. "I mean, good."

"What else?" he asked, like he was in a hurry for her to be gone.

She walked farther inside and stepped over a pile of clothes. She gathered underwear from the back of the chair, held it between two fingers, then said, "Despite your Neanderthal ways, the least you could do is clean up."

Ben looked her up and down, then he leaned forward, gathered up a few T-shirts, then tossed them in his still mostly unpacked suitcase that was lying on the floor. "How's that, cupcake?"

At the best of times, she wasn't patient. With all six feet of this chiseled piece of granite pushing her, her patience levels were dipping like mercury on a freezing cold day. "I don't need a smart-ass like you making fun of me." Then instantly she cringed. "Damn," she muttered.

"Tell me," he said with a wide grin, "are you even capable of being sweet and patient?"

She glowered at him. "Are you capable of doing anything besides surf the Internet?"

Every trace of amusement disappeared from his arrogantly chiseled face. "I'm working."

She rolled her eyes. "Okay, that's another thing. I've got to know. What exactly is it you do?"

Finally, the question was out there. She thought of Rita and her odd response to how Ben knew her husband.

What could the youngest son of a very old and rich family do for a living that entailed people dying and him getting shot?

Ben, however, wasn't nearly as relieved that the question was out there. She could see it in the way his jaw tightened and he stood. A shiver of concern raced down her spine, but she held her ground. When he stepped toward her, she held a wad of T-shirts up to her chest like they might keep her safe.

When he stopped in front of her, he looked at her for a long second. "Why do you want to know what I do?" he asked.

"You don't seem to work!" The words blurted out of her. "And after the way Rita was acting, something seems wrong."

"Wrong?" He tugged the clothes from her hands, then tossed them onto the chair. He was close, too close, and his heat wrapped around her—hard, hot, and nearly overwhelming. Her heart leaped in her chest. And she felt panic—like she never had before. Not when her father died; not when she learned the extent of the debt KTEX was in. She had simply gotten to work and moved forward with determination and confidence.

"Yes, something seems wrong. Tell me this: What respectably employed man gets shot in the first place? And coming out of a bar, at that?"

His eyes narrowed dangerously, but she couldn't seem to stop herself now that the words were tumbling out.

"Are you going to tell me you were in the wrong place at the wrong time? Just so you know, I don't buy it. What respectably employed man is referred to as Benny the Slash? Benny the Slash," she moaned. "What are you, a drug dealer?"

The minute her suspicion left her mouth, she gasped. If he was a drug dealer, it probably wasn't a great idea to confront him about it. She grimaced.

He had this strange look in his eyes, like he wanted to tell her something—or maybe he was just trying to decide if he could rub her out and get away with it—before he threw his head back and laughed.

"Sorry to disappoint you, but I'm not a drug dealer. Nothing so sinister. Whether you believe it or not, I am in the import/export business. Brass elephants, wicker baskets . . . you name it, I import it—legally. On top of that, I'm as lazy as they come. So I work only when I feel like it. I haven't felt like it."

He made it all sound so reasonable, and true. Her doubt wavered, but she wasn't about to cave in that easily. "But what about the shooting?" she probed.

He shrugged. "I've been to my fair share of bars in south El Paso. This time I took a bullet. Just bad damn luck."

She stared at him and considered. But she didn't know what else to say. She started to turn away, then stopped abruptly. "Hey, you said a minute ago that you were on the computer, *working*. But then you said you haven't felt like working. Which one is it, Ben?"

She might as well have said, *Aha! Caught!* for how dramatic she was acting. Ben just smiled at her. "I only go into the office when I feel like it. But I work from the computer all the time."

She snorted. "You have an answer for everything."

And it all made sense the way he told it. Besides, there was no way Chloe would allow a drug dealer to move in with her. He had to be legit.

She pivoted on her heel, but he stopped her when he caught her arm.

"I have a question for you this time," he said, his dark eyes boring into her. "What's up with that prissy bun you've been wearing?"

Her hand flew to her hair. "It's nothing, really. I was . . . hot, so I pulled it up."

His smile slid into sensuality and he took a step forward. She took a step back.

"What are you doing, Ben?" she asked, wishing her voice had been steadier.

He planted his hand on the wall above her head. His gaze drifted from her lips to her throat. He probably could see the wild flutter of her pulse. "You used to be hot. What happened to that woman—the one who grabbed me by the balls playing doctor? She had steel in her spine."

That woman had lost everything.

But she didn't say that.

"If you'd like the ball grabber, I could take care of that right now. Though it seems a little old hat now. Not to mention that your private parts haven't been all that private recently. Sorry, but the mystery is gone."

Liar.

His lips quirked at one corner. "You got an eyeful, have you, cupcake?"

"Believe me, you have more than an eyeful."

Her mouth fell open, and his did, too. Then he laughed even louder. "Now there's the hell on wheels I know. Didn't take more than a few minutes to bring her out of hiding."

"Damn you."

"No doubt I already am," he drawled, his gravelly voice a purr.

His dark eyes flicked down to her mouth then back, before he leaned down and kissed her—though not on the lips.

His mouth brushed over her forehead, then her temple, before trailing back to her ear. She had never felt such a kiss, intensely sexual despite the fact that he never touched her lips.

He pressed into her with a barely perceptible groan, the hard chiseled length of his body feeling like granite against her. She forced herself to keep her own hands at her sides, even as she itched to touch him.

She had kissed a lot of men, but none who possessed this sensual expertise. He had her hot and wanting in seconds, her body shivering and flushed at the same time.

She wanted to give in. Would it really be so bad to touch—just a touch?

Suddenly all the reasons for keeping her distance were clouded and indecipherable. Giving in, she reached up and placed her hands on his chest. His groan deepened as he nipped the shell of her ear. Seemingly of their own volition, her palms skimmed higher, and Ben slipped his hand between her and the wall, pressing her close.

His mouth continued its magic. She started to feel a frustrated yearning. She gave in completely and moved her hands to the bare skin between the edges of his unbuttoned shirt. He was hard and hot.

Too hot.

Desire and passion ticked to a jarring halt.

"Ben." She tried to push back.

He pressed closer, holding her secure.

"Ben! You're hot."

His deep, sexually charged chuckle rumbled in his chest. "I am hot—hot for you."

She snorted. "Do men really think lines like that work?"

"You tell me, is it working?" he asked in a gruff whisper against her ear.

With this man, she silently conceded, on another day, it might actually have worked. But not today.

"Ben, I'm telling you, you're hot. Not *hot* hot. You feel *fever* hot."

That got his attention, and he stepped back. "I don't have a fever," he stated, as if by simply saying the words he could make them true.

"Ben—"

"I'm telling you, I'm fine."

She ignored that. "Did you get the bandage changed?"

He glowered at her. "Pretty much."

"What kind of an answer is that? Let me see it."

"I don't need you to see."

She planted her palm on his chest, his hot chest, and backed him up to the bed. "Lie down," she instructed when he grimaced. "I'll help you with your jeans."

"I can do it."

He did, though barely, the effort sapping him too easily. Then he relaxed against the pillows with a groan. He hardly moved when she pulled the gauze and tape away, even though it had to hurt like crazy. When it came free, her face darkened.

He craned his neck. "It looks the same to me."

"Really?" She sounded doubtful.

"Really. If you'd just bring the hydrogen peroxide—"

She leaped up and in seconds returned with the bottle, plus more bandages. When he tried to do it himself, she brushed his hands away. With relative quickness, she had the wound cleaned and rebandaged.

"I'm going to get you some cool water and some Advil. Then you've got to rest. Take it easy on that leg. You are not allowed to get worse!"

Before he could protest—not that he looked like he would or could for that matter—she dashed to the kitchen, retrieved some water, then hurried back.

He was lying just as she had left him, but now his eyes were closed.

"Great, just great. I've killed you. Chloe made me swear I wouldn't—and that was just when she thought I'd strangle you."

"Just give me the water."

He gulped it down in one long chug. When he finished, his head fell back. He didn't extend the crystal glass to her, he just dropped his hand, the empty glass hanging loosely in his fingers.

"Ben, let me call the doctor."

"I'm fine," he mumbled. "They said I'd have good days and bad days."

Then his breath sighed out of him and he was asleep.

For the next five hours, Julia wore a trail in the carpet from going back and forth between her room and his. Around nine-thirty that night she fell asleep in the chair next to his bed. A half an hour later a noise jerked her awake.

Disoriented, she pushed up to see Ben on the bed, a cover draped over him as he slept, but he was groaning and muttering.

She went to him. "Ben," she said softly.

But he didn't wake.

"Ben," she said louder.

He thrashed his head to the side, his moans increasing.

"Ben." Louder. Then she placed her hand on his shoulder.

And everything changed.

He sat up in bed like a lightning bolt, a ragged moan ripped from his throat as he grabbed her wrist with deadly force.

Fear raced through her, strangling her as she tried to pull away. But he held on tight, his eyes wild as he stared at her. She could see the moment he realized what had happened. Where he was. What he had done.

"Fuck," he croaked, his face burning with fever.

"Ben, it's okay."

She thought he might yell—or break down. The thought surprised her. He only held her hand so tightly that she felt a strange need to cry. For this man, for something she didn't understand at all.

Sitting down on the edge of the bed, she forced him to look at her. "We need to go to the hospital."

"I don't—"

"Ben, you're getting worse."

He stared at her forever, and when she pulled the covers off, he didn't stop her.

He was weak, and she knew he'd never get his jeans on. Hurriedly, she fished through underwear and T-shirts in the suitcase that he still hadn't unpacked until she found what she was looking for. She helped him into a pair of navy blue warm-up bottoms.

Julia felt like she was dressing a child when she pulled a sweatshirt over his head. She was worried and moved at the same time.

Ten minutes later, she had him in her car. With Ben passed out next to her, she flew down I-10, careened off the Schuster exit, then barreled up toward the mountain and the medical center. As soon as she circled into the emergency bay, an orderly came out. In seconds, they had Ben in a wheelchair. Julia had never been so glad to see Ben grumble. Despite his reluctance to get in the chair, he did.

When they told Julia she had to move the car, the old Julia surged and she tossed the guard the keys. "Put it anywhere you want, sugar."

The guard's eyes went wide in surprise. But she didn't wait around for him to say yes, no, or get the hell out of his hospital. She hurtled through the whooshing mechanical doors, following her best friend's brother-in-law, whom she had sworn she wouldn't kill.

Please, please, please, she prayed, *don't make a liar out of me.*

No one wasted a minute. In seconds, the hospital staff had Ben on a table and surrounded like a lab experiment in science class. When Julia inched closer, a stern-looking nurse scowled at her, then pushed her firmly but gently out of the room.

When the door closed behind her, she hated the strange emptiness that she felt. Or maybe it was just fear.

Please let him be okay.

She tried to sit in the waiting room, but wound up pacing. Fortunately, they wheeled him out of the emergency room thirty minutes later.

The doctor came up to her.

"Are you Mrs. Prescott?"

"Ah, n—" She cut herself off. If she wasn't a family member, they'd no doubt kick her out. "Yes."

"Not to worry," he said then. "He's going to be fine. The wound is aggravated and slightly infected, but it's nothing antibiotics won't clear up quickly. I think his biggest problem is that he's exhausted. It doesn't look to me like he's been sleeping."

It seemed like he had been sleeping, but when she thought about it, she had to wonder. More than once when she woke up in the middle of the night, she had heard him rustling around, working at that computer.

"I'm going to keep him overnight just to make sure. I'm giving him intravenous antibiotics to clear up the infection quickly. I suspect he'll be ready to go home in the morning."

"I'm so glad," she said on an exhale of breath. "Is there anything else?"

"He has to take it easy on that leg."

"I'll do my best to see that he does."

"Good. For now, there's nothing you can do. Best to go home and get some rest yourself."

"I can't leave him here!"

The young doctor debated. "You can sit with him for a bit—how about that?"

A nurse led her to a private room. Ben was already sound asleep, an IV hooked up to his arm. As soon as she was alone with him, she walked over and stood at the edge of the bed.

"You gave me a pretty bad scare," she whispered.

He didn't respond, just lay there looking far more angelic than she knew he was.

Regardless of who or what he was—an import guy, a drug dealer, or just a spoiled rich boy—she couldn't resist reaching out and running her finger over his forehead, combing those locks of hair back.

"From now on, you have to take it easy," she added, sitting down on the mattress. "Okay?"

She straightened the covers, smoothed the wrinkles, then told herself to leave. In a minute, she assured herself. But she couldn't seem to take her hand off his chest—as if somehow she could make sure he didn't stop breathing.

chapter seven

He felt pressure on his chest. Though not a bad pressure. He felt warm. Soothed somehow. And rested.

He hadn't had one of the dreams.

Slowly, he came out of that comforting place, out of a deep peaceful sleep that he didn't want to let go of. But when he opened his eyes, the first thing he saw was Julia sound asleep, curled at his side, her arm over his chest.

He couldn't have been more surprised, and for half a second he wondered if they had gotten drunk and made the very big mistake of sleeping together.

But then he became aware of the tube stuck in his arm, the stark walls, and the metal side pulled up on the bed.

What the hell?

It took a second to remember. He was in the hospital after collapsing last night. Damn, he hoped it was only last night.

Whatever, he had to admit he felt better than he had in days.

He smiled at the hazy memory of Julia as a warrior, poking and prodding him into her car, then bringing him here. The woman clearly was great in an emergency. No falling apart for her. Which wasn't a surprise.

He felt the start of a chuckle, but held it back. She looked as exhausted as he had felt.

Unable to help himself, he laid his hand on her hair. That damn bun she'd suddenly been wearing was barely holding on now. And when he allowed himself to stroke the nearly black strands, he couldn't have been more surprised when it tumbled down completely.

His hand went still when he saw that all that beautiful long hair was gone, cut to her shoulders.

"Why?" he asked softly.

But he knew. Her determination to make herself over, as if cutting her hair could help her change.

"Ah, Julia," he whispered.

The door opened, and a doctor walked in.

"Mr. Prescott, I'm Dr. Levin."

Julia was startled awake. She sat up groggily, and Ben could see that she was trying to figure out where she was, much as he had done seconds before.

When she focused on him, then back at the doctor, then on the way she was curled next to him on the mattress, she did something that if asked, he would have sworn she never would have done. She blushed.

"Mrs. Prescott, I see you didn't make it home last night," the doctor said with an understanding smile.

Ben glanced at Julia and mouthed, *Mrs. Prescott?*

If possible, her blush got worse.

"But that's all right," the medical man added. "I'm always happy to see couples in this day and age who are so devoted."

Julia started to scramble off the bed. But Ben caught her hand, holding her there. "Yep, that's us, Doc. Hopelessly devoted."

Julia's mouth dropped open, then she mouthed her response. *Hopelessly devoted?*

"Wow, you two really are a couple of lovebirds."

Ben and Julia shared a look, a single moment of harmony that they hadn't experienced during the month and a half they had known each other. But both of them knew how wrong the doctor's assessment really was.

After a check of all vitals, the doctor allowed Ben to be discharged. But not before providing strict instructions that he was to stay off the leg until Thursday, when the doctor wanted to reexamine the wound.

An hour later, they finished with the business office and were in the car headed for home. They didn't say a word for the first few miles.

"Thanks," Ben finally said.

"Not necessary."

"Sure it is. And I'm going to try to be nicer. Clean up. Put the toilet seat down."

Julia smiled, staring straight ahead. "Based on doctor's orders, you won't be cleaning up anything."

"What?"

"You have to stay in bed," she said with a wry grin.

"That's crazy."

"I am not going to make another mad dash to the hospital with you practically comatose in the passenger seat. I am not letting you out of bed until your appointment on Thursday."

"I am not an invalid."

"You are not going to overdo it on my watch! The doctor said Thursday!"

"Forget it, I'm outta here."

"Then I'll have to call Sterling and Chloe."

That got him and he glared at her.

"I can't believe I woke up and actually had a single nice thought about you," he muttered.

"Welcome to the club of regrets! I can't believe I actually felt badly for you. You are ornery and stubborn—"

"And you're not?"

When she reached the house on Meadowlark, she turned into the long driveway. "Just get inside. All you have to do is take it easy for a few days. A few days! That's it."

Grumbling, he conceded. "And no mention of this to Sterling or Chloe."

"Fine."

"Fine."

They got inside and Julia helped Ben to his room. He started to resist, then seemed to think better of it. Based on the look on his face, she thought the adrenaline that had carried him this far was deserting him. With effort, he stepped out of his sweats, then got underneath the covers that she held back for him.

Nothing else went that smoothly.

Over the next two days, Ben Prescott ran her ragged. He made liberal use of the intercom, buzzing her every few minutes.

He was thirsty.

He was hungry.

The covers were in a twist.

At the end of the second day, after the umpteenth trip, she snapped.

"What is it? I've brought you food, drink. I've plumped

pillows, retrieved the remote from the floor, adjusted the curtains. What now?" she demanded.

A sheepish smile tugged at his lips. "I'm bored," he said.

"You're running me ragged because you're bored?"

"Maybe. And even you're better company than none at all."

She slammed the door behind her as she exited. She didn't answer the intercom after that. She checked on him at reasonable intervals. But that was it.

On the third day, she did her best to focus on her own work. When she booted up her computer, she found another e-mail from the new station manager at KTEX TV. When Andrew Folly had sent an e-mail asking to meet to discuss her plans, she hadn't been ready. She had explained that while she was caring for Sterling Prescott's brother, she wasn't in a position to leave the house. As soon as he was better, she'd drop by the office.

He had sent her a slew of e-mails since, all of which she had avoided. She hadn't even met the man and already she didn't like him.

But the more pressing, obnoxious man was in this very house.

"Julia!" she heard him call.

Since she had stopped answering the intercom, he had resorted to ringing a bell he had found. When she hadn't answered that, he started hollering down the hall. She answered only when she couldn't take the racket anymore.

She groaned and dropped her head onto the desktop. Once Ben got used to the idea of being waited on, he had taken to it like a duck to water. He'd barely set foot out of the bed, and then only to use the restroom. But fortunately, she would have sworn he was finally, truly healing.

So she no longer felt guilty when she ignored him.

A few minutes later the telephone rang. She glanced at the caller ID and didn't recognize the number. She had seen Andrew Folly's work and cell numbers, so she knew it wasn't him.

She picked up the phone. "Hello?"

"I'm sorry for being difficult."

"Who is this?"

"Your patient."

"Why are you calling on the phone?"

"It was the only way to get your attention."

Julia sat back in her chair and couldn't help her smile. "You're not forgiven."

"Fair enough."

"Is there anything else?"

"Since you asked—"

She could practically see his smile.

"Is there any more of that chocolate pudding left?" he asked.

She had made pudding for dessert, the kind out of a Jell-O box, since she was strapped for time. Ben had loved it better than the crème brûlée she had made yesterday, or the strawberry shortcake she had made the day before that.

"I can't believe you like that stuff so much. Didn't you get tired of it as a kid?"

"Vendela Prescott doesn't serve Jell-O pudding in her home," he stated.

"Oh, yeah, I keep forgetting that you're Sterling's brother."

"Be nice."

"I am being nice. So nice that I'll bring you the last of the pudding."

They hung up and she stared at the receiver for a few minutes, smiled, then went to the kitchen. When she walked into his room, she could tell he'd just had his first good shower since their hospital run. He looked fresh and clean and incredibly handsome in a rugged way.

He took the fluted dish, spoon, and napkin. When she started to leave, he stopped her.

"So," he began, "how's it going?"

Turning back, she looked at him with a raised brow. "How's it going?"

"Yeah. Tell me what's happening with you."

"You're bored again."

"I am not bored."

"Then it's worse." She marched over to his side and reached out to touch his forehead. "Your fever's back."

"It is not."

"It must be. The only time you've been nice was when you were half dead."

He laughed out loud. "That's not such a nice thing to say, *Mrs. Prescott.*"

Damn, she had hoped he'd forgotten that little slip.

Her lips pursed.

"Not to worry, Julia. I thought it was kinda cute. Though I didn't know you harbored those kinds of aspirations."

"A real comedian."

"I'm not laughing." Though he did have a big wide smile spread across his face like a banner.

"I only said it because I didn't want you to be left

alone in the hospital, and I knew if I wasn't a relative they'd kick me out."

"Admit it, cupcake, you really do like me."

"I do not!"

"Sure, sure. But just think, you could have said you were my aunt."

She reached out and grabbed the pudding away.

"Now that is mean," he said.

But when she would have left, he caught her wrist. Slowly, he pulled her down to the mattress until she sat on the edge. Taking the dish away from her, he set it aside.

"Just talk to me. For a little while."

He looked so sweet and endearing it was hard to resist. She reminded herself that he looked like a bear. Sweet and cuddly on the outside, an animal on the inside. Though in truth, he didn't really look like a bear at all, not like anything a person could cuddle up to. He was more like a sleek, finely honed predator.

"I can't stay," she said. "Really. Besides, I don't want to take you away from all that important surfing you do on the laptop."

A surprising darkness flared in his eyes, then it was gone just like that.

"I need a break," he said.

For reasons she didn't understand, she believed him. "Okay," she sighed. "But just for a second."

The darkness fled completely, and he whipped out a deck of cards. "I found these in the nightstand."

She smiled despite herself, her mind circling back in time.

"What?" he pressed her.

She shrugged. "When my dad was in town, we used to stay up for hours playing."

"What did you play?"

She glanced over at him. "Go Fish."

Ben laughed strong and deep. "Then Go Fish it is."

With strong expert hands, he dealt.

"You know how to play?" she asked.

"You bet. I'm not bad, either, so guard your pennies, Mrs. P."

Telling herself she could relax just for a few minutes, she pulled a chair up next to the bed. "So we're playing for pennies?" she asked.

He considered her for a second. "No, I think we should play for secrets."

"Secrets, eh? Seems like you're the one who has all the secrets. Aren't you worried about telling them?"

He got a twinkle in his eyes. "I don't plan to lose."

Never one to walk away from a challenge, she said, "We'll see about that. Deal."

He dealt seven cards each, then spread the rest out facedown on the bed. Each of them arranged their cards, then Ben gestured for her to go first.

"Do you have any threes?" she asked.

"No." He grinned. "Go fish."

She picked a card out of the pile, then smiled wickedly. "Got what I wished for." She set a pair of threes down with a flourish.

Ben grumbled good-naturedly.

The round went fast, Julia relaxing as they made their way through all fifty-two cards. Though she wasn't nearly as happy when he won.

"Now," he said, rubbing his hands together. "What do I want to know?"

He considered her, and she started to squirm. "No secrets."

"Fine. If you'd rather, we can switch to strip poker."

She perked up and gave him a sultry laugh. "Sounds perfect." But then she froze. *Not perfect! Not anymore!*

"No, telling secrets is fine," she responded glumly.

He laughed. "All right, if you'd rather not take off those hideous warm-ups you're wearing, then tell me what you were like in high school—really like."

She'd rather take off the warm-ups, since she didn't like them a whole lot more than he did. But they were safe and not wild. Which was the point.

"All right. What was I like? Hmmm." She considered. "I was just like I am now—or who I was two weeks ago."

He settled back against the pillows and looked at her, his smile hitching at the corner. "Nope, I don't think so. I don't think you grabbed anyone's balls when you were a kid. Hell in Heels in training, maybe, but if I had to guess, I'd say you were"—he tilted his head in consideration, and she felt a very foreign blush creep into her cheeks—"loud—"

She had been.

"Funny."

"Maybe a little." She loved making people laugh.

"Smart."

"I didn't do bad."

"Straight A's."

"I got a B once."

He laughed, the sound craggy. "And you were cute. Maybe even sweet."

The word instantly made her think of her father, and

she felt those damn tears threaten. He had called her pumpkin.

"I'm right, aren't I?"

"Maybe. A little."

He looked at her for a long time, and she grew uncomfortable. Then he asked, "What made you think cute and sweet weren't good enough?"

Her breath caught in her throat, surprised at the question. Its accuracy stunned her.

"Come on, Julia," he said. "Tell me."

She pushed up from the bed and moved away before he could catch her.

"Julia?"

She stopped at the door, but she didn't look back. "My dad always told me I was cute and sweet. But none of the slew of women he dated were cute or sweet."

"They were wild and outrageous," he predicted with a wealth of caring in his voice, which made her throat tighten.

She stood there remembering, hating the way those memories made her feel. "Yeah," she said truthfully, "they were."

"But why would you try to be like women he dated?"

"Putting it like that, you make it sound weird. And as an adult now, I can see that it wasn't such a great idea. But as a kid, with my mom gone and no one to teach me any better, all I saw was that the only people my dad paid attention to were the women who were wild and sexy. There, you got your secret. Now let me work in peace."

She left then, before he could say anything else. But when she got back to her office, her father's old office with that space under it where she used to play, she couldn't breathe.

When the phone rang, she picked it up without thinking.

"Hello?"

"Thanks for playing cards."

She sat back, not understanding what she felt. "No problem. Anything else?"

"Yeah. I miss your hair."

Then he hung up with a quiet click, leaving her there with a soft smile pulling at her lips.

To: Julia Boudreaux <julia@ktextv.com>
From: Katherine Bloom <katherine@ktextv.com>
Subject: Station Manager (Resume DOWNLOAD FILE)

Jules, I know you've been swamped dealing with Ben, but I really think you need to make an appearance at the station. Andrew Folly, is . . . well . . . energetic. He's determined to make his mark in TV, and he's taken over your office. He's also been asking about you. I'm afraid if you don't show up here, or at the very least answer his e-mails, he's just aggressive enough to show up at your house. I've attached a copy of his résumé with photo so you'll be prepared.

Kate

Katherine C. Bloom
News Anchor, KTEX TV, West Texas

To: Katherine Bloom <katherine@ktextv.com>
From: Julia Boudreaux <julia@ktextv.com>
Subject: My office!

He's taken over my office? Though I guess it only makes sense since the station isn't mine anymore. Though it gives me more reason to work from here. Did I tell you I've set up shop in my dad's office?

Plus, I can't believe that photo. He looks like a kid. Then I found his birth date and he is a kid! Twenty-four!

xo, j

To: Julia Boudreaux <julia@ktextv.com>
From: Katherine Bloom <katherine@ktextv.com>
Subject: re: My office!

What a great idea about your dad's office. I used to love it when we'd play house underneath his desk.

As to Andrew Folly, Chloe and I were even younger when we started at KTEX. And need I remind you, we're only three years older than he is now.

K

To: Katherine Bloom <katherine@ktextv.com>
From: Julia Boudreaux <julia@ktextv.com>
Subject: Defending him

How can you defend him?! He's probably spilled Gerber baby carrots on my leopard-print sofa. In fact, what kind of man would work in an office that is filled with purple kiss pillows and a chair like a throne?

xo, j

To: Julia Boudreaux <julia@ktextv.com>
From: Katherine Bloom <katherine@ktextv.com>
Subject: re: Defending him

I'm not defending. Just giving you the lay of the land. I mean it when I say he could get it in his head to show up at your house. He asked for your address. When I said I didn't think it was appropriate to tell him, he scoffed and headed for the personnel files.

Be on the lookout . . .

K

p.s. Your purple kiss pillows have disappeared.

chapter eight

By Thursday afternoon, Julia started going through the list of vendors who had responded to her classified ad. The open call interviews for her Primal Guy were scheduled to begin first thing Saturday morning. It felt good to be working, finally, after she had taken Ben to the doctor and he had gotten the word that he was definitely on the mend. Getting him to stay off his leg since Sunday had done a world of good.

Now it was time to focus.

She was worried about getting everything done in time because the clock was ticking and she'd been way too distracted by Mr. I'm-Perfectly-Fine. She was also worried about Andrew Folly. She had every intention of putting together a great show—or she should say, a great local show. But after reading Folly's résumé and seeing the extensive network programming he had been involved in, she just hoped that he understood the sort of programming KTEX TV could realistically produce.

Julia pulled out her notes. The only interruption she

expected was from her former housekeeper, who was supposed to stop by. Zelda was returning the house key, and Julia knew it would be an emotional experience for both of them. Zelda had always been more surrogate mother than employee.

Julia smiled at the thought that if Zelda had stayed, the woman would have whipped Ben into shape in no time. There were times when Julia's father had lamented that he didn't know which was worse—having Zelda there, or not having her there. The woman was a short, stocky general who had always run the house and its occupants with military precision. Though if anyone could have charmed the orthopedic shoes off the woman, it was Ben.

To prove just how wonderful he was doing, when she glanced up, he stood in the office doorway. He looked hot, sexy, and disreputable in a T-shirt, jeans, and bare feet. She resolutely wouldn't allow a single shiver of yearning to race down her spine and settle low at the sight of him.

And it worked, too. Almost. But almost was better than not at all, so she gave herself points.

"You're looking chipper this morning," she said.

Ben leaned up against the doorjamb, crossed his arms on his chest, and studied Julia. He was all about solving mysteries. But the longer he was around this woman, the more he couldn't figure her out.

When they had played that kids' game, he really had wanted to learn her secrets, since he knew people well enough to know that Julia Boudreaux wouldn't give up any information willingly. He wanted to understand what made her tick. But her answers only made her more of a puzzle.

When he had come to the door of the office a few minutes ago, she had been working intensely, not realizing that he was standing there. Even in the conservative clothes she was wearing now, she looked hot. Today she wore a capped sleeve sweater, though instead of the woolen pants she had taken to wearing, she had on a pleated plaid woolen skirt—only a step away from a girls' school uniform. And he still couldn't get used to her hair. Short and conservative. All she needed was a velvet headband to complete the picture.

But somehow she still managed to look sexy. Both the clothes and the hair were like a good-girl veneer over what he knew to be a very bad girl. Sweaters and pearls hiding a body that he knew was hot as hell with an attitude to match.

The window dressing made him want her all the more.

When he had stepped inside the office, she looked up. It was in those few seconds of surprise that the old Julia flared—the heat in her eyes that she wasn't yet used to hiding, the way her lips parted. Though she was getting better at portraying her new image. It didn't take her long to find the prim expression. That's what bothered him the most. If she kept it up, would she actually succeed in wiping out the bad girl?

"May I help you?" she asked formally.

This from the woman who had seen just about every inch of his body. Though he smiled at the thought that she was the one woman who wasn't a nurse or an emergency room doctor who had seen him naked who he hadn't slept with.

He felt his dick swell at the thought of solving that.

"I can think of something you could help me with," he said, his gaze running over her.

He saw the way the pupils of her eyes flared until they were nearly a deep dark purple. He could tell that her nipples drew into tight buds underneath the cashmere. His cock swelled even harder at the sight.

He walked over and sat on the edge of the giant desk. The office looked every bit as formidable as Sterling's office at Prescott Media. "Something hot and wild," he added.

She scoffed, though he could tell she didn't really have her heart in it.

"Absolutely not," she stated after she cleared her throat. "Now that you're on the mend, we need to stay in separate corners. Really."

"Why? I think we both could use a little tension relief—in the form of a good old-fashioned, no-commitment fuck."

"If you're looking for tension relief, I suggest you sign up for yoga."

He laughed. "I'd rather have sex."

"Then find a date."

"I'd rather have sex with you."

"You're not my type."

"What type is that?"

"You thrive on being bad and edgy."

"Hey, I'm as nice as the next guy."

"Only if you're standing next to Colin Farrell or Sean Penn. You are so far from being a sensitive guy that you make the Rock look like a pussycat."

"You exaggerate."

"Do I? Let's see. How often do you buy women flowers?"

"Flowers?"

"Yes, you know. Those things that grow in gardens and are given as gifts."

He couldn't remember the last time he had given a woman flowers. Truth was, he couldn't remember ever giving a woman flowers. "Maybe I don't do the flower thing," he said, a tad on the defensive side, "but I've doled out my share of jewelry."

"What was the occasion?"

When he remembered, he swore he might have blushed.

"A parting gift?" she asked disdainfully. "Appreciation for a really great night of inventive sex?"

"Hey, I'm not here to talk about me."

"You started it."

"Then now I'm stopping it."

"Too late. Do you own a sports jacket or pair of khaki pants?"

"What does this have to do with anything?"

"You said you weren't a bad boy. I'm testing that. Sports coat? Khaki pants?" she prompted.

"I've got a sports jacket."

"One? For emergencies? And the pants?"

He glowered.

"I won't even ask if you have ever worn any sort of pleated pants. You probably don't even know what a pleat is."

He glanced down at her skirt. "Believe me, I'm very aware of pleats—or I was until you went off on your little lecture."

"See, you have a one-track mind."

"And that is?"

"Sex. All you care about is sex."

"And you don't?"

"No."

"Liar."

"Go away." She *humph*ed.

Instead he stood and pushed her swivel chair back from the desk with her in it. Then he stepped in front of her. Reaching out, he grasped her arms and pulled her up.

"I'm not sure in what country *Go away* means *Grab me out of my chair.*"

The corner of his mouth twitched as he tugged her close until her body lined his. The soft cashmere made her breasts even more of a mindblower than the tight Lycra had. High, soft nipples distended. He wanted to touch and suck. Heat slid between his legs.

Her lips parted, pink and full, and he saw desire flash in her eyes. He could tell she was fighting a battle with herself. The need to flee doing hand-to-hand combat with the need to satisfy the itch they both felt.

He slid his arms around her, gathering her close.

She made a sound, part start of surprise, part purr of pleasure. When he kissed her neck, she shuddered with the passion he knew burned barely contained just beneath the surface of her donned propriety.

He kissed her ear, trailing across to her temple, then hairline. Then back to her neck, where he sucked with gentle pressure. Finally she gave in and slid her arms around him with a moan, her hands slipping down the muscles on either side of his spine.

Her head fell back, allowing him better access to her neck. They didn't bother kissing anymore. They searched for skin, each seeking. He pulled up the sweater top and felt a swift spear of heat at the knowledge that at least underneath she hadn't resorted to prim. She wore a sheer violet bra that hooked in front. He could see her nipples through the gauzy material.

He cupped her breasts, pushing them high, running his thumbs along the tender skin. The sensation of material between her nipples and his thumbs made her moan again, low and throaty.

"Yes," she whispered when he unsnapped the bra.

Leaning down, he kissed her on the full mounds, getting closer and closer to the peaks, but holding back.

She groaned in frustration when his lips came to the very edge of her nipple, then stopped.

"Damn you," she whispered.

He chuckled, and only then took her deep in his mouth.

He sucked and pulled to the rhythm of her panting breath. First one breast, then the next. She ran her fingernails down his back, making him arch closer.

It was like she had been holding on to prim until she couldn't take it any longer, then all the wild came rushing out of her. His arousal pressed against his jeans, and she boldly reached down between their bodies and cupped him.

This time the wild broke through him. When she tugged at the 501's fastenings, he groaned. And when she reached inside, she curled her fingers around his dick.

"God," he managed, gulping air.

His jeans fell down around his thighs, then lower, and he kicked them away. He wrapped his hand around hers, making her grip him tighter. Dragging in a ragged breath, he moved her hand on him until she found the rhythm. When she cupped his balls, a hard, driving sensation ran through him, and he knew he couldn't take much more. Reaching down for the hem of her schoolgirl skirt, he ran his hands underneath. Awareness burned through him at the feel of the same sort of wispy material of her thong. It wouldn't take more than one sharp tug and it'd be gone.

Her butt was round and elegantly firm, and he pressed his erection into her. She clung to him like she was starving for intimacy. He didn't think about consequences. He didn't think about his wound and that maybe he was pushing too quickly, yet again. He couldn't have turned back then if he wanted to. In that second he would have gladly spent another night in the hospital if it meant that first he could slip hard and deep inside her.

He wanted her. He couldn't think of anything else but having her. He ripped her sweater off, then cupped her fullness at the same moment she palmed his sack.

In some distant recess of his mind, he became aware of the doorbell ringing. His brain registered that fact, but then she squeezed him gently and a shock went through him like an electrical current, making it hard to care.

"Don't answer it," he commanded gruffly.

He pinched her nipples, and suddenly she didn't seem any more interested in answering it than he did.

It rang again.

"They'll go away," he added.

Either the sound wasn't registering with her at all or she agreed, because she let the straps of her bra fall down her arms before the slip of violet gauze drifted to the floor.

Triumph and pleasure roared through him. Holding her, bringing her body to life, made the wound and everything that had led up to it fade to the back of his mind. He wanted relief. Though he knew he didn't deserve it.

Closing his eyes, he held her tightly, burying his face

in her neck, reveling at the feel of her breasts pressed against him and the silken brush of her hair.

But all of a sudden she stiffened.

"Miss Julia? Where are you?"

He wrenched up at the same moment her eyes went wide.

"Oh, my gosh! I forgot Zelda!"

Julia scrambled for her clothes. When she tried to fumble into her bra, she couldn't get it snapped.

With calm efficiency, Ben moved her hands away and had her snapped up in seconds. Then she slapped at his hands.

"Get dressed," she demanded.

"I will. But you've got to get out there and distract her while I do."

He reached for his jeans, but they were caught under the rollers on the chair.

"Miss Julia!" the woman called out again. "There is a visitor here to see you!"

That's when he heard two sets of footsteps coming down the hall.

"Great!" Julia cried in a frantic whisper, tugging the sweater over her head. "You've got to hide."

"I do not hide from anyone," he stated firmly, wrestling with the denim.

"Yes, you do!" she hissed, pushing at him to get under the desk. "You owe me after I saved your sorry ass, dragging you to the hospital—"

"I am not going to—"

"Miss Julia, it's a Mr. Folly here to see you."

Julia gasped. "The new station manager! My new boss!" She cocked her head. "Me, with a boss." Then she blinked and focused. "You owe me, Prescott. Get under the damn desk."

"At least let me hide in a closet."

"Hello?! Do you see any closets?"

"Fuck."

Then he disappeared under the massive expanse of hand-carved walnut just as Julia got her sweater adjusted and made a dash for the door. But she was too late.

"There you are, *querida,*" the woman said, clasping Julia's cheeks with command as if she were still running the Boudreaux household. "You look hot. Are you sick?"

"No, no. I'm fine. Really."

Zelda tutted, then added, "Lucky I got here and found this nice man at the door. He was about to leave. He says he's the new boss of the station."

The man Julia had seen in the résumé photo appeared in the doorway.

"Ah, Julia, I'm Andrew Folly."

"Andrew—"

"Sit, sit," Zelda instructed as she always had. "I'll bring something to drink."

"Zelda, that really isn't necessary."

Andrew Folly didn't agree. "That's very nice of you. A cup of tea would be nice," the man said.

Zelda headed down the hallway, her rubber-soled shoes squeaking on the hardwood. Ben was sure he heard heavier footsteps come into the office even farther. "So this is Philippe Boudreaux's inner sanctuary."

There was perfect silence after that.

"Oh, I apologize, Julia. I didn't mean to upset you. I'm sorry for your loss."

Ben had wondered about her father. Julia said she had been close to the man. But something didn't add up.

"You didn't upset me, Mr. Folly. Let's go into the living room."

Instead the heavier footsteps walked closer, and there was a squeak of leather as the man sat down in one of the chairs opposite the desk. "I won't be here that long. Just a question or two."

Ben could feel Julia's ire.

After a long, tense pause, she walked over to the desk and sat in the swivel chair.

Ben would have been pissed at being stuck there, his jeans still caught under the wheels of the chair, if he hadn't gotten an amazing look at her legs that disappeared up into the dusky recesses underneath that pleated skirt. He was glad she hadn't worn pants today. If he had to hide like a wimp under a desk, then he damn well was going to enjoy it.

"We'll need to make it quick, Mr. Folly."

Suddenly she was all formality. And really pissed.

"Okay, fine. We need to discuss your . . . situation at the station."

"What situation is that?"

"The type of show you're developing. I really have to insist that you tell me your intentions."

Julia's heart pounded so hard in her chest that she felt light-headed from the rush of blood—this on the heels of one of the most erotic encounters with a man, the experience no doubt compounded by her abstinence from so much as a kiss over the last week and a half.

All of a sudden, Andrew stood and came over to look at a row of photographs on the wall. Quickly, she scooted her chair forward, and her knees ran into Ben.

"Fuc—"

"Ssh!" she hissed.

"Pardon?" Andrew said, turning back from the line of autographed pictures of her father with famous people.

"I didn't say anything," she said with a tight smile. Then she had no choice but to spread her knees if she didn't want to sit far back from the desk. Which would look odd—not to mention she'd run the risk that Folly would see Ben.

She was all too aware of the tiny wisp of thong she wore, and while she had never been shy, she wasn't a *Penthouse* sort of girl, who spread her legs to give a show. She prayed it was dark under there.

Though if it was that dark down there, Ben was playing Helen Keller.

"Ack!" she squeaked, slamming her thighs together when she felt his finger tracing the seam of her underwear.

"Ugh" was his muffled response when she no doubt caught his head between the vise of her knees.

"What?" Andrew asked, a frown marring his pale features.

"Ugh, ugh, ughly," she managed, casting him a big fake smile. "I just think that those photos are . . . well . . . ugly. That's it." Then she shook her head. "This really isn't a good time, Andrew. Let's schedule something, then we can discuss—"

The words cut off, as did her breath, when Ben ran his finger between her legs and over the material, brushing erotically along the most intimate part of her. She drew in a ragged, gasping breath.

"Is something wrong?" Andrew asked.

"Asthma," she managed.

She tried to lever her knees together, but Ben had them firmly propped apart. All she could do to stop the sensual torment would be to jerk away from the desk. But between Ben underneath and the pair of men's jeans tangled at her feet, she wasn't willing to take that chance.

"I'm sorry to hear that," Andrew said. "And I'm sorry that this isn't a good time for you to talk. Unfortunately, this can't wait." He returned to the chair across from the desk.

She felt skewered on the double prongs of need—the need to strangle the man across from her and to yell at the one who was toying with her under the desk. Toying with her in a way that made her head spin and her knees want to widen traitorously.

Then she felt the thong disappear, the sheer material ripped away in one easy stroke. She really couldn't breathe when she realized what was coming next.

Despite the foolish anticipation, her body rocked when she felt Ben's finger against the seam of her. She also felt how she instantly got wet.

Her fingers clutched the edge of the desk and her head came back. Andrew's eyes went wide. "Are you sure you're okay?"

"Okay?"

Ben's finger slid between the folds and she could no longer talk, speak, or even think.

Andrew must have taken her *okay* as an okay to talk, because he launched into a spiel about numbers and demographics. She barely caught words like *change* and *younger, hip*. Like this twenty-four-year-old who dressed and spoke so formally knew the first thing about hip.

But then Ben's finger slid even deeper and all she could think about was her *hips* and the way they were straining to move.

She tried to reach under the desk to grab something, preferably Ben's hair. But he stayed out of reach, and short of falling to her knees and taking him to task, she knew she was at his mercy.

He must have known it, too.

He stroked her with an expert's ease, pulling out, then sliding deep, his thumb finding the secret nub. She felt hot and tight, and at the same time he kissed the inside of her knee.

"God," she whispered, her eyes closing.

"What?"

She jerked to attention. "God, this is fascinating stuff."

She would have sworn she heard Ben chuckle.

Andrew looked more grim by the second. But he didn't give up and go away. He launched back into his recitation of facts.

Ben launched two fingers, sliding deep, then deeper. Unable to help herself, she widened her knees. He kissed her inner thigh like he was doling out points for being a good girl—or being a bad girl. *Damn, damn . . . ahhh,* when his finger found the sweetest spot.

He'd pay for this dearly, she promised herself.

He slid and stroked, making her body hum, the tiny hairs on her arms standing on end as vibrations sang through her flesh. She forced herself to look at Andrew as he went on and on about who knew what at this point. What little part of her brain had been functioning gave up completely.

Ben nipped and kissed her skin as his fingers brought her higher. Sensation seemed to consume her, pooling between her legs. She felt the beginning of the tremors, starting deep, swelling, teasing until she thought she couldn't bear it another second. Then finally the intensity came rushing forward like an avalanche.

Her mouth fell open and she bent partially over the desk the minute her body orgasmed, the sweet rolling waves washing over her. She was afraid she might have moaned.

Andrew stopped speaking, then he stood. "Are you all right?"

"What?"

He grimaced. "I'm not sure what is wrong with you. I was trying to do this the nice way. But since you clearly want to play games with me, I'll lay out the hard, cold truth. Unless you can provide some quality programming that brings something different to this market, then you provide no added value to KTEX that I can see. And regardless of what Sterling Prescott said, I'll have no choice but to let you go."

Her mind reeled in time with her body. And then she realized that Ben must have heard, because she could feel that he was trying to push her away.

This time she did reach under and grab something. "No," she bit out.

"No?" Andrew gasped.

"I wasn't talking to—" She stopped, then shook her head.

"Mr. Prescott said you had to stay. But it's my job to turn KTEX TV around. Or *I* get fired."

She had to fight to keep Ben down. "I can deal with this," she stated, no longer caring.

Andrew pushed out of his seat. "You can deal with this? How? Can you honestly say that you can bring in something that looks more like New York produced it rather than El Paso?"

"Yes," she said before she could think.

He studied her, then nodded. "I hope you can." He

stopped at the doorway. "Let me know when you have something on tape."

Then he left.

Ben started to come out, but Zelda entered with a tray of tea things.

"What happened to the nice man?" she gasped.

"He had to go."

"Oh, *madre mía*." She tutted, then left again, the tray in hand.

This time Ben did come out, stretching and groaning.

"Are you okay?" Julia asked, thinking of his wound for the first time.

"I'm fine." His dark eyes narrowed with a barely contained anger. "Though I wish you'd let me have a piece of that guy."

Everything rushed in on her. She was utterly spent. Physically and mentally. She felt unsettled, and the precarious footing she'd had in this new world got even more precarious. She hated this new vulnerability she felt—combined with this rugged man being protective. She had never relied on a man. And she never would.

"I don't need you to defend me, Ben. And I certainly didn't need you playing fast and loose with my body."

Ben stared at her hard for long seconds before he grabbed his jeans, pulled them on, then headed for the door. At the last minute he stopped. "My guess is that you need a little bit of both."

Then he was gone, walking out on her. She had to stop herself from running after him—not to punch him, but to throw herself in his arms and have him tell her everything was going to be all right.

She sat down and curled her fingers around the arms of the chair instead.

chapter nine

"Are you sure you want all these strange guys coming to your house?"

Kate Bloom sat in Julia's kitchen with a cup of tea in front of her, her froth of soft dark curls framing her face, her mouth agape after Julia told her of the plan for her show.

Julia laughed and squeezed Kate's hand. "I can handle a few strange guys."

"True. If anyone can, it's you."

They sat for a few companionable moments, each sipping her tea. Julia looked at her dear friend. While Kate still wore the same conservative clothes and her hair was still the same, there was something different about her.

"Love suits you," Julia said, realizing that was the difference.

Kate smiled dreamily. "Yeah, who knew?"

Julia laughed, then grew serious. "I take it everything is still going great with Jesse?"

With her elbow planted on the table, her chin cupped

in her palm, Kate sighed softly. "Yes, it's still going great." She looked around, then leaned closer, her voice lowering into a stage whisper. "The other night, Jesse pulled out all those idiotic sex games you sent over for the sex products show you forced me to do."

Great. Sex talk.

Julia held back a wince. "Oh, wow." She tried to sound enthusiastic.

"*Oh, wow* is right. Who knew sex could be so fun?"

Kate laughed. Julia tried to do the same. But they had been friends too long for her to hide anything from one of her best friends.

"What's wrong?" Kate asked.

"Nothing."

"Jules? Spill."

Julia set her cup down and grimaced. "I'm thrilled that you and Jesse are doing great. But right now, with me having to work so hard to change, just mentioning sex is like talking about a big fat slice of chocolate cream pie in front of a woman who's on a diet."

"Oh, I forgot!" Kate leaned closer, her eyes glittering. "How's the resolve going when you have that big strapping hunk of man living under the same roof with you?"

"Hey," Julia barked, but she was smiling as well. "Shouldn't you be apologizing for talking about sex in front of me?"

"Sorry. There. Now tell me, how's it going?"

Julia rolled her eyes. "Great. Fine. Nothing is going on."

Kate raised a brow.

"Okay, maybe I had a little setback in the resolve department." She glanced at the closed kitchen door, then this time she leaned close. "It involved me, that Cro-

Magnon man"—an involuntary shiver ran the length of her—"and the most amazing orgasm of my life."

Kate about choked on her tea. "What?!"

"I kid you not. The guy is a sexual genius. And genius should be in all caps. And get this, it happened with Andrew Folly standing on the other side of the desk."

Kate went red in the face, then coughed and choked, looking like she might have some sort of a fit right there. "You had sex while Andrew Folly watched? I'm not sure whom I'm more worried about, you or him. Tell me I didn't hear you right."

"You heard right. I had an orgasm right in front of him, though he didn't know what was going on. He thinks I have a bad case of asthma."

"How could you have an orgasm in front of someone and he doesn't know?"

Kate wasn't as inhibited as their friend, Chloe, but while she had talked big about the sex game a few minutes ago, Kate had always been exceedingly circumspect about bedroom matters.

"I'm talking about me in my desk chair, Ben under my dad's desk, and Folly sitting on the other side. Ben should be shot." Then she smiled.

Kate's eyes went wide. "You liked it!"

"So sue me." Then she pursed her lips. "But it will never, ever happen again."

"*You* should be shot. Folly has it in for you, Jules. He wants you out of KTEX so bad, the entire office can taste it."

"Why? I don't get it."

"Neither do I." Kate's eyes narrowed. "Did you ever date him?"

"Folly?" she gasped.

"Yes, Folly."

"No way. I've never seen him before in my life."

"That's what I thought. But the only men I've seen who have it in for you are men you've dated and dumped. So I thought maybe that was the case with Folly. If that's not it, then it has to be who he thinks you are."

"The former station owner's daughter?"

Kate grimaced. "No. It was like the minute he saw your office, he had it in for you. He doesn't like fluff."

Julia blinked. "I'm not fluff." But she knew that was what people thought. And she also knew that that was part of what had driven her to this place where she was determined to change. She was determined to show everyone that she was more than fluff.

"Speaking of not being fluff," Kate said, "what's with the bun, anyway?"

Julia pulled out the pins and let her hair fall.

"No way! I can't believe you cut it."

"Neither can I."

"You hardly seem like the short-hair type."

"The point is to not look like me."

"Julia, I worry about you and these extremes you're going to."

"Don't worry about me. Haven't you and Chloe always complained about me and my assortment of men and wild clothes? Didn't you just get through telling me that Folly has it in for me because he thinks I'm a fluff doll? Well, I'm through with both—wild men and wild clothes. As soon as I find a nice, sensitive guy, then I'll start dating again. And while I'm at it, I'm going to blow Folly's argyle socks off with the show I put together."

When they finished their tea, the women hugged and Kate had to run. Once Kate was gone, Julia returned to her office and thought about her show, Folly, Ben Prescott, and a certain orgasm she had under the desk.

It was understandable that she would falter, she reasoned. They were living under the same roof. They were attracted to each other even if they really didn't like each other. And Ben Prescott was the sort of man who needed a woman . . .

A woman.

One of the long line of women who called here at all hours. Then he would be preoccupied and not making her life such a . . . challenge.

She tapped her pen on the blotter of her desk as she considered. Why wasn't he dating or having under-the-desk fun with someone else?

Only one person could answer that question.

Julia picked up the phone and dialed. She could just make out the faint sound of a cell phone ringing on the other side of the house.

"Slash."

"That's how you answer your phone?"

She heard him groan.

"I never should have given you this number," he lamented.

"You didn't. I have caller ID. You called me, remember? Back when you were being the patient from hell."

"I wasn't that bad. And it's unfair that your number is 'Unavailable.' "

"It's great. You should try it if you don't want people to have your number."

"I do want people to have my number. Just not you."

"Why are you in such a bad mood?"

"I'm not," he stated.

"Sure you are, and I think I know why."

"This should be good."

"You need to go out on a date."

"What?"

She leaned back in the chair, put her feet up on the desk, and crossed her ankles. "You have an assortment of women calling around the clock, but you're not seeing any of them. I think you should."

His deep, sensual laugh sizzled over the airwaves. "I take it that orgasm really rattled you."

She dropped her feet to the floor and planted her elbows on the blotter. "I am not rattled."

"Sure, sure. So what's the question again?"

"Dating. Why aren't you?"

"I'm not interested in anyone right now."

"You've got a good dozen to choose from. Surely one of them is interesting?"

"Nope. Anything else?"

"Well, ah . . ."

"Then I'm busy. Gotta go. But if you can think of anyone who might be interested in a little home-office fun"— he chuckled—"let me know."

A deliciously decadent shiver ran through her at the thought.

Then he beeped off and was gone.

The doorbell rang at three-forty that afternoon. She pushed up from her desk, but by the time she got to the door, Ben was already there.

"Hey!" he said to two teenagers standing in the courtyard. "It's good to see you."

Julia was surprised at the enthusiasm, since Ben didn't strike her as the gushy type. Plus, the gush seemed pretty strained.

Hmmm, Ben trying too hard. She wondered what this was about.

"Come in," he said to them.

When he turned around, he saw her.

"Julia. This is Todd and Trisha. They're practically my niece and nephew."

The teens looked almost identical, with brown hair and brown eyes. They looked at her, then looked at their feet. "Hi," they mumbled.

"Hello, Todd and Trisha."

"Let's go to the kitchen," Ben said.

Earlier he had asked if she minded that he wanted to use the kitchen when the kids arrived.

"Nice to meet you," Julia said, then returned to her office.

She finished up some calls and e-mail, then curiosity got the better of her. She made her way down the hall to the kitchen. Ben, who still wasn't allowed to drive, had ordered groceries and had had them delivered.

She was stunned. The entire counter was covered with every sort of ice cream known to man, along with every topping, every nut.

The beeper on the microwave went off.

"This is going to be great," he enthused, waving an oven-mitted hand.

He pulled out what could only be hot fudge. Her mouth salivated at the smell.

"Hey," he asked her, "do you want a sundae?"

"Well, I really shouldn't. I don't eat ice cream."

"Worry about that hot—" He cut himself off and looked at the kids. "Worry about your girlish figure another time."

"Like we don't know what you were going to say, Uncle Ben," Trisha said, rolling her eyes.

Todd laughed and dug into a container of ice cream.

Julia relented and pulled a stool up to the middle island in the kitchen she loved so much. They each made their own sundae. Julia went for one scoop of vanilla ice cream with hot fudge and pecans, and another scoop of chocolate with toffee chunks and plain Hershey's chocolate. She put plenty of whipped cream over the whole thing, with a cherry smack dab in the middle.

When she was done and looked up, Ben, Trisha, and Todd were staring at her.

"What?"

They burst out laughing, then dug into their own creations, none of which had the photo-op quality of hers. Though from the looks on their faces, she knew they tasted great.

"So tell me, *Uncle* Ben," Julia said, forcing herself not to sigh in decadent delight over her first bite, "how are you related to these fabulous ice-cream professionals?"

Todd laughed, though Trisha did the eye roll thing again. Instantly, Julia pegged Todd for a nerd. Trisha, on the other hand, had cool-girl-wannabe written all over her.

"Our dad was a good friend with Ben, so he's not really our uncle," Trisha said disdainfully. "And the only reason he wants us over here is because he feels obligated."

"Trish!" Todd said.

"Trisha," Ben said, his tone both caring and forceful, "that's not true."

Tears welled up in the girl's eyes, and Julia felt horrible for having stepped into it. "I'm sorry, Trisha."

"So am I," she noted bitterly. "My mom is making him see us. I know it."

"Trisha," Ben stated like a commander in the army, "that isn't true."

Every ounce of the man who was trying too hard vanished. He turned into a Terminator type who would scare a Green Beret.

"Listen, you two, your mom came over here, and she asked me to talk to you. No question. But it sounds to me like you both need talkin' to."

He might have started out on the right foot by serving up ice cream, but he was fast turning into a stern adult.

Trisha got a stubborn look on her face, and Todd looked really uncomfortable.

"Ben," Julia said kindly.

"Not now," he said with an autocratic snap.

Julia had to force herself not to snap right back. But she managed to swallow hard, and then felt foolishly pleased that she hadn't given in to the knee-jerk old Julia reaction.

More progress. She mentally congratulated herself.

"But whether your mom talked to me or not, once I found out what you two had done, I would have been knocking at your door."

Now Todd really looked uncomfortable, and while Trisha still appeared belligerent, she seemed a tad on the scared side, too. Julia wondered what in the world they had done.

"I hate like hell that your dad's gone. But you're doing a disservice to his memory when you start doing stupid things."

She realized that their mother must be Rita, and that

their father was the deceased Henry. Her heart went out to them.

Julia opened her mouth to protest Ben's exacting approach. But he didn't give her a chance.

"You can't go around stealing cars or money and not end up in juvie or worse."

Stealing cars and money?

Julia couldn't believe it. Trisha might not look like a Goody Two-shoes, but she also didn't look like a thief. And neither did Todd.

Trisha's chin jutted out. "You don't know anything, Ben. I didn't steal the car. I borrowed it."

"You don't *borrow* cars when you don't have a license. Did it ever occur to you what could have happened?"

"Nothing happened!"

"Like hell it didn't. You wrecked the car!" He turned his glower on the boy. "And you! What the hell were you thinking stealing money out of your mother's purse?"

Todd planted his elbows on the countertop and hunched over the melting ice cream.

"No answer, huh?"

Okay, that was it.

"Ben—"

"Julia, I'm in the middle of something."

"Yes, I can see that. Regardless, could I speak to you a moment? It's an emergency."

"Like I said—"

"Ben. Like *I* said, it's an emergency."

Glancing between her and the kids, he stood, muttering, and followed her out of the room. If the brother and sister were smart, they'd make a run for it while they had a chance.

"What?" he demanded.

"Who turned you into such a jerk? Those are two kids in there who lost their dad. Seems like you could do the discipline thing a little nicer."

"They're getting into trouble," he enunciated with barely held patience.

"But you acting like an idiot isn't going to help matters."

He scowled at her, but he didn't cut her off.

"I can see that you want to help," she added. "Really I do. It's just that the way you're acting isn't going to help anything."

"What makes you such an expert?"

"I'm not. I just have an ounce of common sense and I've learned that being too much of anything—too nice, too mean—doesn't get a person anywhere. And as soon as they got here, you were way too nice, and then like a light switch was flipped, you flew into the mean zone—"

"*Mean zone?*"

"You need to take the time to have a rational discussion with them. Show that you care and that you're concerned."

"They're kids, Julia. Kids don't need all that psychobabble crap."

"Ah, so instead you'll just give them a *psycho.*"

They both froze, stared at each other, then smiled, before Ben quickly glowered again. "This is no joke."

"I know it isn't. I'm the one who brought you out here. But if you don't lighten up, you're never going to help those kids."

He grumbled. "So what are you proposing?"

"Be nice, but firm. Ask them why they did the things they did. Ask them how they're feeling—"

"Not that feeling crap."

"Do you want to help or not?"

He muttered, glowered, muttered some more, then stalked back into the kitchen. Julia followed.

"Okay, let's talk," he announced.

Julia shot him a look.

He rolled his eyes in a decent imitation of Trisha. "Sorry," he stated. "I'm floundering here, guys. I need some help."

Trisha rolled her eyes this time. When Ben started to say something about it, Julia ran her finger across her throat, cutting him off.

Swallowing back a weary sigh, he persevered. "I know this is a rough time. And I just want to be there for you. You've got to be hurt and confused."

He actually said the words softly, and Julia was amazed at how this big bear of a man really did sound like he cared. Trisha must have thought the same thing, because the belligerent expression on her face started to waver.

"Todd, tell me what happened with the money," Ben said.

Todd looked reluctant, then said, "I really wasn't stealing it, I swear. I was going to pay my mom back. But she freaked out when she couldn't find the money, then wouldn't listen."

"So you're saying she's wrong?"

Trisha snorted. "Mom goes racing into Todd's room and he's standing there holding the money. No, she's not wrong."

"Hey!" Todd belted out. "You're one to talk. I might have wanted to borrow the money, but I had a good reason. And if I'd had the chance, I would have paid her back every cent. Besides, before Dad died, he promised I could apply for the video workshop they have at the college this summer. I did all the stuff I could at school, and Dad and my teacher said I was really good. But you have to turn in a video résumé with your application. And I don't have a camera. Dad promised to get me a video camera!" The boy was choked up, and his face turned a splotchy red. "But when I told Mom that I needed the money, she wouldn't listen. She never listens anymore. She just acts all crazy and like she's the only one who misses him! I miss him, too!"

At the words, Trisha's face went red, her eyes blinking back tears of her own.

Ben stared at the two kids in horror. He glanced hastily back and forth from the kids to Julia, then mouthed, *Look what you've done!*

She sighed, then gestured to him to go over to them.

Clearly he didn't want to, but Julia was impressed when he walked across the kitchen.

"Hey," he said placing a broad hand on a shoulder of each of them.

That's all it took before both Trisha and Todd turned into his embrace. Awkwardly at first, then more easily after a few seconds, Ben held the two teens. Julia felt a lump in her own throat, thoughts of her own father coming to the surface. But she wasn't lost.

Or was she?

She scowled and shook the thought away. She wasn't lost; she was simply finding a new way.

"So your dad said you could enroll in a video workshop," Ben said, "and your mom said no."

"She didn't say no. She just ignores me."

"She pretty much ignores everything," Trisha explained. "Not that I don't understand. Heck, she's upset like crazy, cries all the time, and has so much to take care of now that Dad is gone." The teen's eyes burned again with tears.

"So you took the car to get back at her?" Ben probed. "You were cruising around the Coronado High School parking lot late at night and crashed into the wall with your girlfriends because you wanted to get your mom's attention?"

Trisha's face got even redder. "I'm turning sixteen in three months and I don't even have my learner's permit."

"Exactly, so you shouldn't have been driving."

"But if I don't learn to drive, I can't get my license on my birthday. Everyone gets their license on their birthday unless they're a geek or a moron. Even Todd got his license on his birthday."

"Hey, I'm no geek or moron!"

"Whatever," she snorted. "But you get to drive, and you're even driving Dad's car."

"Someone has to take us to school."

"No one is going to talk about geeks and morons around here," Ben stated.

"Fine."

"Whatever."

"I just don't get it. You were driving when you didn't have a permit or even any lessons."

"Exactly!"

Julia could tell Ben was really confused. As was she.

"With my dad gone," Trisha added, her voice breaking, "who's going to teach me? I had to find a way to practice. And CeeCee has her permit, has been through Driver's Ed, and we thought she could teach me how to do it. With Mom the way she is, I was sure we could be

back before she ever woke up and knew we were gone."
Trisha was crying now. "Dad promised I could take
Driver's Ed this semester. But after he . . . he . . . died,
Mom said no. It's like she wants all of us to sit around
and be miserable and unhappy just like her. I am mis-
erable! I am unhappy! I hate that Dad is gone. . . ."

Todd had finally lost his battle and was crying now,
too.

"But me not driving or Todd not being able to do the
video stuff doesn't bring Dad back!"

Julia saw Ben's throat work as he fought back emotion. She felt it, felt the very real pain these kids were
experiencing. She didn't want to feel their pain; she
wanted to turn away before she started crying. But
she couldn't move. Couldn't walk away. And her heart
swelled when Ben in his own gruff way looked at each of
the teens and said, "I can't bring your dad back, but I
can get you a video camera and teach you to drive."

Both kids' faces lit with surprise. "Really?" they asked,
dashing their hands across their eyes. Then in exact unison added, "But what about Mom?"

"I'll talk to her. But there's a condition attached."

"What?" they muttered, their expressions dubious.

"No more getting into trouble. The minute either of
you does anything wrong, the deal's off."

"That's it?" they asked.

"That's it."

"Awesome!" Trisha cheered.

"This is so great!" Todd enthused. "Once I get the
camera, all I have to do is put together a video résumé!"

Julia studied the boy. "What are you planning to put
together?" she asked.

"I don't know yet. Everyone does some kind of lame

minimovie. When Dad and I were talking about it last summer, he was saying I should do something different."

"Really?" Julia said, her brain going into high gear. "I have an idea that might help."

Todd, Trisha, and Ben looked at her oddly. "You do?" Todd asked.

"How would you like to help with my new reality show?"

"What?" Ben demanded.

"A reality show?" Trisha asked, wide-eyed.

"Cool!" Todd said.

"Actually, you would be a big help," Julia continued. "I'll use a cameraman from the station to do the main work, but right now KTEX is low on staff. I was trying to figure out how I could be on camera, direct the segments, and provide the backup work a cameraman needs. Todd, you can be on-set to provide support, plus you can use the camera Ben gets you to tape what's going on. Sort of like documenting the process. I would think that would not only show that you have experience, but give you something really unique."

"That sounds great, but Todd goes to school," Ben interjected. He turned to the kids. "Can you two wait for me in the living room?"

"Ah, man," Todd lamented. "I can do this. I want to do this. It'll be perfect to get me into the workshop."

"Come on, Todd." Trisha grabbed his arm. "Let them talk it out." She glanced at Julia and smiled. "I think you'll get to do it."

Ben didn't look at Julia until the kitchen door swung shut. Then he turned an ominous eye on her.

"She thinks you have me wrapped around your finger." He was incensed.

Julia swallowed back a smile. "We both know she's wrong. Completely wrong."

He growled. "Either way, Todd can't take off school to work on your show. And I thought you gave up on the reality show business."

"One, tomorrow is Saturday, and I'm starting then. Plus Thanksgiving break starts next Friday at noon. We can do a lot of the work over the holiday. And two, I did not give up on my reality show."

He put his hands up in surrender. "You think you have it all figured out. But why would a teenager want to work over the holiday?"

"To take his mind off his dad? To get a different sort of video résumé?"

Ben grudgingly conceded. "So what kind of show did you come up with this time?"

"I never changed it. I'm still doing *Primal Guy.*"

"I said no."

Julia looked at him for a long second, then started laughing. "Glad to know that you finally admit you *are* a primal guy."

"I'll show you primal."

He started for her, but all she could do was laugh. She laughed so hard that the kids came running, stopping Ben in his tracks. It was even more amusing to see the wild man put himself in check with two impressionable teens in the room.

"Does this mean I get to do the show?" Todd asked excitedly.

Julia looked at the man in question. "I'm doing *Pri-*

mal Guy without you. I start interviewing bad boys to-morrow. Right here."

"Here?" Ben demanded.

"Starting at nine a.m." She turned to Todd. "Can you be here at nine?"

"Sure!"

"This is going to be great! Part MTV, part NBC. We'll be edgy and professional at the same time. I'm going to create a hit, and you are going to help Todd. We'll have it in the can, ready to go, the first week of December."

Todd cheered. Trisha looked happy for her brother, but a little wistful.

Ben must have noticed. "Trisha, why don't you come over with Todd. I'll talk to your mother tonight. If she agrees, we'll start driving lessons while these two are making their show." He looked at Julia. "Their crazy show."

"You just don't think I can do it," she said.

"Do what?" Trisha asked.

"Turn a bad boy into a sensitive guy."

Ben snorted. "She wants to turn guys into wimps. Todd, if I were you, I'd be careful around her. And no matter what you do, don't take any of her advice to heart. Just help tape, get what you need for your résumé, and keep your ears and mind closed."

To: Rita Holquin <rita@yahgoo.com>
From: Ben Prescott <sc123@fastmail.com>
Subject: Kids

Dear Rita:

I had a good talk with Trisha and Todd. When you get home from work, give me a call and we can discuss.

Ben

To: Ben Prescott <sc123@fastmail.com>
From: Rita Holquin <rita@yahgoo.com>
Subject: re: Kids

Dear Ben:

Thanks for talking to them. They called me at the office and I haven't heard them sound this happy in a long while. Thank you. Trish said you're going to teach her to drive. And Todd told me about the video work.

I know you will do right by the kids, so I'm not worried. You have my permission to teach as you see fit.

Warmly,
Rita

To: Rita Holquin <rita@yahgoo.com>
From: Ben Prescott <sc123@fastmail.com>
Subject: re: Kids

Rita, Trish and Todd need you in their lives. Don't shut down on them. They need their mother. —Ben

chapter ten

The doorbell rang in the distance.

A rush of excitement and maybe even a little fear flooded through Julia at the sound. Day One in the actual creation of her new show was about to begin.

For half a second, she sat in her chair, closed her eyes, and sent up a silent prayer. *Please help me make this work.*

"Julia!"

It took her a second to recognize Todd's voice.

He came bursting into the kitchen. "You should see the line outside! There are guys everywhere."

"What?"

A short, stocky man with red hair and freckles followed Todd inside. "Hey, Julia."

"Hi, Rob. Thanks for helping me with this."

Robert Krynowski was one of the KTEX cameramen, and Julia knew he wouldn't mind working in a crunch to get this done.

She raced to a front window. Sure enough, the entire

length of Meadowlark Drive was lined with cars. An assortment of men had already formed a line at her front door.

"Okay, okay, think, Jules," she said to herself.

Ben appeared and he didn't look happy. "Who the hell are all those guys lining up outside?"

Then he noticed Rob. "And who are you?"

Julia made quick work of the introductions, and the men shook hands. Ben continued on toward the kitchen.

"Wait!" She leaped after him. As soon as she caught his arm, she found a smile that she hoped covered her nerves. "I need your help."

His eyes narrowed.

"Please." She batted her eyelashes.

"Batting eyelashes won't get you anywhere with me."

"Okay, how about you owe me."

Ben grinned at her, that frustratingly sexy lock of dark hair falling forward on his forehead. "You already used that one to get me under the desk. Remember?"

Blood rushed to her cheeks. She doubted she would ever forget. She stared at him, feeling the heat slide through her. It had been two weeks since he had arrived, a week tomorrow since they had made their mad dash to the hospital. He still walked with a hitch in his step, but it was easy to forget that he had ever been wounded.

"I'm sorry," she said. "I shouldn't have asked. It's just, who is going to send those men in one at a time? I never dreamed I'd have this kind of turnout."

His smile fled and he studied her. After a second, he shook his head. "All right, tell me what to do. But after this, *you'll* owe *me*." The eyebrow with the slash in it rose ominously.

*   *   *

Julia set up shop in her father's office. She had a stack of résumés that she had gathered. Rob would move around the room, taping everything that went on. Todd would help, shooting footage with his own brand-new video camera whenever he got the chance.

Ben maintained order over what had to be at least seventy-five men waiting in the living room and dining room. A quick glance at the rank and file revealed an assortment of leather-clad men, leather-faced men, and even a couple who were carrying leather whips. Julia ruled those out after deciding that any man with a whip was beyond even her help.

At nine sharp, Ben came to the office door. "Are you ready?"

She must have looked like she felt, scared out of her mind, because he laughed and shook his head. No words of encouragement, no *You can do it*. He turned to the living room and called out the first name.

"Jones, Bo."

Rob set up to capture the guy walking into the office, but had to quickly pan up because the man was so tall.

"Mr. Jones," Julia said, standing and extending her hand.

The guy about crushed her fingers in his grip.

"All right," she said, pulling away when he didn't let go. Instead he eyed her up and down.

"Prim, but hot," he announced.

"Hey, buddy, shut up and sit down."

This from Ben, who stood in the doorway like a prison guard. If she hadn't been so relieved that he was there, she would have bristled at his command.

Like he owned her.

Another traitorous thrill raced down her spine.

"So, Mr. Jones, tell me about yourself."

He sat, slouching in the chair, crossing his ankle on his knee, which pulled the already tight jeans so tight on his crotch that she could make out the line of his balls.

Ugh.

"The ad said you wanted bad boys. I'm bad to the bone, candy lips."

Candy lips?

He leaned forward, planting his elbows on his knees, and looked at her in a hot, piercing way. "No need to bother with all the other twerps out there. I'm your man."

No, he wasn't, she thought instantly. Not even if she had to pose as the man herself to get the show done. "Great, thanks. I'll keep that in mind." She stood. "Next!"

Bo Jones grumbled, but thankfully he departed without making a scene. In fact, when she caught a glimpse of his face as he was leaving, he seemed to deflate, and she wondered if the whole production hadn't been a show. Maybe he wasn't a bad boy at all, but an actor playing a part.

She didn't want an actor. She needed an authentically *bad* bad boy.

Richard Paxton entered next. He genuinely seemed rugged and archaic, but she sent him on his way in seconds.

Ben poked his head in. "That was fast."

"He wasn't right."

"You could tell that quickly?"

"If you have to know, I need a cute guy."

Ben shook his head. "You talk about men being bad. I swear, women are worse.

"Next!" he called out.

They went through quite a few of the men by midday. They stopped for lunch only because she had a recovering patient and a teenager to think about. But even then they stopped for only twenty minutes.

It was during those twenty minutes, however, that Julia met Sonja.

The woman was stunning. Gorgeous in a tall, blond, blue-eyed, Nordic sort of way. Her lips shone with pink gloss, her nails painted to match. Her clothes were short, tight, and expensive. Just the sort of attire Julia used to wear.

She felt a twinge of envious longing, then pushed it away.

"Can I help you?" Julia asked when the woman entered the office.

After a quick introduction, Sonja said she had heard about the show.

"I want to offer my services. I'm a hairdresser," Sonja said. "Services rendered for publicity. I'm trying to grow my business, and this feels like the perfect way to do it."

They talked for a few minutes, and Julia was surprised by how much she liked the woman. By the time she was ready to get back to work, she had struck a deal with Sonja.

Julia already had arranged for clothes through the Fashion Place. Now she had a hairdresser. Another piece falling into place. Now she just needed the guy.

Sonja left her phone number so that Julia could call once she was ready to start taping. Then Julia got back to work.

"Who was that?" Ben asked, coming into the office.

"My new hairdresser," she stated proudly.

"You're going to cut your hair again?"

"No." She chuckled. "My hairdresser for the show. Now please send in the next contender."

It took several more hours to get through nearly half the candidates, but by five-fifteen, they had to put the remainder off until tomorrow. Rob stretched the small of his back, and Todd collapsed in the interview chair. Even Ben looked worn out, and Julia was too exhausted to think.

"Thank you all so much for your hard work. I couldn't have done it without you."

Todd smiled. "I got some really good stuff on my camera. And I know Rob got tons of great official stuff. When can we edit?"

"We'll wait until the end. Then we can sit down at the station and you can experience professional editing."

Pushing up, energy renewed, Todd beamed. "Cool! I better get home. I'll be back in the morning for the last of the interviews."

He headed for the door with Rob right behind him.

"You're bringing Trisha with you tomorrow, right?" Ben called after Todd.

"Oh, yeah. I guess. But dragging her out of bed any time before noon on a weekend is, like, totally impossible."

"She wants to learn to drive. She'll be up," Ben predicted.

The next morning, Ben still looked exhausted. At least that's what Julia told herself the darkness was in his eyes.

She had heard him up at all hours last night, working on the computer and pacing. It was like he didn't want to go to sleep. More and more she got the feeling that there was something wrong underneath his sensual smiles. But what?

No question he was upset about his friend's death, and he was worried about the man's children. But something in Ben's eyes told her that it was beyond that.

When the doorbell rang and Todd arrived with Trisha in tow as Ben had predicted, Julia said, "I still have forty-five minutes before I start the last round of interviews for the show. If you'd like, I can teach her if you don't want to."

On top of his sleepless nights, yesterday had taken its toll on him, and she felt horrible that she had thought only of herself.

"I'm fine. I'll show her the basics, then next week I'll take her out on the road."

"I can do it, really."

"You've got your hands full. It'll be a piece of cake to show Trish the ropes, then drive up and down your driveway. I blocked it off."

"How did you do that?"

"With lawn chairs."

"You shouldn't be lifting those!"

"I'm not an invalid, Julia," he said, his voice edged with an impatient ruthlessness.

He took one last sip of coffee, set the cup in the sink, then headed outside.

Since they had time before the interviews started, Todd and Julia found themselves watching Ben and Trisha through the window. The pseudo-uncle and teenager sat in Rita Holquin's car, which had a long scrape down the side. Julia could see Ben explaining about the gearshift and pedals.

Trisha must have gotten impatient and tried to hurry him along, because Julia could see when he turned into the stern guy. The teen relented, and more explanation ensued. It seemed like forever before Ben handed Trisha the keys. Reluctantly. Grimly.

"I think I should catch this on tape," Todd said. "No telling what she'll wreck this time."

Todd went out the back door to the wide, turn-around drive. Julia followed. Todd started the video recorder just as the car lurched forward. Brakes, then gas. Then stopping altogether.

Todd was amused; Ben was getting frustrated. Then suddenly the vehicle started going backward. Julia felt her heart leap into her throat when she realized where they were headed.

"Stop!" she blurted out.

But it was too late. The car backed into the yard, running over a plant that had been the one present that she had always cherished. A rosebush from her dad.

She became vaguely aware that Todd had turned the video on her. She felt weak-kneed and light-headed, like a dam was about to break inside her.

"Hey, Julia?" Todd said. "Are you okay?"

She blinked and focused on him. "Me? Sure. I'm great." She tried to laugh.

Trisha had gotten out of the sedan and now stood in the driveway while Ben straightened the car. When he finished, everything looked back to normal. Only the rosebush lay scraped and broken on its side, the roots pulled up, some still clinging to the ground.

Ben got out of the car and looked at her. "I'm really sorry about this."

"I'm so sorry, Julia," Trisha added, on the verge of tears.

Julia saw the genuinely desperate sadness in the girl who had lost so much and tried not to show it.

Julia found a smile. "It's just a rosebush. Don't worry about it. Now get back on the horse—or in the car—and show yourself that you can do this. You can drive."

"Really? You're not upset?"

Julia was aware of the way Todd looked at her oddly.

"Not upset at all. But if I don't get back inside and start interviewing, I'll have a bunch of upset men on my hands."

"I'll finish up with Trisha," Ben said, "then I'll come in and help."

"No need. I've gotten the hang of it. I can do this round by myself. Todd, it's time to get started."

chapter eleven

*E*ven though she told him she didn't need any more help, and despite the fierce darkness Julia saw in his face, as soon as Rita picked Trisha up, Ben was back inside running roughshod over the *Primal Guy* hopefuls.

After she had interviewed nearly seventy-five men over two days, she got a little worried that she wasn't going to find the perfect man. That man who was ruggedly handsome and arrogantly alpha—but also had some glimmer in his words or his eyes that told her that he was a man who had something inside of him that spoke to kindness. She was looking for a diamond in the rough. So far all she had interviewed was chunk after chunk of coal.

There were only five men left, and she was determined to find her guy today. Though, as usual, the only male in the house she noticed was Ben.

After he let the first guy in, she saw Ben flip open his cell phone and go outside to talk. After he let the fourth guy in, she noticed that he went to the front door and retrieved some sort of a package from a man. Yet again she was reminded that she knew very little about Ben Prescott.

He didn't have the package when he walked into her office.

"There's only one more guy left to interview," Ben said. "But he's not worth your trouble."

"What? Why?"

"He's a jerk."

"How do you know?"

"Trust me. I can tell these things."

"It's my show, and I'm going to interview everyone." But then she smiled at him. "Though if you would be my Primal Guy, we can send this last candidate packing."

His brows slammed together. "Russo," he bit out loudly. "You're up."

The last man entered, and Julia had to force herself not to gasp. He was stunningly gorgeous. He was also a contrast. He had blond hair and blue eyes, but the hair was much too long and his eyes blazed with danger. His leather jacket was soft and worn, his jeans so tight that she could see the outline of his thigh muscles. His black boots were scuffed, and he held a motorcycle helmet in the crook of his arm.

She stood to shake his hand, and he immediately gave her the once-over. Ben started to step forward, that scowl on his face, until Julia held up her hand. "Ben," she warned. "I can handle this."

His eyes narrowed, but he didn't leave the room. He stood behind Rob and Todd with his back against the wall like some sort of security detail, while the camera crew got this guy on tape.

"Mr., ah, Russo, is it?" She glanced down at his résumé. "Rocco Russo?"

"Yeah, that's me," he stated.

On the surface he was more than perfect. He had the looks, the attitude, the potential to clean up nicely. But did he have anything underneath that would show her he had potential to be kind?

"Have a seat," she said. He sat down before she did, and she grimaced. But manners could be taught.

"So tell me about yourself, Rocco."

Using a lot of grunts as he slumped in his chair, he told her about the business he owned. He had started a kitchen remodeling company.

He was looking better by the second. Looks, and now a good job. Please let there be some kindness somewhere in there.

"I'm impressed," she said truthfully.

Ben made some sort of a noise. She ignored him.

"But I'm curious," she continued. "Why are you interested in becoming the Primal Guy?"

He sat up in his chair, leaned in, and planted his elbows on his knees. He looked at her with intensity blazing in his blue eyes. "I want to do this show because I want to be transformed."

"Really?"

"Really. I'm in love with a woman, Fiona Branch." He said her name with a reverence that sent a thrill down Julia's spine. "But she won't give me the time of day." He sat back. "I can tell she thinks I'm rough around the edges. But if you can turn me into a sensitive guy, I know I'll be able to win her over."

Julia's breath caught and she placed her hand on her pounding heart. "That is so sweet," she breathed.

Ben cursed. "That's the biggest load of crap I've ever heard."

"Ben!"

"I'm out of here," he said, and walked out of the office.

It was hours later when Julia called down the hall. Everyone was gone by then and it was safe to come out. Like he had been hiding.

He grumbled because he had been.

Ben wished he hadn't promised Sterling he would stay here. And he might have been tempted to break a promise for the first time in his life if his new apartment had been ready before the end of the month. But that wasn't happening. And as much as he didn't want anything to do with Julia, the thought of staying on the floor or a couch in some buddy's apartment didn't sound appealing.

Besides, a promise was a promise.

He found her in the kitchen, surrounded by pots and pans. Some people exercised or drank when they were stressed. Julia, he had noticed, cooked. She had changed out of the prissy clothes she had worn for the interviews, putting on those ugly warm-ups again. If he hadn't known better, he'd have no idea what kind of a body she had under all the baggy material. And she still managed to look great.

"Mmmm," he said, coming up behind her, "something smells good."

"Must be the prime rib."

"Something's prime in here."

She craned her neck to look at him. "If you're in any way referring to me, and that is a line, I really have to reassess my thought that you are a bad boy—or at least a smooth-talking bad boy."

Ben threw his head back and laughed. He did that a lot with Julia. Laugh, and laugh in a way that had the ability to drive the darkness out. Which, when he was truthful with himself, was at least part of the reason he was still there. He could afford a hotel. He could make Sterling understand his need to leave. But the thought of the dreams haunting his sleep made Julia the better alternative.

But she did something else for him as well. With her television show, smart mouth, and deep violet eyes, she provided him with some kind of reprieve from his thoughts about Henry.

The truth was, he wasn't getting anywhere with his search for his partner's killer. He felt no closer to finding answers as to why Henry was in that alleyway than he was when he had started. None of his online searches in "need cash fast" and classified sections had panned out.

He had come up with another avenue to check out, and had already started posting notes. On dating sites. At first it had seemed crazy. But after he had made a list of attributes of people who might be open to dealing drugs, one had popped out at him. People who were lonely; people who were looking for any means to interact with others to feel wanted or important. And people who were lonely might very well frequent dating sites. But he knew he was running out of time.

What he hadn't wanted to acknowledge was that the brass in the department thought something wasn't right. Whatever Henry had been involved in had gone bad, everyone agreed, but there was more to it—more than just Henry going into the alley to get the goods on a dealer.

Henry had done something wrong.

That was the secret unspoken concern that was drifting through the department. Ben sensed it. And Ben intended to prove Henry had only done his job. But did he believe it?

Ben dragged his hands through his hair at the traitorous sentiment, and when he glanced up, Julia was studying him. She started to say something, but he cut her off. "I'm starved," he said. "Let me help you put dinner on the table."

Fortunately, she didn't question him. And in minutes they were sharing a meal of prime rib, Yorkshire pudding, roasted potatoes, green beans with almonds, salad, and rolls.

After the first bite, he moaned his pleasure. "You definitely can cook." He took another bite, swallowed, then added, "I had you pegged for a Cordon Bleu type, not an all-American meat and potatoes type."

She considered that. "I've never been crazy about saucy foods."

"Saucy?"

"The kinds with sauces and are stuffed and, well, fancy."

"You're always a surprise."

He watched her while she ate. When she finished, she sat back and smiled. "I can't believe I'm finally done with the interviews."

"What happens now?"

"I've got to pick a winner."

"What about finalists?"

"I don't have time. I have to have a show done by the time Sterling and Chloe return."

"You don't have to hurry. There's no way in hell Sterling will listen to that chump, Folly."

"That isn't the point. I want Sterling to keep me on because I deserve the job. Not because I'm a charity case."

He finished the last of his dinner, then sat back as well. "So tell me how you expect this mind-blowing show of yours to work."

Her nearly violet eyes went wide with excitement and she sat up. "Really? You want to hear about it?"

"Sure, why not?"

Anything not to have to think about his doubts about Henry.

She pushed her plate away and started to talk enthusiastically. "It's going to be great. It will be a one-hour show. I'll start with one man, then work on getting a lineup of other men ready to go once the first episode gets the green light."

"You're optimistic."

"Why shouldn't I be?" she said with the sort of confidence that he couldn't help but admire in her. "The idea is inspired. What woman doesn't wish for the experience, looks, and confidence of a bad boy, combined with a man who knows how to treat a lady like a queen?"

"That guy is a figment of your imagination."

"Maybe, maybe not. But it's just that sort of thing that will play into the success of the show. Viewers will want to see if I can make it happen! They'll be asking, *Will she succeed? Can she do it?*"

"But if they don't believe a man can be experienced,

good-looking, confident, *and* sensitive anyway, why would they be disappointed if you can't make it happen?"

"Because they *want* to believe it's possible. It's like a happily-ever-after ending. This show will tap into women's deep down hope that Mr. Wonderful is out there."

He shook his head. "So how's it going to work?"

Julia clasped her fingers together. "I'm going to divide the hour up into four segments. After the Primal Guy is introduced, for the first segment I'll do hair, clothes, hygiene . . ."

Ben grimaced.

"I'm going to take my rugged-looking guy and clean him up. I'll make a big visual difference right there."

"Hell, after seeing most of the guys who interviewed, you have your work cut out for you."

She gave him a look, and belatedly he realized he hadn't shaved since yesterday.

"Yeah, yeah," he grumbled, "what's after that?"

"The second segment will be on manners."

"Manners, as in eating with the right fork?"

"Yes, but also dancing, pulling out chairs, not sitting until a lady has sat, opening doors. The sort of questions he should ask a woman. In general, how to treat a woman."

"You're setting yourself up for failure. I'm telling you that for your own good."

"Why do you say that?"

"You can't change anyone."

"Sure you can. It's like leading a horse to water."

"I guess you don't remember the point of that saying."

"Of course I do. But you can't make him drink. In my

interviews, I made sure that I searched for men who were thirsty."

After a startled second, Ben laughed again. "You're priceless."

She started to preen, then physically stopped herself, which really made him want to get her to loosen up all the more. He had the urge to reach out and pull her into his lap. But he held back.

"After the manners section of the show," she continued, "I'll go to the guy's house or apartment and fix it up."

"That's a lot going on in an hour."

"And I'm not even finished yet. But remember, we are taping hours and hours that will be edited down into highlights. It's how all the reality shows are done. Heck, at *The Apprentice*, they have something like twenty-three cameras taping hundreds of hours of footage. For each hour-long show, they tape for a week, then cut it down into about forty-four minutes of programming. That's all I'm doing. Taping, editing. Which brings us to the last segment of the show. By then, the Primal Guy will be cleaned up, polite, his house will have been transformed, all in preparation for the grand finale with his date."

"You're going to show them going to bed?"

She scoffed at him in disbelief. "No! He's going to serve the lucky woman a fabulous dinner. Appetizers, champagne, the whole deal. I'll have the entire episode complete by the time Thanksgiving vacation is over."

Ben was impressed. And he told her so.

"Thank you," she said.

They sat there for a moment, sharing a surprising ease.

"So," he said after a while, "have you decided which guy to choose?"

She looked like an imp. "As a matter of fact I have."

"Why do I get the feeling I'm not going to like the answer?"

"Because I chose Rocco."

"You've got to be kidding me."

"Nope. He's perfect."

"Why is that?"

"Because he's thirsty." She smiled coyly.

"How the hell do you know that?"

"He told me. He said that there was a woman he had been trying to win, but hadn't been able to get her attention. I'm going to turn him into a man who can win her over. He's perfect."

"He's a mistake."

"If you're so convinced he's the wrong man, then you can be my Primal Guy."

"I am not a primal guy," he groused. "And I'm sure as hell nothing like Rocco."

She snorted, their quiet moment evaporating.

"Let us review a few of the questions I included on the questionnaire. Favorite pants? Rocco said jeans." She tilted over and looked at what Ben was wearing. "Surprise! Jeans."

He grumbled.

"Favorite jacket? Rocco said"—she acted out a drumroll—"leather. And what is the only coat I've seen you wear? Leather. Thank you very much. Question three—"

"Just because we dress the same doesn't make me like him."

"Let's see." She leaned forward and skewered him

with those violet eyes. "He's ruggedly masculine, outra-
geously arrogant, and thinks women were invented to
do nothing more than spread their legs to please him.
Sound familiar, big boy?"

He wasn't sure, but he might have sputtered. Shaking
it away, he leaned forward as well. "The only pleasing
that has gone on in this house is me pleasing you."

Red flared in her cheeks. Even more proof that all that
worsted wool and baggy warm-ups were starting to take
hold.

Damn.

Though why he cared he didn't know.

"Please stop!" she said. "The desk episode was a mistake." She lowered her head and mumbled. He could
have sworn she said, "An amazing mistake," but when he
pressed her, she said, "Are you angling for a compliment?"

He grinned at her.

"Anyway, Rocco is going to be perfect. I'm going
to turn him into a great guy, and Rob and Todd are
going to capture the whole thing on camera. By the
time Sterling and Chloe return, I'll have a show, Rocco
will have a date, and Todd will have a video résumé. A
win-win-win."

"So Todd hasn't been in the way?"

"No! He's great. In fact, he left some of the tape he
shot here. I looked at it on my dad's machine and it was
really good."

Her mood changed with the words. A darkness came
into her eyes, and Ben didn't think it had anything to do
with Todd, the tape, or even the show.

"You never talk about your dad," he said.

She focused, then abruptly she stood and started gathering plates. "There's nothing to talk about."

She took a handful and headed for the kitchen. Ben took the rest and followed her.

"What happened to him?"

"Why do you want to know?"

"Because you're so weird about it."

"I am not weird about it."

"Sure you are."

She scowled. "There is nothing to be weird about. He was killed in a climbing accident."

"Your father was a climber?"

"My father was an amateur adventurer. He traveled all over the world, finding new ways to get an adrenaline rush. His last adventure was on Mount McKinley. He slipped on some ice, his crampons or pitons or whatever weren't secured properly, and when he fell, there was nothing to stop his fall. End of story."

Ben stood there and studied her. He had witnessed his share of grief in people who had lost loved ones unexpectedly. With Julia it was different. She didn't give in to grief, she held on against it, as if by sheer will she could make sure she wasn't upset. Like glass about to shatter.

"I'm sorry," he said.

"Yes, so am I."

"What about your mom? Was she with him?"

"What are you doing? Going on a little fishing expedition? Trying to find out about me and my family?"

"Just curious."

She started rinsing the dishes. Ben stacked them in the dishwasher.

"No, my mom wasn't with him. She died when I was in junior high."

He felt something twist inside him for this woman. He had more family than he knew what to do with and was always complaining about the way they meddled in his life.

"What about grandparents?"

"What about them?"

"Do they live close by?"

"They died when I was little." She started to scrub the pans that couldn't go into the dishwasher.

"Aunts and uncles? Cousins?"

"My parents were only children."

"Then you're all alone."

She skewered him with a glance, her hands wet with suds. "I am not alone. I have Chloe and Kate."

"Who are busy with their own lives these days."

She scowled and scrubbed even harder.

"Sorry," he said. "You probably don't need me reminding you."

She nodded, but didn't look at him.

"Tell me about your mom."

That surprised her. "You don't want to hear about my mom."

"Sure I do."

She hesitated, then renewed her scrubbing without saying a word. But he could tell something had shifted inside her. After another pan, she actually wrinkled her nose and smiled softly.

"She wasn't anything like me. She didn't wear much makeup or girlie clothes. The most dressed up she ever got was to put on those prim suits like Nancy Reagan used to wear. She was into causes and charity work— but not the social aspect of it. Behind the scenes. On the surface she seemed boring, but more than once I caught her dancing to Donna Summer disco tunes when she thought she was alone." She laughed out loud. "Once when she saw me, I was terrified that she'd get mad that I was spying on her. Instead she pulled me into the room and got me to sing and dance 'Hot Stuff' with her."

"You knew the words?"

"No, but it didn't matter. I just danced along and moved my lips. It's the most fun I ever had with my mother."

"She sounds great."

"Yeah, I guess. I always wondered why she didn't go on trips with my dad. I used to get angry that she wasn't doing a good enough job to keep him home. I realize now that she didn't go because she wasn't invited."

She shook herself.

"If your dad was traveling all the time and your mom had died, then who raised you?"

"Everyone, no one, whoever was around."

Ben paused in the middle of drying the oversized roasting pan. "What does that mean: Whoever was around?"

"My dad had a revolving-door policy regarding the women in his life. There were a lot."

"All those wild and flamboyant women you mentioned?"

"Exactly. And they were all totally opposite of my mom. I liked some more than others. Though I'm not sure if I could drum up their names now if my life depended on it."

"So if I've got this right, your mother died when you were young, you had no relatives, and your dad was gone most of the time, leaving you alone."

She waved the comment away. "I had Zelda."

"The housekeeper?"

"You have a problem with the housekeeper?"

"Well, no. But it seems like . . . Never mind."

"Good."

Which made him chuckle. Most people couldn't stand a response of "never mind." They had to probe and dig out what had been left unsaid. Not Julia.

She looked at him and said, "Now it's your turn."

"My turn?" He finished the last pan and set it aside.

"Yes, your turn. Tell me what you were like as a kid."

He waggled his eyebrows. "I was bad to the bone and as cool as they come."

She snorted. "Unfortunately, I believe you."

"I thought you were reassessing my bad boy status—remember the prime rib remark."

"Oh, yeah, hmmm—"

He tossed the terry cloth towel onto the counter and took a step toward her.

Julia stammered, "Wh-what are you doing?"

"What does it look like I'm doing?"

He took a second step toward her, and she bit her lip.

"Tell me about your parents," she managed.

"Both my parents are living and still married."

He took another step closer, and she moved backward until she bumped into the counter.

"You met my grandmother, who is a ball of fire and keeps us all on our toes."

If he was concentrating on what he was saying, Julia couldn't tell. His gaze traveled the length of her. She couldn't seem to move away.

"You've also met Sterling and my sister, Diana."

That's when he touched her. Just barely. The tips of his fingers on the tip of her shoulder, then trailing down along the outline of her arm. A shiver ran through her.

"And, of course, you know me."

He smiled at her, a big, crooked smile that burned away any trace of darkness on his face.

"Close your eyes," he commanded softly.

"I don't think that's a good idea."

He chuckled. "Do you trust me?"

She hated to admit that despite everything she did.

"Then close your eyes."

Foolishly breathless, she did as he instructed. She had the feeling that he just looked at her for a second. Then she felt his warm hand close around her fingers, pulling them to his lips. Then his mouth pressed against her palm in a gesture that was at once innocent and intensely sexual.

She breathed in a slow and ragged breath. Heat flooded her. Then she felt the sharp bite of something else. Immediately he closed her fingers over whatever he had placed in her hand.

Her eyes flew open, but he wouldn't let her look.

"What is it?"

"A thank-you. For the mad dash to the hospital. For saying you were my wife so I wasn't left alone. And an apology for the ones that were ruined," he added cryptically.

Then he was gone, leaving her alone to open her palm. And there he had left a tiny wild pink rose made of glass.

chapter twelve

Julia had three very bad qualities. Or so her father had been fond of telling her.

She was overly curious, easily bored, and patently rebellious. Growing up with her dad after her mother died had only fanned the flames of her personality. But while she and her father had butted heads whenever he was home, she had always known he loved and cared for her. And while he was gone a lot of the time, he never once forgot her birthday. No matter where he was in the world, he always remembered to send her flowers. Red roses. Not her favorite, granted, but it was the thought that counted.

With her birthday looming just around the corner, Julia was all too aware that this would be the first year ever that she wouldn't receive roses.

Her throat tightened. She didn't care about the roses. She just wished she'd get to see her dad again. Even once. Even for half a second. Just so she could tell him she loved him.

She had always taken it for granted that he understood. Just as she had always known he loved her. But now she wondered. If he had loved her so much, why had he been so careless with his life? And why would he leave her with so much debt?

She didn't care about the money, just as she didn't care about the roses. But she cared that her father didn't seem to care for her as much as she had thought.

Which was ridiculous. He had cared. Those roses had been proof that he thought about her and wanted her to know that he loved her. And surely he had known how much she loved him.

She knew Ben wondered why she was so determined to change. Why now? Her father's death didn't seem to be answer enough. And of course it wasn't that simple. She had been wild and willful for as long as she remembered. After her father's death she felt the need to be . . . better.

She rolled the glass rose around in her palm.

It was beautiful, tiny, and delicate. And unexpected, coming from Ben.

She finished up in the kitchen, turned out the light, then headed for the opposite side of the house. Ben's light was on. She told herself to keep going, but like a moth drawn to a flame she knocked.

"Come in."

She peeked around the door. Ben sat at the desk, the laptop computer going. At the sight of her he sat back and smiled.

"What can I do for you?" he asked.

She shrugged, then entered. "I love the rose."

"I'm glad."

"It was really considerate of you."

"It was the least I could do. I wish I could have saved that damned rosebush."

She held back a grimace at the reminder of the plant that was drying up and dying. Despite his wound, and despite all her protesting, Ben had tried to replant it. But the poor bush was wilting like it didn't know how to hang on after getting torn from its nice comfortable place.

She shrugged instead. "It's just a bush."

He tilted his head and studied her. She figured he was too smart by half and might start asking questions she didn't want to answer about that bush.

"What are you *not* working on now?" she asked, with a teasing smile.

It took a second, but finally he blinked, then looked back at the screen. "Just the same old, same old," he offered. "The same old nothing."

"At least you're consistent."

As usual, Ben looked great in jeans and a T-shirt despite the November cold. He appeared a zillion times better than he had a week ago, but he still didn't seem like he was a hundred percent.

Standing, he walked over to retrieve his boots, then returned to the chair to pull them on. She could tell he swallowed back a grimace of pain. When he stood again and slipped into his leather jacket, she looked at him in confusion.

"What are you doing?" she asked.

"I've got some things to take care of."

"Things?" She jammed her hands on her hips. "You're going out?"

"Yep."

"Is someone picking you up?"

"Nope."

She shook her head as if she could shake comprehension into it. "You're driving yourself?"

"Yep."

"Did you ask the doctor about this?"

"Nope."

With a screech, she skewered him with a glare. "Yep, nope, yep, nope—can't you say anything else?"

"Nope."

She nearly launched herself at him. "The doctor said you had to wait until next week before you could drive. So you need to wait until next week."

He continued to find his keys and wallet. "Sorry, cupcake, no can do."

"Which means you are going out, driving yourself, without consent from your doctor."

He stopped in the middle of sliding his wallet into his back pocket. "Good work, Nancy Drew. Now let's go out and have a cherry soda at Woolworth's."

"Funny."

"I aim to please."

By then, she stood by his computer, more to get out of his way than anything else. She gaped at what she saw on the screen. "A dating site? You're surfing a dating site?"

That got a reaction from him, though not a good one. All that dark moodiness came surfacing in his eyes like a tsunami heading for the shore.

But just as quickly as the intensity had flared, he held it back. "Yep, dating sites."

Her eyes narrowed. "Why do you need dating sites? Why not date any one of your slew of admirers?"

"I've told you, none of them are for me."

"And a stranger on a dating site is?"

"You never know." He winked at her. "Hope springs eternal."

She hated the foolish anger she felt, anger that she had been moved by the dinner they had shared and by thinking he was kinder and deeper than she had believed. But no, she reminded herself, he wasn't deep. He was a man who got himself shot coming out of a bar and now was heading out for some kind of late-night rendezvous with a woman he'd found on the Internet.

Only a half hour after he had given her that rose!

He reached around her, logged off the computer, then headed out.

"Fine. Drive, date, find some wacko stranger online. But don't come crying to me when you're back in the emergency room or . . . or . . . dead."

He cocked his head, then came back to her, stopping so close that the tips of his boots nearly touched the tips of her sneakers. There went her pulse. There went all that liquid heat pooling in places she was trying to keep out of her mind.

"Who would have guessed that Julia Boudreaux would ever be jealous? And over me," he added, the words a sensual caress of sound.

"Dream on, Prescott. I'm not jealous, I'm disgusted."

She barely got the words out of her mouth before he leaned close. She could tell he was going to kiss her— prove her wrong—and her heart about leaped out of her chest. She had to fist her hands at her sides to keep from launching herself at him.

He nipped at the delicate skin on her neck, and she felt that amazing tingle race through her, her knees going weak when his lips trailed to her temple, then down.

But when he bypassed her mouth and went to her collarbone, she pushed away with a start of surprise.

"Why is it that you never kiss me on the lips?"

That actually startled him, then he smiled. "See, you do want me to kiss you."

"I do not." The *liar* sign was flashing off the chart in her head. "I just find it strange that you kiss me all over, do what you did under the desk, but you steer clear of kissing my lips."

"So I'm not a lip man. Sue me."

"I think you're afraid of intimacy."

He raised one dark brow, the one with the slash through it. "Need I remind you what went on under that desk?"

"That was not intimacy. It was fun, great, wow! But not true intimacy. It could be argued that kissing on the lips is more intimate in ways than having sex."

"I think you've been reading too many self-help books."

"I've never read one. I just happen to be a great student of men. You're afraid of letting people get too close."

"You're crazy. I'm not afraid of intimacy. I'm not afraid of getting too close."

Who was a liar now? she wondered with a snort.

But clearly he wasn't a man to be pressured into anything—even a kiss on the lips. He backed away to leave, though not before tapping her on the nose like she was nothing more than a pesky golden retriever.

*　　*　　*

Ben was stiff when he pulled himself into his Range Rover, but nothing that he couldn't handle. He turned around in Julia's wide drive, then headed toward downtown.

After he had posted an assortment of notices to several dating Web sites, the only thing he could do now was wait. But he wasn't good at waiting. So he decided this was a good time to pay an unexpected visit on Spazel Petralis, or Spaz as he was called on the street.

Ben knew he wasn't supposed to be driving yet, but he couldn't very well ask the slimy informant to pay a social call at Julia's. And he couldn't ask Julia to make a trip to the south side with him.

He cruised down to Pax's Cantina on Santo Domingo Avenue, where he knew he'd find Spaz. Sure enough, practically the first person he saw when he stepped inside was the thin, lanky man with the big glasses who made a big production of acting like a cool tough guy.

"Hey, Spaz."

The minute the man saw Ben, his eyes went wide, and he slunk away from the group of women he was no doubt filling with a bunch of lies.

"Hey, if it isn't Benny the Slash," Spaz said with bravado. "How's it going, my man? Long time, no see."

The grimy underbelly of this world startled Ben—which it shouldn't have. This was his world, the one he had cultivated, the one he moved within easily to get drugs off the streets. He'd never given it a thought before. But tonight, it felt like he was stepping into a shoe that no longer fit.

He told himself it was because of Henry. That this world had taken on a new edge. But Ben knew he was lying. It felt wrong because he had spent six weeks outside of this world. He had done the bodyguard gig and now was staying with Julia.

He hated the thought that the new life he was leading held some appeal.

Fuck.

"I've been tied up," Ben said coldly.

"Yeah, I heard about your dance with the wrong end of *una pistola*. I said my prayers every night for your full recovery, man. I'm glad to see they worked."

"Thanks," Ben said with sarcasm.

"So what brings you to my part of town, Slash?" Spaz sat down on the edge of a vinyl booth, crossed his legs at the knees, and ran his arm along the back of the seat bench.

"Have you heard of anyone named the Lion?"

Spaz looked confused. "The Lion? What kind of name is that?"

"Yeah, I forgot. 'Spaz' is a whole lot better than 'the Lion.' "

"Hey, don't be insulting, man."

"Cut the crap. Have you heard the name?"

"Not ringing a bell."

Ben considered the con man, could tell he was speaking the truth. "Then tell me what you've heard about Henry Baja's murder." Henry had always dreamed of going to Baja California, had used it for his street name. The fact that Ben's partner would never see the place made Ben's frustration tick even louder.

"Henry, Henry." Spaz sighed dramatically, then extended his hands in an exaggerated shrug. "I've heard nothing."

Ben picked him up by his too shiny suit and then

crowded him against the wall. "I'm guessing you have heard something. I want to know what it is."

"Look, Slash. I tell you, I haven't heard nothing other than he was stupid."

A fury that felt hot and deep raced through Ben, and before he knew it, he had Spaz pinned against the wall.

"Watch the suit, man! You're ripping the lapels."

Ben banged him again, and the bar crowd started to give them a wide berth.

"It's cheap material. Now tell me what you know or I'll rip more than the suit."

Spazel's eyes darted around. "Outside. We'll talk outside."

Ben debated, then loosened his grip. As soon as his feet were back on the ground, the lowlife hurried toward a back door. Once the men were in an alley, Ben felt a sense of déjà vu. But he didn't feel fear. He felt the same crazy need to lose himself. Spaz must have seen it, because he started spilling his guts as fast as he could.

"I really don't know nothing, man. But whoever killed Henry wasn't playing by the rules."

"There are no rules."

"Sure there are, and you know it. The killing was too harsh. Everyone says so. Too messy, making everyone nervous. Though I tell you, I blame Henry, too. He was careless and stupid."

A fissure of foreboding ran down Ben's spine.

"Why was he stupid?"

"Because he was cramping Morales's style. From everything I hear, Henry was letting it be known that he was in charge in the barrio. Crowding Morales's territory. Everyone knows Morales owns this city, especially the barrio. Henry had to know it, but didn't care."

Ben absorbed the information. He couldn't imagine that Morales would risk everything to off someone he thought was an inconsequential dealer. But if he thought that dealer was becoming a serious player, that was a different story. Ben headed for the street.

"I'd be careful if I were you, *amigo*," Spaz called out.

Ben stepped back and smiled. "But that's the thing. You're not me." He shoved a fifty into the man's shirt pocket. "And you're certainly not my friend."

Ben left the alley, every nerve ending tingling with adrenaline. He knew what he had to do next. Convince Taggart that he needed to go to Morales. Walk into the dealer's lair and see what he could find out.

To: Ben Prescott <sc123@fastmail.com>
From: j.taggart@eppd.gov
Subject: Morales

Ben, the chief has agreed to your plan to get inside Morales's hacienda. But it's just going to be done as a preliminary step, to see the lay of the land, to find out if the guy will say anything about Henry's murder.

Call when you're free and I'll fill you in on the details.

Tag

chapter thirteen

Friday, November 19.

It was nearly noon, *Primal Guy* was in full swing. Todd was getting out of school for Thanksgiving vacation, and Rob, Todd, and Rocco were scheduled to arrive at one sharp to start taping *Turn That Primal Guy into a Sweetie Pie.*

She had finalized arrangements with the hairdresser, Sonja, to come over and cut the Primal Guy's hair. Julia had surfed the Internet and thumbed through magazine after magazine to find the perfect style for Rocco's long blond tresses. He still had to look sexy, but he also had to look respectable and responsible. She had landed on the perfect style—a cross between a young Pierce Brosnan and a not-too-messy Tom Cruise. Only blond.

She'd also gone to the Fashion Place and gotten a whole slew of men's attire.

Julia paced back and forth excitedly, ready to get started. When the doorbell rang, she raced to the door and yanked it open before the chimes stopped ringing.

*   *   *

Ben hung up the phone. Everything was set. He was going to attempt to get into Morales's compound Saturday night. The plan was for backup to be in place by eight p.m., and Ben would show up shortly after that.

For now, all he could do was work the online aspect of this.

Over the next hour, he read through more than fifty responses to the posts he had placed Sunday night on the dating sites. Some were funny, some were pathetic, and several were disturbing. He decided that several of them needed further inquiry—though not regarding his pursuit of Henry's killer.

He forwarded the e-mails in question to a buddy in sex crimes division. Then he focused on three e-mails that brought up the need for money. He sent e-mail responses back, probing the issue. He'd find out soon enough if they wanted money from him, or if they were offering him ways to make some extra cash.

He had just fired off the last response to the three e-mails when the doorbell rang. He heard Julia talking to another woman. Seconds later he heard Todd and Rob arrive, and shortly after that he heard another man's voice.

He didn't know why Julia's choice of Rocco pissed him off so much. Something about the man bothered him. Despite what Julia said, he didn't have anything in common with Rocco. Just because the guy answered many of the questions on the questionnaire as he would have wasn't what bothered him. So he liked jeans, leather, and boots. And so what if he liked hot and fast women, and wasn't interested in settling down. There was more to him than that.

But seeing Russo strut around and eye Julia really got his blood boiling.

Though that wasn't why he headed for the other side of the house. Really. He wanted to see Todd.

When he walked into the kitchen, Todd was video-taping while Rob loaded his own camera. Rocco sat on a high stool without his shirt on, looking Julia over. Julia was eyeing him back.

The woman who had shown up offering her hair-styling services was there as well. Sonja. No question she was a knockout. Drop-dead gorgeous. And the minute he walked into the room, she stopped what she was doing and looked at him. She ran her eyes over him, then smiled at him with promise. Six weeks ago he would have been interested. But a lot had changed in six weeks.

"What do you think of this style?" Julia asked the hairdresser.

Sonja smiled for one last second before she turned to Julia. "It's perfect. He'll look like a totally hot banker."

Rocco grunted. Ben would have sworn Julia grimaced over the grunt.

"When you finish his hair, I'd like you to give him a manicure and a facial," Julia instructed.

"I don't need no wimpy manicure," Rocco scoffed.

Julia got a look on her face—the kind the old Julia used to get. "You signed a consent form saying that you would do whatever I said as long as I didn't cause you any bodily harm."

"All right, all right," Rocco conceded. "But no pansy-assed polish or any crap like that."

Julia whipped out a notepad. "Work on cursing and appropriate language."

Rocco groaned, and for half a second Ben actually felt sorry for the guy.

"And we wonder why men make such lousy dates," Sonja observed.

Julia eyed her curiously, then put her hand on the woman's arm. "You just haven't met the right man yet."

"Hey, Ben!" Todd enthused, his new camera rolling.

Ben instantly put his hand up. "I'm not the one you need to be filming."

Todd laughed. "Don't tell me you're camera shy."

"That's me," he responded, using his fingers to pry a cinnamon roll off of a plate—causing Julia to slap his hand and Todd to laugh as, despite instructions, he caught it all on tape.

By Saturday morning, Julia's excitement had grown tenfold. The audience was going to be wowed by the before and after shots of Rocco Russo. After less than twenty-four hours of cleaning him up, he already looked like every mother's dream date for her daughter. That is, as long as he kept his mouth shut and his eyes staring straight ahead instead of ogling female body parts.

Today she was going to work on the rest of him. After doing a great job with his hair, Sonja had returned, offering to do whatever else she could to help in the mornings that she had free. Julia was happy to have her around. She missed her friends, missed the time they spent laughing and talking. While Sonja would never take Chloe's or Kate's place, she was a lot of fun and made Julia laugh.

"What's on the list for today?" Sonja asked.

"Dancing. Speech. Polite behavior. By the end of the

day, our newly groomed bad boy needs to know how to treat a lady."

Sonja arched a brow. "Good luck. Yesterday all he had to do was sit there and get pampered. Today he'll have to do some work." She smiled at Julia. "But if anyone can do it, you can."

"Thanks. I hope you're right. I haven't been so great dealing with men recently."

"Like who?"

"My boss, for one. Ben, for another."

Sonja looked toward the door, as if she expected someone to walk in at any second. "How long have you and Ben been together?"

"Together?" She about spit out a sip of tea. "You mean as in *together* together?"

"Is there any other kind?"

"Well, ah, no, we aren't together. He's just staying here for . . . a while."

Sonja glanced back at the doorway. "Really," she said with a purr. "I bet he's a handful," she chuckled, "which is a good thing. He's handsome, elusive. Just the sort of man who gets a woman interested."

Sitting up in her chair, Julia felt yet another bite of what she swore to herself wasn't jealousy. First the dating site, now Sonja acting interested in Ben—

Interested in Ben!

The anger, jealousy, or whatever evaporated when a thought occurred to her.

Sonja was interested in Ben!

Julia had seen the way Ben looked at the beautiful woman, his heated gaze taking in her clearly great body. And now Sonja said she was interested in him. The question was what, if anything, should Julia do about it?

The doorbell rang, and Julia heard Rocco call out when he entered.

"Good morning, Rocco," she said when he walked in the door.

He pulled out a kitchen chair, slouched into it, his knees spread, his grin wide and predatory. It gave her a chill. And not a good chill.

"Hey, babe, how's it hangin'?" Then he gave Sonja a serious once-over. "Mmmm, mmmm, you're looking mighty fine this morning."

For a second, Julia thought Sonja, in all her Nordic glory, was going to body slam Primal Guy into the tea-cups on the table. But in the end, she just smiled at him like he was a troublesome child.

She might be a good match for Ben.

"Yep, that's the perfect way to impress a woman," Sonja said.

Rocco muttered something unintelligible. Julia leaped to her feet.

"That's the perfect segue into our first lesson of the day. Appropriate forms of speech."

"Great. You're going to complain about something else?"

"Now, Rocco, you want to be transformed, don't you? You said you wanted to be the sort of man who can sweep Fiona Branch off her feet."

"Yeah, well," he grumbled. "God, she's hot."

"Rule number one, no more *God, she's hot*. You can use words like *pretty, beautiful. You look fabulous* would work really well."

Rocco muttered something, but when she questioned him, he just grinned. "You're the boss."

"That's right," she stated.

In preparation of the day's work, Julia had made a meal to serve Rocco, one that he could eat while she watched and pointed out his flaws.

"Rob and Todd, are you ready?" she asked.

"Yep. Everyone take your places," Rob called out.

They worked on the place setting first, which fork to use when. She had to slap his hand when he did the same thing Ben had done. He reached over to pick up a cinnamon roll with his fingers.

"Men," she muttered.

When Rocco dragged his wrist across his mouth instead of using a napkin, she bleated, "No wrists!"

"No fingers, no wrists, no regular talk. How do you expect me to remember all of that?" Rocco complained.

"I know there's a lot," she consoled him. "So I prepared index cards for you. Between now and the big day, I want you to memorize each instruction and practice. Practice, practice, practice."

"Oh, man."

"Fiona," she reminded him.

That changed his tune, and instantly he yanked up the napkin and dragged it across his face.

Ben spent the entire day in his bedroom, finalizing the plan to meet Morales that night. By the time everything was set hours later, he could hear Julia still working. He stood, stretched, and went in search of her like he could do nothing else.

It was seven-fifteen when he found the small crew in the grand living room with the furniture pushed back and the rug rolled to the side. Julia looked exhausted. Rocco looked like he'd been run over by a Mack truck.

Sonja's perfect hair was no longer so perfect. Everyone looked beat.

He didn't have much time.

"Okay, Rocco," Julia said, drawing a deep breath. "I want you to tell me everything you do on a typical date. Then we're going to refine that. Plus I'm going to teach you how to dance."

"Ah, man. I'm worn out. Can't we do this another day?"

"No, we can't. We have to finish manners and etiquette today or we'll never wrap up the show in time."

Rocco muttered, then grunted his agreement.

"No more grunts!" Julia screeched, her exhaustion washing over her.

Rocco sighed, then said in a deep, cultured voice, "My apologies, Julia."

She actually gasped, leaped up, and clapped her hands. "See! You can do it! I knew it!" Her exhaustion was pushed back just a bit. "Now, how do you ask a woman out? How do you pick her up? Where do you go? How do you end the date?"

Rocco shrugged, jutting his head forward, and seemed to consider, then instantly forgot his good manners. "I call up some babe and say, 'Ya want to do something Saturday night?' Then I tell her where to meet me. We slug back a few brews, then I take her back to my place for a little undercover hide the hockey stick."

Rocco clearly thought that was funny.

Julia, clearly, did not. Ben had never seen such outraged disbelief on any one person's face.

"Undercover hide the hockey stick?" she sputtered.

Rob chuckled, Todd said, "Cool!" and Sonja covered a laugh.

"Yeah," Rocco said, looking pleased with himself. "I made that up."

"Why am I not surprised?" Julia said with more than a little sarcasm. "It's getting late. We've got to get to dancing."

Ben refused to think about the time he had called having sex Horizontal Hockey. He had been kidding. Really.

He wanted out of there bad. He felt anger ticking through him that was disproportionate to what was going on. But this guy was really pissing him off.

No way was he like this obnoxious guy.

The thought surprised him. Which was the only possible reason for what happened next.

When Julia asked Rocco to stand and show her how he danced, the guy took her hand and pulled her to his chest with a jarring thud, his hand running down her back until he cupped the rounded curve of her butt. A second later, Ben had Rocco up against the wall.

"Ben! What are you doing?"

"Holy crap!" Todd gasped excitedly.

"I'm showing this bastard how to treat a lady."

"Last I heard, *How to Pin Someone Against a Wall* wasn't a chapter in *Emily Post*."

Once she had pried them apart, Ben couldn't believe what had just happened.

"Geez, man," Rocco gasped, "what the hell is wrong with you?"

Ben wondered the same thing.

"He's just trying to show his own form of bad boy behavior," Julia supplied.

"You want to see a bad boy?" The words were out

of his mouth before he could think about what he was doing. Or why.

When she started to walk away, he caught her arm. Her breath snagged in her throat as her lips parted. Slowly he pulled her to him, her eyes going wide, and then he started dancing her around the room.

He held her close, could feel his own heart pounding inside him in a way that he didn't begin to understand. He guided her around the hardwood in a smooth Texas two-step. Reality faded away, and all that was left was Julia in his arms. It felt like he had been waiting for this. And the minute Rocco had touched her, he unraveled.

What he realized in that second was that he wanted her. He wanted her in a way he had never wanted a woman. Forgetting they weren't alone, he pulled back and looked at her. They stood facing each other, and he reached out and ran the backs of his fingers along her jaw.

"Wow, who knew you could dance?"

Todd's voice, and Ben felt like he'd just been doused with a bucket of ice water. It took him a second to understand what had happened.

Todd, Sonja, Rob, and Rocco stared at them.

"Oh . . . well," Julia said, the palm of her hand pressed to her cheek as if she were flushed.

Rob had the decency to stop filming. But Todd zoomed his camera in on her face.

"Todd, please," Julia said, holding her hand up to shield herself from the lens. "This isn't the sort of thing you're going to get points for on a video résumé."

"What the hell is going on around here?" Rocco wanted to know. "I'm the Primal Guy, man. Not you. So buzz off."

Ben tensed again, but it was Sonja who really got Julia's attention. Sonja looked at her with a raised brow.

Julia started to move away from Ben. "You *are* the Primal Guy, Rocco."

But Ben cut her off when he grabbed her hand and pulled her toward the front door.

"What are you doing?" she asked.

He didn't answer until the *Primal Guy* crew couldn't see them anymore. Then he turned around to face her.

"I'm going to regret the hell out of this, I know."

"Regret what?"

"This."

Then he did what he hadn't done in years. He cupped her jaw and leaned down to touch his mouth to hers.

The simple kiss of lip to lip stunned him with its intimacy. It must have been the same for her, because she clutched his arms, her fingers curling into his shirt front. Then he gave in like a starving man.

He parted her lips with his tongue, the world around them forgotten. He groaned into her mouth, tasting her. Sheer hunger drove through his body. And when her hands slid up his chest he fell into desire, giving in. He brushed his thumbs over her nipples, and her tiny moan nearly undid him.

Yes, he wanted her. So much that sense left. So much that all he wanted was to carry her back to his room and finish this. But he couldn't. Not then.

Reluctantly, he pulled back. Her violet eyes were nearly purple, her lips full and swollen from his kiss.

"I've got to go," he stated.

At first she looked disappointed. Then those eyes of hers flashed their ire.

"Go? Go where?" she asked.

"Out."

"Again?"

"Yes, again. I have work to do."

He opened the door to leave, but at the last second he turned back and cupped her cheek. When he leaned close to kiss her one last time, she couldn't have pushed away if her life depended on it. She melted into his heat, curling her fingers into his jacket.

After a second he pulled away. "Damn," he said, but he was smiling.

Then he turned around and was gone.

Dazed, she barely noticed that Todd was standing there until he spoke.

"You're not as smart as I thought you were if you like him," the teen said with surprising venom.

He shook his head and started away. She grabbed his arm. "What was that supposed to mean?"

"Nothing," he practically snarled.

"Todd? What do you mean?"

He cursed angrily. "Him and his work. Just like my dad."

A shiver ran down her spine. "What is just like your dad?"

"He was always leaving." He nodded toward the door. "Just like Ben."

She couldn't imagine where this was coming from. "But Ben had to leave. He said he had work to do."

The boy scoffed. "Yeah, work. Just like my dad."

Her stomach clenched. "What did your dad do?"

"He was a businessman." He snorted. "And he traveled a lot."

"What kind of business, Todd?"

"He sold stuff."

"What kind of stuff?"

He shrugged. "I don't know. Hard to get answers from a guy who was never around. Not that I would believe whatever he said anyway."

"Why do you say that?"

"Hey, don't look at me like that. My mom didn't believe him, either."

"How do you know that?"

"I heard her tell him." He rolled his eyes. "I heard her yell it at him. Like a thousand times."

She searched her brain for any kind of a response. "All parents fight, Todd."

"Yeah, right, that was my parents. Just a couple of regular joes." He retrieved his video case. "It's late. I gotta go."

"Wait. Talk to me."

"No way. I just want to get my video résumé done so I can get into the workshop."

To: Katherine Bloom <katherine@ktextv.com>
From: Julia Boudreaux <julia@ktextv.com>
Subject: Men

Who needs them? Especially to marry. With the exception of
Sterling and Jesse, I can't think of a single man who is simple
and straightforward.

xo, j

To: Julia Boudreaux <julia@ktextv.com>
From: Katherine Bloom <katherine@ktextv.com>
Subject: re: Men

Where did this come from?

Kate

Katherine C. Bloom
News Anchor, KTEX TV, West Texas

To: Katherine Bloom <katherine@ktextv.com>
From: Julia Boudreaux <julia@ktextv.com>
Subject: re: Men

A teenage boy.

xo, j

To: Julia Boudreaux <julia@ktextv.com>
From: Katherine Bloom <katherine@ktextv.com>
Subject: No!

Tell me you aren't dating boys now!!

K

To: Katherine Bloom <katherine@ktextv.com>
From: Julia Boudreaux <julia@ktextv.com>
Subject: re: No!

No, I'm not. You forget that I've sworn off dating anyone but appropriate, responsible men. Which means I'm not dating at all because that man doesn't exist. It's enough to explain why a vibrator is all a woman really needs. Forget men. But a vibrator with extra-long battery life is priceless.

xo, j

To: Julia Boudreaux <julia@ktextv.com>
From: Katherine Bloom <katherine@ktextv.com>
Subject: The problem . . .

. . . with vibrators is that they don't send you birthday cards or take you out for a romantic dinner. And you certainly can't cuddle up to one in front of a fire.

To: Katherine Bloom <katherine@ktextv.com>
From: Julia Boudreaux <julia@ktextv.com>
Subject: re: The problem . . .

I could try.

xo, j

To: Julia Boudreaux <julia@ktextv.com>
From: Katherine Bloom <katherine@ktextv.com>
Subject: Another problem

Yeah, you could try, but it would probably melt. <g>

chapter fourteen

It was dark when Ben drove west on Country Club Road toward Santa Teresa, New Mexico, and the sprawling golf course Lee Trevino had developed decades ago.

He didn't wear a wire or carry a gun, despite the fact that he was going in to see the biggest drug lord in the region. Carlos Morales.

Ben couldn't risk it since they would undoubtedly frisk him when he entered. That is, if he could get inside.

Ben knew it was crazy to walk into the Morales camp alone. But he felt crazy these days, felt something deep and burning pushing him on. But he wasn't worried about the danger. All Taggart wanted was for him to get the lay of the land, poke around a little bit. All Ben wanted was to see Morales's reaction when he asked about Henry. The reaction would tell a lot.

He took the fork in the road that turned into Westside Drive. He headed north now, along the two-lane road that was lined by a private tennis club and the adobe shacks that had remained resistant to gentrification. The Morales compound was a sprawling hacienda just before the New Mexico border. A tall adobe wall surrounded the house, and thick wooden gates blocked an interior view. And the placement of guards around the perimeter made it look more like a prison than a home.

Years ago an infamous lawyer, reported to have unsavory ties, had lined his walls with curled barbed wire in an attempt to stay safe. But the man's enemies didn't have to get to him at home. He was gunned down in his office on a holiday when no one was around.

Morales, it was said, wasn't going to make the same mistake. The man rarely left the hacienda. Which, Ben had often thought, explained why he did insane things. Imprisoned behind his own walls, Morales had drug money and drug power, bringing him a long way from the days of growing up on poverty-filled dirt streets in Juárez. But money hadn't bought him freedom.

Ben pulled up to the gate. Surveillance cameras buzzed over to focus on him. A second passed before the intercom beeped on.

"Yes?"

"It's Slash. Benny the Slash." He wouldn't have suspected he had backup if he didn't know they were already in place—not that they would do any good once he was inside. "I'm here to see Morales."

"You *estúpido*! No one comes here looking for *Señor* Morales."

"There's a first time for everything." He bit back his own desire to give the twerp behind the intercom a sharp set down. He wanted to get inside. "Just tell him I'm here, and I'll disregard the *stupid* remark."

The man took a few seconds, as if debating, then said, "*Señor* Morales is busy."

Now that was original.

"I'm sure he is. I'm busy, too. But I need to talk to him—"

"I told you, you stupid—"

"Look, buddy, I'm having a bad day. I really don't have time for this. I have a lucrative business proposition that I think he'll be interested in. Now, are you going to tell Morales I'm here, or do I have to sit here until he notices something's going on at his front gate?"

The man on the other end cursed colorfully in Spanish, then beeped off.

A full five minutes passed before the gate swung open, the slow, graceful sweep revealing the sprawling adobe mansion at the end of the long curving drive made of crushed terra cotta. The entire compound was flooded with light.

Sweat ran down Ben's back. He was going in. But he relished it, relished going in, relished doing something productive rather than sitting in a frilly bedroom surfing the Internet in hopes of catching a break. Posting notes, getting responses from a variety of crackpots and lunatics, but finding not a thing that led him to hold any hope of solving Henry's murder.

He didn't see a soul as he drove up the drive. But he knew he was far from alone. It was eerie how isolated he felt, watched but cut off from the rest of the world as the gates closed ominously behind him.

He parked in front of the main house in a wide area filled with BMWs, Mercedes, and a Hummer. Nice cars for a man who rarely, if ever, went out.

The minute Ben put the Rover into park and opened

the door, he was met by a big man with an even bigger gun. Ben doubted the firearm was registered. A lot of firepower for a man who claimed he was a simple merchant who imported *pintas* and sold them around the world.

"I'm here to see Morales," Ben said.

The big guy grunted and used the tip of the machine gun to direct him. A wordless, not to mention dangerous, *This way*. Ben assumed there was no *Please* tacked on to the silent command.

Two more guards met them at the front door, both wielding guns. A third appeared out of the shadows and frisked him. Finally, when Ben was nudged into the house, he stepped into an indoor courtyard filled with birds, a fountain, and thick green flowering plants. The only sound that reminded him that he wasn't in a South American jungle was the buzzing of the surveillance camera following him along the brick path that ended with another guard waiting at an archway leading into the house.

For all the people he was encountering, not a single word was uttered. He could think of a few people back on Meadowlark Drive who could stand a lesson or two in silence.

Which made him think of Julia. Which made him feel a moment of regret that he had walked into this crazy situation with an unpredictable drug lord.

And suddenly the thought of not finishing off what he had started in her office made him wish he had waited a few days before setting out on this insane path. Sex first. Die later.

Which was idiotic and proved just how much Julia Boudreaux had rattled his brain. He might want Julia, and want her more than he had wanted any woman, but it was in a purely sexual way. She made his body burn, his balls get tight, his dick go instantly hard. But he wasn't about to change his life for any woman, least of all a woman who didn't know the first thing about who she was anymore. Though he had to admit he was impressed that she was trying to make something different out of her life after she decided she needed to change. Most people stayed as they were, taking the path of least resistance. But not Julia.

"If it isn't the infamous Benny the Slash."

Ben cursed his lost concentration. When he focused, he saw that they had come to a study of sorts. A room filled with books and paintings and artificial light since there wasn't a single window on any of the four walls.

Morales was a short man with a full head of thick, curly dark hair. He sat behind a massive hand-carved desk, smiling at Ben when he entered. He had seen the man in surveillance photos before, but in person he looked smaller.

"You must have very big *cojones,* or you are very *estúpido,*" the drug lord said with a high-pitched noise that sounded like a giggle.

Ben shrugged with an indifference he didn't feel. "I guess we'll find out which by the end of the visit, you think?"

Morales laughed even louder, then stood. He was a good foot shorter than Ben, and he wore a western shirt with turquoise snaps tucked into tight western pants that ended in overly pointed cowboy boots made of alligator skin. A cowboy hat with a matching alligator band hung from a hook by the door.

Morales didn't offer to shake Ben's hand. He came

around to the front of the desk and leaned back against the edge. "Why are you here?"

"I want to do some business."

"What kind of business?"

"I need someone to move product for me."

Morales's black eyes narrowed dangerously. But Ben forged ahead.

"I'm having trouble distributing. I have a backlog of quality product, all because street dealers are nervous these days and lying low. I was told that if anyone could move product, it was you."

Morales crossed his arms on his chest, tucking his fingers in his armpits. "I heard you were a ballsy one."

"I'm not ballsy. I'm just a supplier whose business is suffering because Henry Baja was shot, making everyone on the street nervous."

The dealer's eyes narrowed, and Ben could see the wheels turning in his head. Morales was smarter than most dealers. He had pulled himself up through the ranks of hundreds to become the most successful of them all. But he had started making mistakes. And Morales was smart enough to know the mistakes were costing him. Ben could see it in his expression.

"Who cares about one dead street punk? There are plenty more where he came from," Morales said dismissively.

Fury burned through Ben like a wildfire. But he held it in check. Ben could tell Morales's tone was forced. And something else occurred to him. Standing in the middle of a ruthless killer's fortress, Ben realized that Morales didn't know anything about Henry being undercover EPPD.

Ben's eyes narrowed as his brain spun. "He might

have been just one guy selling dope on street corners, but the killing seemed random to the rank and file. If it happened to that guy for no apparent reason, it could happen to them just as easily. You've gotten everyone worked up. It's hard to do business in this climate. No one's sure who to worry about more, you or the police."

Morales jerked away from the desk, his nearly black eyes flaring with anger. The guards in the room leaped to attention as well, their guns drawn.

Either Morales didn't notice or he didn't care. He started cursing and muttering in Spanish. Ben had lived in Texas long enough to get the gist of the conversation. The man wasn't pleased about the killing—which surprised Ben.

Morales cursed, banging his fist against the desk, every ounce of playing it cool gone. "I know this has screwed everything up. If I find out who did it, I will make them pay."

"Then you didn't do it?"

"Hell, who are you? The *policía*?" He sneered. "The police couldn't solve this crime if their lives depended on it. But I wish they would so we could get back to business." He spat. "And no, I didn't do it. There was no finesse."

"Then who did?"

"I don't know." He spewed profanity. "But rumor has it that Henry Baja had woman trouble, the sort that got him killed by some jealous husband or something. Can you believe it! You're not the only one suffering from this. Some dumb fuck does something stupid, and no one will move my product!"

Ben stared at Morales, the hairs on the back of his neck standing up.

"What?" the dealer demanded.

"It's just that I heard Baja went down doing a deal. I didn't hear anything about a woman."

"There was no deal going down. Though I wouldn't be surprised if some *puta* was *going down* on him." He laughed with a wicked sneer. "Now get the fuck out of here before I decide I'm really pissed off that you showed up uninvited. Until things settle down, no one's doing any business, *comprende*?"

Ben didn't breathe again until the massive wooden gates closed behind him. He retraced his path along Westside Drive, flipping open his cell phone and checking in with the team of ghosts shadowing this operation. He hardly heard what was said. He felt numb.

Henry. What the fuck had he been doing?

His thoughts were chewing through his head, and he blew right by the turnoff to Julia's house. He didn't think. He drove. He drove until he pulled up to his old apartment, then finally remembered he didn't live there anymore.

He pulled back out of the parking lot, then found himself heading to the alleyway where Henry was killed. The bloodstain was still there—no rain in weeks to wash it away. But that was all there was. No people, nothing to give him a clue what had gone wrong that night.

It was late when he finally returned to Julia's. The small light over the stove was still on, like a night-light in the dark. All traces of Primal Guy and the show were gone.

He was quiet. He didn't want to see Julia because he knew he was tired and his thigh hurt like hell.

When he finally got into the shower, the question that had been at the back of his mind finally came to the forefront. Had Henry's murder been about more than poor judgment and pushing too far? Had Henry started to live the life he was only supposed to pretend to lead? Had he gotten caught up in something illegal? And if that was true, Ben wondered if he had played a part in his partner's fall from grace.

Julia paced the length of her office. She had tried to write off what Todd had said. But it hadn't worked. She had heard Ben come home, heard him walk quietly past her darkened office, then disappear back in his bedroom.

She told herself to go to bed, to talk to Ben in the morning. But her stomach churned with anger and worry. It also churned with disappointment that she was wrong about Ben.

When she couldn't stand it anymore, she marched down the hall, across the entry hall, then down the opposite wing. She pushed through Ben's door without knocking. Which was a mistake.

She froze at the sight of him. He looked wild and fierce and sexy as hell. There was one other thing that had her rooted to the spot.

"You're naked," she said, her voice barely audible.

It took a second for him to bank the wildness. But finally he appeared like an animal back on the leash. Barely.

"I generally take off my clothes when I shower."

She noticed the damp shoulders and the towel tossed aside.

"What do you want?" he asked, his tone seething.

"Oh, ah . . ." She tried to remember. "We need to talk."

"I'm not interested in talking. So leave."

"Sorry. Can't."

His expression shimmered with barely contained anger. His sex was full but not hard, hanging down against his thigh, the nest of curls at the base as black as midnight. Every inch of his body was strong and finely chiseled. His chest was no exception.

Her heart hammered away as he looked at her through heavy-lidded and intent eyes. His gaze raked over her face, to her throat, then down to her breasts.

Her throat went dry and she had to forcefully clear her thoughts. "If you're dealing drugs, I don't want you in my house."

She blurted the words out, and his head jerked back as if she had hit him.

"What the hell are you talking about?"

"You, and whatever it is you do."

"We've been over this, Julia."

"I know. But I can't keep my head in the sand anymore. I mean really. Benny the Slash—the import/export guy?" She shook her head, picked up a discarded towel, and threw it at him.

He caught the terry cloth, and after a fierce second, he wrapped it around his waist.

"I tried to believe you," she continued, finally able to breathe, "partly because I couldn't believe you'd be involved in anything . . . well, illegal—"

"Hell."

"—and partly because I don't believe for a second that Chloe or even Sterling would put me in danger. But I've reassessed. They wouldn't *knowingly* put me in danger. I doubt Sterling Prescott has any clue that you do the majority of your business at such odd hours."

"You don't know what you're talking about."

"Don't I? I don't believe you really hang out in bars in south El Paso just for grins, any more than I believe that your getting shot was just you winning the *unlucky* lotto."

If he looked dangerous before, he looked really dangerous now, the leash long gone.

"Is that what you think?" he asked ominously. "Let me start by saying I have gotten plenty of *grins* while I was drinking in seedy bars. In fact, in the weeks between playing babysitter to Chloe's show and the night I got shot, I was lost in a haze of alcohol and seedy bars—just me in a bar, hanging out, getting as drunk as I could."

He took a step toward her. The danger in him grew worse. He looked caught and cornered.

"But you're right," he added. "That isn't why I got shot. I got shot looking for a killer who never should have had the chance to shoot Henry."

She blinked in confusion, and her dread grew. "Henry, as in Todd and Trisha's dad? He was murdered?"

"Yes. My partner was murdered."

"Partner?"

"I'm a cop. Obviously not a good cop, since my partner was all alone when it happened." His jaw tightened. "I should have been there."

Julia tried to absorb the words. Ben was a cop?

A cop whose partner was killed and who didn't know how to move beyond that. That explained the odd work hours and his inability to sleep. It also explained the darkness that was never far from his eyes.

The pieces fell into place like the one section of a puzzle that finally gives meaning to the whole. It made sense. And it filled her with relief. She hadn't been completely wrong about him. He was a bad boy, yes, but he wasn't a drug dealer or worse.

"If I had been there, it never would have happened."

She looked at him in disbelief. "Were you supposed to be there? Did you sleep in and fail to show up on the job?"

He muttered an oath.

"I'll take that as a no. Which I'm sure is the truth since you are a lot of things . . . ornery, arrogant, difficult—"

"Is there a point coming up any time soon?"

"Sorry, got a little carried away."

She smiled. He didn't.

Clearing her throat, she continued. "It's just that you're many things, but irresponsible isn't one of them. If you weren't there for him, there was a reason. I'm certain of that."

He glowered at her.

"And let me add this, Mr. Thinks He Needs to Carry the World on His Shoulders, if you had been there, who's to say you wouldn't both be dead?"

She felt the cold hard edge that swept through him, but no denial. He was furious, but she also saw that beneath the anger was a palpable vulnerability. If she hadn't seen it with her own eyes, she never would have believed it possible of this man. On the surface he was a hard-ass cop. It all made sense now. But there was a kindness beneath it all. Which explained why he had taken the job as bodyguard for Chloe's show. And why now he was trying to be a father to two teenagers. He was trying to be a good man even if he didn't know the first thing about two lost kids.

He started to turn away from her, and without thinking, she crossed the room. When she touched him, he flinched.

"Ben—"

But the look in his eyes stopped her cold. A fathomless pit of darkness and anger swelled in his eyes.

"Julia," he warned ruthlessly.

A shiver of concern raced down her spine, but she wasn't about to let him intimidate her. She raised her chin.

"You'd be wise to go to your own room," he added a second later, but with no less determination.

She suspected he was right. But she didn't see how she could walk out on him when he was clearly hurting.

"That's the thing," she said. "I never seem to do anything wise when it comes to you."

"Fuck."

"Hey, hey," she said with a smile she hoped would be catching, "I wasn't thinking that, but a little friendly conversation wouldn't be inappropriate."

She got more than she bargained for.

With a fierce growl, or maybe a cry, he pulled her close so quickly and easily that she didn't have a chance to think, much less react. The towel dropped away and he held on to her, his face buried in her hair. When she tried to talk, he kissed her.

All those times that he hadn't touched her mouth—as if it was an intimacy beyond what he was willing to give. Now it was like he consumed her. Finally giving in and not able to get enough.

She felt his groan, the sound rumbling through him as he took her hand and pressed it to his chest. If she had wanted to, she could have pulled free. But she couldn't seem to do it despite the fact that her mind was screaming alerts like a ship going down.

She couldn't seem to help herself when her hand drifted lower. She swallowed hard at the feel of his flat stomach, and her breath caught at the hungry look that stirred to life in his eyes. He wanted her. She sensed it.

It felt like a taste of sugar after being deprived of sweets. Or maybe it was like a taste of water after a long desert journey. She had lived a lifetime with men appreciating her. But she had done without. Wanted to do without. But like a dieter giving in, she relished the feel of the desire that she could see in his eyes.

Then he pressed his hand to hers, lowering it even farther.

She inhaled deeply when her fingers wrapped around him and he swelled hard in her hands. She stroked him, cupped him.

"Do you feel that? Do you feel how much I want you?" he asked, his voice hoarse and gravelly.

But before she could answer, he took her hand away and kissed her again. She leaned into him, feeling a mix of desire and confusion. She didn't understand why she couldn't resist him—what it was about this man who made her forget all her good intentions.

But right then she didn't care.

His hands trailed back to her shoulders, then down her spine, molding her to him.

She moaned, hot and pliant in his arms as she closed her eyes. Heat flared between them, the heat that was never far away, smoldering. Clinging to him, Julia kissed him back boldly.

The last of his restraint vanished. He brushed his thumb over her lips, touched her body, savoring her. He sucked her lower lip in his mouth, his teeth nipping, before he slid his hands into her hair. Gently he pulled her head back to expose the arch of her neck. And when she reached up and wrapped her arms around his shoulders, she felt as if he had been waiting for this forever.

The intensity grew, his erection pressing against her.

"Julia," he murmured with a ragged voice.

With infinite care, he kissed her again, the sound of a soft mewling coming from deep within her. Gently, he coaxed her lips apart until their tongues intertwined. She wanted to make love. Consequences be damned.

But that was the problem.

Just as suddenly as the intimacy had started, she stopped it, pushing away from him.

His eyes flashed dark, and he would have grabbed her back if she hadn't leaped away.

"We can't do this."

"Why?"

"Because."

"Not good enough."

He started for her again, but she held out her hand. "I promised myself that I wouldn't have any more . . . casual affairs." What else could she call the relationships she had had with men? They might not have been casual, but they had never been committed. She made a point of picking and choosing, then moving on when they became too attached. She didn't want attached. But somehow with Ben, she couldn't think in those terms any longer. She couldn't think of picking and choosing, then moving on. But she also couldn't imagine them working together long term. "Can you possibly think this, you and me, would ever be anything more than casual?"

That stopped him.

"I didn't think so," she said, inwardly cringing at his unspoken acknowledgment of the truth, even though at an even deeper level she was grateful for it. She hated men who lied. Ben Prescott didn't lie.

"What's wrong with two consenting adults who clearly want each other finding a few hours of oblivion?" he asked, all that darkness that was never far away surfacing in his eyes.

If she hadn't liked his unspoken acknowledgment of the truth a few minutes before, she hated the reality that this man thought of her as nothing more than oblivion. But why shouldn't he? She was the one who had cupped his balls in the middle of World's Gym. She was the one who had exaggerated her experience with men—not that she was some lily-white virgin. She only had herself to blame that he would think mindless, unattached sex would be perfectly fine with her.

She moved away. "If you're seeking oblivion," she said tightly, "I suggest you go back to one of your seedy bars . . . or do some more surfing on those Internet dating sites. I'm sure you could find plenty of women seeking oblivion there."

His eyes narrowed dangerously.

But she didn't care. She left the room, swallowing back ridiculously hurt feelings.

To: Ben Prescott <sc123@fastmail.com>
From: j.taggart@eppd.gov
Subject: Report

Ben, your report feels incomplete. There's plenty of description of Morales, his compound, and the weaponry, but there's very little about the conversation you had. You were in there for a good thirty minutes. All he said was that he didn't know anything about Henry?

Also, I just found out that they found two blood types in the alleyway. Henry's and another. No ID on the second type, but we suspect someone else was wounded that night.

Tag

To: j.taggart@eppd.gov
From: Ben Prescott <sc123@fastmail.com>
Subject: re: Report

Tag, thanks for letting me know. I'll do some legwork on that today. Hospitals, morgues, etc. Can you run reports on missing persons?

As to Morales, he wasn't interested in talking. Sorry I didn't get more.

Ben

To: Ben Prescott <sc123@fastmail.com>
From: j.taggart@eppd.gov
Subject: re: Report

Why do I find that hard to believe? Why do I think you learned something you are keeping to yourself? Let me tell you, Benny, if I find out you are doing anything crazy, I'll have you taken off the case so fast your head will spin. I don't want two dead cops on my hands. Understood? Don't piss me off, Ben.

Taggart

To: j.taggart@eppd.gov
From: Ben Prescott <sc123@fastmail.com>
Subject: re: Report

Me, piss anyone off? <g>

chapter fifteen

She could no longer deny she was obsessed with Ben Prescott. Nor could she deny he still believed she was an easy, wild woman. But how to explain at this point that having fun and living boldly in the past didn't mean she was easy, especially when she wanted—no, craved—to leap into bed with a man whom she didn't even like that much. *That* would be wild, easy, and idiotic.

Sure, she had a better understanding of him now. He was a cop. But still, his predatory arrogance appealed to her only on a sexual level.

And that was the thing—she was bigger than that, more mature, not ruled by lust or her body. Despite what Ben thought.

The new Julia Boudreaux didn't give in to every whim just because she felt like it. She was responsible now, and quite frankly, she was rather proud of the fact that she hadn't given in to the draw of simple, unattached sex with a man who was sure to be dynamite in bed. She was above that now.

But more than that, she had to prove to herself that she could follow something through—that she could succeed with something she had set out to do. Ben, however, was proving to be a distraction that was too tempting to ignore.

Which meant she had to come up with a way to effectively make Ben off limits.

But what?

Since she couldn't kick him out of her house, the only other solution was to find him a date. If he became interested in some woman, then he'd be out of her hair, taken . . . off limits. And if there was one thing she knew about herself, it was that she never wasted time with taken men.

But he had told her flat-out that he wasn't interested in any of the women who called regularly. He needed to find someone new. And while he was all over those dating sites, he didn't seem to be finding anyone there.

Her brain started to grind until she came up with a solution. *She* would find him a date. She'd find him a wonderful, available woman who would consume his interest.

And she already knew who that person was.

Sonja.

It was perfect . . . or at least it was as perfect as her setting up a man like Ben on a date was going to get.

She fell asleep encouraged, and by the time she woke the next morning, she was convinced that it was the perfect plan. But when she went in search of him to tell him what she was going to do, he wasn't there.

A frisson of surprise raced through her at the thought that he'd finally had enough and moved out. Was she happy? Was she disappointed? She didn't have a chance

to study her conflicting emotions. Although the Range
Rover was gone, she found that his clothes and belong-
ings were still strewn about like party decorations. He'd
be back. Which meant she still had to do something to
get him out of her mind.

Julia decided to go over to Sonja's house right then
and put her plan into action. Picking up the phone, she
called the number Sonja had left. But the answering machine picked up.

*"This is Sonja at Sonja's Salon. I'm working and can't
come to the phone right now. Leave a message and I'll
get back to you as soon as I can."*

Not wanting to wait, Julia found her keys and headed
for the address Sonja had given her for the salon.

Julia drove to a small residential area by Putnam Ele-
mentary School. The address Sonja had given was for a
tiny house on a busy corner. Julia pulled up along the
side of the house where the salon entrance stood. A sign
over the side door read *Sonja's* in a fancy script.

Rather than going around to the house's front door,
Julia went to the salon entrance on the side. The smell of
hair spray and shampoo greeted her when she opened
the door.

"Julia!" Sonja exclaimed, clearly surprised. She held
a curling iron in her hand away from the head of a
woman whose hair was done up in a 1950s beehive.
Sonja had just finished curling tendrils that now hung
down the woman's neck.

Julia stared and wondered what kind of woman wore
beehives in the twenty-first century.

"What brings you here?" Sonja asked, setting the
curling iron aside and taking out a can of Aqua Net hair
spray.

The whole thing had a definite 1950s feel to it.

"Well," Julia began, "I actually came by because I wanted you to . . . come to dinner."

"Me?"

The woman in the chair pulled off her smock, paid, then left.

"Yes, you. And Ben."

"Ben?"

Sonja was breathless with anticipation. Which reassured Julia that she was doing the right thing—even if her mind flashed green with an emotion that she refused to say was jealousy. It was clear Sonja liked Ben, and that was all that mattered.

"Yes, Ben. It'll be fun," Julia answered. "I was thinking tonight at six-thirty."

"I'll be there!"

It wasn't until Julia was driving away, the reality of her plan on the verge of coming to fruition, that she finally wondered if this date thing was such a good idea.

Ben drove along Paisano Drive in south El Paso. Determination beat through him—determination and the need to find answers.

Two blood types.

Who had been in the alleyway with Henry?

Ben intended to find out if someone else had been hurt badly enough that they had left blood in the alley. He would check hospitals, clinics, and the morgue, while Taggart checked missing persons.

Trolling El Paso hospitals took him until noon. But he found no information on patients with suspicious lacerations or gunshots, no dead bodies with bloody wounds. There were plenty of drownings, not to mention indigent and homeless deaths. But none of those had bled before dying. Standard hospitals proved to be a dead end.

The city morgue provided no help either. By two-thirty, an exhaustion that had nothing to do with lack of sleep ticked through him. But he ignored it. He started on the list of small-time clinics in bad parts of town that might not be as inclined to report mysteriously wounded people as a traditional hospital that wanted to protect its funding. But by six he had to concede that he wasn't going to find a trace of the second person—at least not this way. Either the second person had helped themselves, was dead and not yet found, or someone was covering for them.

At six-twenty, Ben headed back to Julia's place frustrated, his temples pounding, his leg throbbing like a bitch. When he walked through the back door and she let out a relieved *"Finally!"* he wasn't in the mood.

"Where have you been?" she demanded.

"You sound like a wife."

"I do not! But the least you could have done was leave a note. Something, anything. For all I knew you were lying dead in an alleyway somewhere."

He held out his arms. "I'm not dead. Happy?"

He saw the tension drain out of her, and those lush lips of hers turned down in a pout. Julia, pouting. It was a sight to see, and one that eased his own tension.

He stood there for a second, pulling a deep breath at the same time he dragged his hands through his hair. Again he felt an ease try to push through him, push out the insanity that had dogged him for almost two months now. All she had to do was look at him and somehow this new nightmare world of his seemed manageable.

He could tell she expected him to say something, but right then he didn't trust words. He wasn't sure if he would curse or drag her close and never let go. Both of which were crazy, not to mention weak.

"Happy that you're not dead?" she asked with a teasing scoff. "That depends on my mood. Right now I'm just glad you're back."

As usual, she made him laugh.

"Really?" he said. "You're glad that I'm back?"

He took a step toward her and her eyes went wide.

"Yes," she blurted out. "Because I have a . . . surprise. Yes, a surprise!" She ran over to him, turned him around, and pushed him toward the door. "Go take a shower and clean up. But you've got to hurry."

"Why?"

He allowed her to push him out of the kitchen, but the minute he was in the long hall, he caught sight of the dining room.

"What's all that for?" he asked carefully.

Julia froze, but only for a second, before she renewed her efforts to keep him going—this time with little success. "Dinner?" she said with a sigh when she gave up.

"You say it like a question. Dinner for who?"

"You?"

"Enough with the tentative tone. What's going on, Julia?"

The doorbell rang, and she squeaked.

"She's here! And you haven't even showered."

"Who's here?" His tone was ominous.

So much for any improvement in his mood.

"Your date."

"What?"

The word kind of exploded out of him, and Julia

knew it wasn't a good sign. "Well, I was thinking about how you clearly are in need of a woman."

If she had thought he was arrogantly predatory before, all he was now was predatory and dangerous. Ben looked mad as Hades.

"What have you done, Julia?"

"I set you up on a date!"

The look on his face was priceless. A stunned mix of incredulity and the need to murder someone. Namely her. She took a step back and smiled.

"I saw the way Sonja looks at you—"

"Sonja!"

"And you can't deny that you gave her a pretty serious once-over."

The doorbell rang again.

"Ben, really, I can't leave her outside. It's rude."

"I'll show you rude."

"You already are."

He glowered at her. She started pushing him toward the bedrooms once again. "You have to hurry."

"I'm going to hurry, all right. Hurry out of here and not come back down until she's gone."

"You can't do that!"

"Try me."

"Ben, please. She likes you."

Ben rolled his eyes, so she went at it from a different direction. "If you aren't here, it will hurt her feelings badly. Are you really so callous that you'd knowingly hurt a woman's feelings?"

"Yes."

"Yes?" Not the answer she had hoped for. "I can't believe you even try to deny being a primal guy!"

"Believe it, babe. I'm outta here."

He marched down the hall like a furious general. Julia groaned.

"Chicken!" she called after him.

He only grunted.

"I knew you were a Neanderthal, but I didn't know you were . . . were . . . mean!"

He only grunted again.

But fifteen minutes later, while she and Sonja were talking in the kitchen—Julia trying to find a nice way to tell Sonja that her date hadn't been willing to participate— she was surprised when Ben reappeared.

He came through the door like some knight in shining armor, ready to save the day. Even wearing jeans, or maybe because he was wearing jeans, he looked like everything she loved in a man. Deeply sensual and bad to the bone.

Sonja whistled—really whistled—and he laughed and bowed.

Julia was charmed, and after a quick glance at Sonja, she was sure she was, too.

Ten minutes later the three of them sat around the dining room table, eating the feast Julia had prepared. They started with an assortment of cheeses matched with a complementary taste. Blue cheese served with walnuts, Gouda served with dried plums, farmers cheese served with dried apricots, all to be eaten on homemade cranberry walnut bread. Next came salad, followed by rack of lamb, rosemary potatoes, and wilted spinach.

Sonja looked at Julia and smiled shyly. "This is so sweet of you," she said.

Julia was moved by the woman's emotion. "Thank you."

"I mean, who would have thought to pair cheeses

with dried fruit and serve it on a fancy bread. I've never seen so much food."

"You really have outdone yourself," Ben added with a quirk of a grin.

"Well," Julia said, smiling pointedly at Ben, "I spent most of the day worried. Some people eat when they're worried. Others drink or exercise. I cook."

"You must have been incredibly worried," Sonja remarked, awed at the meal.

Julia dismissed the comment. "So tell me, Sonja, what movies have you been to lately?"

That's all it took.

Soon Ben and Sonja were talking about the latest action-packed thriller, laughing over some implausibility.

Julia stood abruptly. "I'm not feeling so well. Could you excuse me?"

Sonja looked pleased.

Ben looked pissed.

Julia bolted before Ben could grab her hand and make her stay.

Once she had made it to the relative safety of her room, she decided to spend what she hoped would be hours by getting ready for the next day of taping the show. Rocco was so primal it was wonderful. But she worried that he would never get it right. And she wasn't sure if all her carefully written-out notes were going to help him or not.

But all thoughts about the show fled when she heard the front door open, then close. A quick glance at the clock confirmed that only a matter of minutes, maybe twenty, had passed since she left the table.

She flew out of her room, careened toward the dining room, and found it empty.

"Ben?! Sonja?"

"In here."

She launched into the kitchen. Ben stood at the counter with the chocolate crème pie she had made, eating right out of the pan. Sonja was nowhere to be seen.

"What happened?" Julia blurted out.

He turned around, a tiny smudge of whipped cream on his lip. She felt an instant jab of desire to wipe it off. Heck, who was she kidding? She wanted to kiss it off.

"What did you do to run her off so fast?"

He took another big bite of pie and chomped with exaggerated pleasure.

She rolled her eyes and groaned. "You probably grabbed her by the hair and threatened to drag her into your cave."

He raised a brow. With good reason, she conceded. In fact, she wasn't sure exactly why she was so upset—unless it was because deep down she was relieved.

"I didn't do anything," he said, then took another bite. "Plus, you might have warned me that she's a talker. Good God, she's worse than you."

She marched over and yanked the spoon—not even a fork!—out of his hand. "Don't try to change the subject. Tell me why she left so soon."

Unfazed and clearly unrepentant, he retrieved another spoon from the cutlery drawer and unabashedly scooped up another bite. "God, this is good pie."

"Do you have the ability to carry on an intelligent conversation?"

"Sure, if it's a conversation worth having."

"This conversation is worth having! Why did Sonja walk out on your date?"

"Not a *date,* cupcake."

"I told you I was fixing you up!"

"I don't need you or anyone fixing me up with a date."

He was right, and she knew she had been out of her mind—and desperate—when she had put her plan into action. But she still felt horrible for Sonja.

"You didn't hurt her feelings, did you?" She moaned. "What was I thinking? This is all my fault."

"A truer statement you have never spoken." Then he grinned.

Julia groaned. "Okay, give it to me straight. How bad was it?"

"It wasn't bad. I told her the truth."

"What truth is that?"

He took one last bite of pie, then didn't answer her until he was finished. Finally he set the spoon and the pie aside and turned to her. When he looked at her, there was so much intense sensuality in his eyes that she sucked in her breath.

"I told her that it was unfair to date her," he said, his tone serious.

"Why?"

"Because the only woman I want is you."

Julia's world tilted on its axis and her head spun. "What?"

He leaned back against the tile counter and grinned. "I had pretty much the same reaction, too."

She muttered her indignation.

"But yes, I want you," he continued. "I want you in my bed, underneath me, dressed in nothing more than those damn stiletto heels that I haven't seen in weeks. I want the real Julia, and I want her badly."

"That Julia is gone," she stated primly.

"That's where you're wrong. She's in there, just waiting to get out. And I'm willing to wait."

He reached out and brushed his thumb over her lips. She couldn't help the shiver that raced through her.

"You don't play fair," she managed.

"That's the thing, Julia. I don't play games. I want to sleep with you. No question about it." He straightened and kissed her forehead, his body brushing against hers.

Then he walked out of the kitchen, leaving Julia stunned and bewildered and desperately concerned that all her good intentions were on the verge of flying out the window.

To: Katherine Bloom <katherine@ktextv.com>
From: Julia Boudreaux <julia@ktextv.com>
Subject: Houston . . .

. . . we have a problem. Ben wants me. Me. He can't want me!

Julia Scarlet Boudreaux

To: Julia Boudreaux <julia@ktextv.com>
From: Katherine Bloom <katherine@ktextv.com>
Subject: re: Houston . . .

Ben and you? Wow. That's some high-octane stuff. But you have bigger concerns right now. Folly has been asking about you again.

Kate

Katherine C. Bloom
News Anchor, KTEX TV, West Texas

To: Julia Boudreaux <julia@ktextv.com>
From: Andrew Folly <andrew@ktextv.com>
Subject: Scenic shots

Dear Julia:

I have been giving some thought to what I would like to see in
terms of programming from you. It is my understanding that you
are working on a reality show. Given the station's recent success
with reality television, I agree that this is the right approach. In
addition to the reality setting, however, I would like to see scenic
shots of the area. Much like Donald Trump's *The Apprentice*
where he has shots of New York City from all angles. It is
interesting to see places that people either know and love or
would like to see. Therefore, in whatever sort of opening you
create, I want soaring shots of the beauty of El Paso.

Sincerely,
Andrew Folly
Station Manager, KTEX TV, West Texas

To: Katherine Bloom <katherine@ktextv.com>
From: Julia Boudreaux <julia@ktextv.com>
Subject: Great

As predicted, Folly is showing his network roots. He said he
wants big sweeping shots of El Paso in my intro. Like Trump!
Like I have the kind of money Trump has! How am I going to get
sweeping shots of El Paso?!

xo, j

To: Julia Boudreaux <julia@ktextv.com>
From: Katherine Bloom <katherine@ktextv.com>
Subject: An idea

What about taking a utility tram up the mountain and getting a shot from there? It would be stunning. Plus, I have a friend who could take you up, and it wouldn't cost a penny because it's not the fancy tourist one.

Let me know if I should put in a call to my friend.

K

To: Katherine Bloom <katherine@ktextv.com>
From: Julia Boudreaux <julia@ktextv.com>
Subject: re: An idea

Any tram? And me? Though it really would be a fabulous shot, and it would impress the pants off the Folly.

If you don't mind, could you set it up with your friend?

xo, j

chapter sixteen

*T*wo days later, Julia sped along Mesa Street on her way to Rocco's house. In hindsight she realized that she had been naïve to think creating a new life for herself would be easy. Though in truth, she wasn't sure that she had *thought* too much about it. As usual, she had simply acted. Her life had been about doing, not spending endless hours thinking and analyzing as so many women did. She had always acted, dove into projects without fear. However, she was quickly learning that while steering clear of leopard prints and stiletto heels might try her resolve, steering clear of bad boys was truly testing her determination—or she should say steering clear of Ben Prescott made her wonder if she would ever succeed. He caused her to think. He caused her to analyze.

And now, in order to please Andrew Folly and give her show network-type sweeping shots of El Paso—even if it had to be achieved on a local station budget—she would be getting on a tram. A tram!

Julia couldn't believe she was going to get in some sort of maintenance metal box with plastic windows in order to get an aerial shot of the city. But if that was what it took to get the footage Andrew wanted, that's what she'd do.

Rob wasn't available to work after hours to get the shots until the following week, and that would be too late. And she certainly couldn't ask Todd to do it by himself. Which left her.

Pride, and not just a little bit of stubbornness, ticked through her and she pulled her shoulders back. Of course, underneath the pride was a huge dose of fear. The fact was, the Franklin Mountains were the southernmost tip of the Rocky Mountains. They were big. Huge. Rugged cliffs and craggy crevasses. And there was a long haul between the tram terminal and the top. Fortunately she wouldn't have to get out of the tram, only use the small video camera she would bring along to tape footage on the way up. Once she got to the top, the tram operator promised to bring her right back down.

However, before she could get on the tram, she had to tape the third segment of *Primal Guy*.

The session was scheduled for that day, with Rob and Todd meeting her at Rocco's house. The photos of the place he had brought to the interview had shown a small cottage with more posters of half-naked women than furniture. Like with Rocco himself, after Julia got finished with his house, she felt certain she'd get some great before and after shots to wow the audience.

Knowing that she had her work cut out for her, she wore a pair of khaki pants, a simple white shirt, a cardigan sweater, and a pair of loafers she had found in the back of her closet. When she looked at herself in the mirror, she saw prim and responsible. She should have been encouraged. But after two weeks of dressing like this, she had to face the fact that the change was only surface deep.

Somehow the change wasn't taking hold on her personality no matter how hard she tried to redo herself. She might look prim and responsible; she might even be acting that way. But she didn't feel prim and responsible in her heart.

She wanted to believe the wildness was just plain hard to tame. But she was afraid that wasn't it. When she looked in the mirror and saw the khaki pants and plain white shirt, she didn't feel prim—she felt empty. And that's what scared her. That's what drained her confidence away. Confidence had always been her anchor. But as she tried to change, tried to be someone else, she didn't feel new and reborn; she felt like someone she didn't know—and didn't want to be.

Running late, she hurried to Kern Place and to the small house where Rocco lived. She cringed at the sight of his front yard. Despite the beautifully manicured late fall lawns on either side of his, Rocco had gravel instead of grass and wrought-iron bars over all his windows. The place looked like a miniature prison.

Todd pulled up to the curb right behind her, Rob behind Todd. Together the three of them stood in the street and surveyed the house.

"Gnarly," Todd announced.

Julia had to agree.

As usual, Rob didn't say much.

"I'll get some potted plants," she said, her mind instantly working on what needed to be done. "We'll put them mainly around the front door and we'll only do a close-up shot. No wide pans of the place."

"Yeah, that'll work," Rob agreed. "Good thing the front door doesn't have any bars on it. Which makes no freakin' sense."

They walked up the cement walkway and rang the bell. It took forever for Rocco to appear. But when he did, Julia felt better. He really was the right guy for her show. With his new haircut and his sky blue eyes, he looked like a dashing poet.

"Hey," he said in a single grunting syllable.

"You mean, *Hello, Julia. Hello, Todd.* Or *Good morning, Rob.*"

The man chuckled. "Yeah, I forgot."

As if to make up for the lapse, he gestured like a gentleman at a ball for them to enter. Julia was impressed and a little relieved that he had it in him—until she entered the house.

She recognized the posters and all the leather. But he must have cleaned the place up for the photos he had taken.

"Rocco, this place is a disaster."

"Maybe a little. I cleaned before you came."

No question they would get those great *before* shots. But she had her work cut out for her if she hoped to get a decent *after* shot. No wonder he had trouble getting a date.

Julia pulled a deep, fortifying breath. She would scrub and scrape and do whatever it took to clean this place up.

"Okay, let's get started."

Rob set up his camera with Todd doing much of the work now that he'd gotten the hang of the professional equipment. But as soon as that was done, Todd pulled out his own video recorder.

Smoothing her hair, she smiled for the camera. "We've come to see Rocco Russo's home. The site for his upcoming big date. But as we can see, no date in her right mind would come within an inch of this health hazard."

Rocco didn't even bother to look sheepish. He smiled for the camera, even flexed his muscles.

Julia broke out in a sweat.

They taped the living room, the dining area off the kitchen, and then both bedrooms.

"All scary," she said to the camera, though she gasped when they came to the single bathroom.

She looked straight into the lens. "*I Know What You Did Last Summer* wasn't this scary. And we certainly know what Rocco *wasn't* doing last summer. Cleaning."

Rob gave her a silent thumbs-up before he ran the camera over the scum in the sink, the hideously dirty and rusty bathtub, the shower curtain that was falling down. And the rot.

Rocco chuckled. "Sorry, babe."

"Cut!"

"What?" he groused.

"You're supposed to have already learned manners. No more *babe*s! We'll have to reshoot that."

They did. And this time Primal Guy smiled and apologized.

Good God, what had she gotten into? But it was too late to turn back now. She only had two weeks left before Chloe and Sterling returned. Two weeks to finish taping and editing the show and prove Andrew Folly wrong.

After the opening shots, Rocco departed, already having scheduled to stay the night on a friend's couch. He was more than happy to vacate while other people did the work.

Julia didn't waste any time. She called up the garden store that had offered goods for promotion and told them what she needed. A pair of large cedar barrels and enough flowering fall plants to fill them. And an assortment of small evergreen plants to decorate the front porch. She didn't want to make the home look girlie, but she needed some sort of decoration on the door. So she had a wreath made of dried autumn leaves, with an assortment of dried autumn flowers and three miniature pumpkins clustered together in place of a bow.

She made the same kind of deal with the neighborhood paint store, a furniture store, and Kabal's House of Rugs.

While she waited for the deliveries, she would clean.

Rob taped it all, while Todd assisted Rob and taped what he could.

Julia retrieved the assortment of cleaning products from home. She pulled on bright yellow rubber gloves with a snap.

"Are you getting all of this?" she asked her crew.

"Every bit."

"Good. I want plenty to choose from when we're editing."

She started in the kitchen. She scrubbed the pans that looked like they could be saved. She threw the rest away. She washed cups and bowls that had who knew what in them. Thankfully Rocco loved fast food and paper plates. Just gathering the wide assortment of paper goods and McDonald's meals, then taking it all out to the trash, made a significant difference in the look of the kitchen.

Next came Soft Scrub, then Mr. Clean on the floors. The kitchen alone took her two hours, but when she was done, Julia didn't remember ever feeling so proud. Blowing a damp lock of hair out of her face, she smiled at the camera. "Just as we did for our Primal Guy, we're cleaning this place up."

The living room was a piece of cake in comparison. Pulling down the posters. Picking up dirty clothes. Mopping, dusting, scraping. She didn't want to think about what it was that needed to be scraped.

Just as she finished the living area, the delivery from the garden store arrived.

The multiple colors of mums made her smile. And the coordinating wreath they had whipped together felt like a sign that it was all going to work.

After providing directions to the gardening crew and instructing Rob to stay with them and for Todd to go back and forth between the gardeners and her, she dove into the bathroom. That's when it hit her.

She shuddered at the sight of the toilet, and for reasons she couldn't explain or didn't want to think about, she wondered if she could do it. This. The toilet. Her new life.

The thought of her father unexpectedly flitted through her mind—his smile, his larger than life laughter.

God, she missed him.

But what she hadn't admitted to anyone was that she was angry at him, too.

"Don't you dare go weak on me now," she whispered heatedly, wiping at the foreign feel of a teardrop in her eye.

"What's wrong?"

She jerked her head up and found Todd standing in the doorway, the camera trained on her, capturing her pathetic moment.

"That won't make the final cut," she warned him.

He only smiled, then focused on the toilet. "I'd cry too if I had to clean that."

"I wasn't crying."

He moved the camera to the side of his face, still taping. "Yeah, right."

"I wasn't," she claimed.

Todd shook his head, his grin wide and happy. This was the Todd she had known for the last week. But she now knew that lurking inside was a teenager who needed to know more about his own father.

No question, it wasn't her job to tell him. But surely she could cajole him into asking his mother or Ben about his dad.

"Hey, Todd," she said, when he started to return to the gardeners.

"Yeah?"

"I was thinking about what you said the other day. About your dad always being gone. And your parents fighting."

His jaw set.

"Maybe you should talk to your mom about that, or better yet, talk to Ben."

"No way. My mom would kill me if I talked to Ben about it."

Her shoulders came back in surprise. "Why?"

"Because she made me swear I wouldn't tell anyone about my dad and his women."

"What?"

His eyes went wide with panic. "Oh, man. You can't tell anyone that." He rushed over to her. "I didn't mean to say that."

"Todd, it's all right. But—but surely you're wrong."

"Wrong?" He scoffed. "Hard to make a mistake when your parents are screaming at each other because your mom tells your dad that she knows about his hookers."

The scrub brush dropped out of her hands.

"Todd, that can't be true."

"Are you calling me a liar?"

"Oh. Well. Of course not. It's just . . ."

Just what?

"You're nice and all, Julia. But face it, you being nice and sweet won't make everything okay. It doesn't work that way."

He left the room and headed back to the gardeners.

Julia's head spun the rest of the day. Was he right? Though right or wrong, what should she do? Should she tell Ben even after knowing that the boy's mother didn't want Ben to know?

She finished cleaning by two in the afternoon and had to get started on the painting. Fortunately, the paint store had taken pity on her and sent over two college kids to help her out. They had the small living area and kitchen of the house painted by six o'clock. They would have to finish up in the morning before the new furniture arrived the following afternoon.

At six-thirty, she locked up the house. She was exhausted.

After making plans to meet back at Rocco's in the morning, Rob, Todd, and Julia headed home.

It was dark on Meadowlark Drive. After flipping on the lightswitch, she dropped her purse, poured herself a glass of wine, then headed back to her bedroom for a nice long bath.

She had rarely seen Ben during the last two days. It still surprised her to think that he was an undercover cop. Having met his upper-class St. Louis family, it astounded her that he had left that life behind. It impressed her as well.

Ben Prescott could have taken the easy way and lived a life of wealth and privilege simply by going to work for his brother. Or he could have been like their sister, Diana, who clearly didn't work at all.

Could she be as good as Ben? Could she rise above her moneyed past and succeed in this new world?

She also remembered his "date" with Sonja that had gone awry. Julia felt horrible about the disaster. The hairdresser wouldn't return any of Julia's phone calls.

She grimaced. Her list of concerns was growing by the day. Sonja. Todd. What to say to Ben about his friend Henry and his hookers.

Ben's door was closed when she walked by, a light burning underneath. She started to knock, but couldn't bring herself to do it. Not yet. She had to think things through.

She kept going.

Before she allowed herself to sink into a tub of warm water, she took a hot shower, scrubbing every inch of grime from her body. Then she plugged the tub, dumped bubbles in, and soaked. She closed her eyes, sipped her wine, and willed all the aches and pains and worries to go away.

She was quiet, and she might have fallen asleep. Which could have explained why Ben walked into the bathroom without knocking.

Her eyes flew open, and Ben froze with his hand on the knob.

In the weeks he had been staying there, the shared bathroom had never been a problem. They kept different schedules and, she had to admit, she always remembered to lock the door leading to his room. But not tonight.

"I'm sorry," he said, his voice deep and gruff. "I thought you took a shower and were done."

She sunk low in the tub, the bubbles covering her breasts, and tried not to think about the tingling that instantly swept through her at the sight of him. She remembered his promise that they would make love. The arrogance appalled her. But deep down she knew that they were inching toward that eventuality. The Sonja setup had been an insane excuse to derail this mad train they were barreling along on.

But tonight there was more in his expression than arrogant sensuality. There was a weariness, his features more ravaged than usual. There was a dangerous edge to him that made it look as if at any second he would lash out.

He backed out and closed the door without another word.

Pulling herself out of the tub, she grabbed a towel and told herself she wasn't disappointed. She tugged on a T-shirt and pulled on a pair of velour warm-up bottoms. Just to be nice, really, she popped her head into his room to tell him the bathroom was all his.

But her heart twisted when she saw him.

He sat on the edge of the desk chair, his head in his hands, his elbows planted on his knees. The minute she opened the door, he straightened with a jerk.

He didn't say anything; he just stared at her, his dark eyes rimmed with emotion, his jaw tight, his shoulders seemingly massive and granite hard underneath his navy blue T-shirt. A cops' T-shirt, she realized in the back of her head. He had been wearing cops' T-shirts the whole time.

"What is it?" she whispered.

"Nothing," he said coldly.

"It's not nothing."

The frustration on his face was palpable. "What do you want from me?" he demanded, his voice tired and despairing.

"I don't want anything from you," she said. "I just want to help. Is it Henry?"

She saw his shoulders stiffen, frustration and tired despair slipping easily into anger. She felt a moment of trepidation. She sensed she had stepped into something that wasn't going to be pretty. Suddenly, pressing him didn't seem like such a good idea after all. But she had never been afraid to face life's difficulties before.

"What is wrong, Ben?" she persisted. "You're chasing demons . . . or they're chasing you, but I can't quite figure out exactly what those demons are."

He stared at her forever. "You want to know?" His tone was ominous.

"Yes, I want to know."

She realized then that without knowing it, they had been headed for this place since the day he came to stay with her.

"Why do you want to know?" he demanded.

"Because I know you're upset about Henry and you are trying to help his family. And while I think that's great, I don't think it's that simple."

He laughed, though the sound held no humor. "Simple?" The question was a sneer. "God," he groaned, raking his hands through his hair, his eyes wild. "It could have been simple. All I had to do was answer the fucking phone."

"What?"

Ben looked her straight in the eye. "He called me that night."

"I don't understand."

"He called my apartment. I was off duty—nothing was in the works. When I heard his voice come over the answering machine, I turned the volume down. Emergencies came over my cell phone. That night I wasn't interested in being disturbed by anything less than an emergency."

"Why?"

His chiseled features went cold and he looked her in the eye. "I didn't want to talk."

The look in his dark eyes changed from anger to predatory.

"Ben, really, tell me," she whispered. "Why didn't you answer the phone?"

Something snapped inside him. "Because I was screwing some woman I don't even remember." He laughed bitterly. "While my partner was getting his brains blown out in an alleyway, I was at home fucking my brains out. How's that for a cheap, sordid-ass story they'd show on some cheap, sordid-ass cable station?"

Her head spun and her heart hammered. "That's why you keep trying to find Henry's killer, half hoping you'll catch a bullet yourself." She blinked as a thought occurred to her. "That's how you got shot!"

He scoffed. But she knew that she had hit a nerve.

"Getting yourself killed isn't going to help Henry. Or his kids."

He pressed his eyes closed, and she could hardly believe the sheer vulnerability she saw in him. She walked over to him and placed her hand on his chest, her palm to his heart.

"You're okay," she whispered.

But she realized that he wasn't okay. He was tormented by a night he couldn't change.

He didn't move, didn't seem to breathe, though she could see grief shudder through his body.

His features grew ravaged, but his chin rose defiantly as an eternity passed.

"After the woman left," he continued ruthlessly, "I finally checked my machine. It was hours later. I listened to Henry's message. '*Hey, Slash.*' Then there was a long pause. I swear he went from a joking laugh to being choked up." He ran his hand over his face. "Henry was upset and said, '*I need to talk, man. If you're there, pick up.*' I was there, but I had turned the volume down and didn't hear him—didn't want to hear him. When I called back, it was too late."

"You can't keep blaming yourself, Ben. We've all turned off our machines at one time or another."

He continued as if he hadn't heard her, his voice cold and void of feeling. "I called him back." His eyes narrowed, then he pressed them closed for one brief second before he swore. "But *he* didn't answer this time. Another detective did and I knew something was wrong. When I asked for Henry, the guy told me Henry had been shot."

The words seemed to paralyze her. This man and his outward strength, never able to show how much he hurt inside. And she didn't have any idea how to make this better. How to fix what was wrong.

No new job, no new idea, no simple makeover was going to fix Ben Prescott.

She took his hand in hers. "You aren't really such a bad bad boy, are you, Benny the Slash? It's just a role you play to cover up how much you care."

His expression hardened, a wildness flaring. She hated to see him hurting, hated to see this strong man holding on by a thread. She wanted to hold him. Comfort him.

When she touched him, a shudder ran the length of his body. "Don't do this, Julia."

She curled her fingers into his shirt and pulled him to her. His moan was deep and savage, melting the anger away completely, leaving only despair. He started to push away.

"No, Ben." She held on with surprising strength.

She could feel the tension in him, the need not to give in—as if giving in made him weak.

"I know you would give your life for Henry if you could. But that doesn't solve anything. You're a good man, and you can't spend the rest of your life trying to make up for someone else's mistake."

"You don't know what you're talking about. The day before he went into that alleyway alone, I asked to be reassigned."

He said the words with cold precision, as if they proved his guilt.

"I've seen how you don't put up with crap from anyone. And if you asked to be reassigned, then I'm sure it was because Henry was on a dangerous course before the night he was killed. And no matter what you keep saying to yourself, Henry went into that alleyway alone. If you didn't answer the phone, he should have come by your apartment or called someone else."

She slipped her arms under his, embracing him. But he didn't give in. With her ear against his chest, she could hear his heart pounding hard. "It's not your fault, Ben."

He stood stiffly, his muscles so tight that it felt like he would snap. Then with a feral roar he gave in. He wrapped her in his arms, crushing her to his chest, his control finally, completely broken.

They clung together, she trying to offer comfort, he absorbing what she had to give. They stood that way, lost in each other.

"You're a strong man who again and again tries to help others."

He scoffed, but he didn't let go.

"It's true. You helped your brother with *The Catch*. Keeping all the girls safe. And now dealing with Henry's kids. But you won't give yourself a break."

Slowly, like he had no will of his own, he reached out and ran his thumb along her jaw. The simple touch sent sensation coursing through her. Then she reached up on her tiptoes and kissed him, kindly, gently. She felt his breath shudder through him. And everything changed.

Suddenly caring turned to heat, comfort turned to need, and he sought her mouth. They came together, their kiss instantly desperate, slanting in need.

"Julia," he breathed against her.

They kissed hungrily, his hands skimming over her body as if he couldn't believe she was really there. She couldn't believe it either, but in that second, she didn't care. Right or wrong, she had wanted this man since the day she first laid eyes on him. And just then, she didn't want to think about tomorrow, or even an hour later. All her good intentions were gone. Consequences weren't even a thought as his palms brushed over her nipples through her T-shirt.

"Damn," he said, his voice strained, defeated, as he cupped her fullness.

She cried out in a soft mewling sound at having him touch her after weeks of doing her best to keep him at a distance. She couldn't have stopped this path if she wanted.

They kissed again, as she tore impatiently at his shirt. In seconds it was gone and she ran her hands over the heat of his skin. She lost herself to the feel of him. When she did, desire erupted and he groaned into her mouth, half cry, half demand.

She moaned when his lips trailed back to her ear, the whisper of breath sending fire carving through him as he grazed a path to the delicate skin on her neck. He nipped and sucked, and she clutched him to her.

With one hand, he tilted her head so he could taste her more deeply as he pressed her body closer. His shaft swelled hard against her body, and she felt him shudder. They were both letting go in some way, each giving in. She had said she wouldn't have sex with him. He had said he would wait until she was ready. Neither of them was ready for this. Each was caught up in a tidal wave that carried them forward.

His hands cupped her round bottom, pulling her up against him, then he rolled his hips, his forehead pressing against hers, their lips only grazing together. Bending his knees, he pressed his erection low, then slowly rose to his full height, the sensation like sin itself.

"I want this." His voice was ragged. "I want you."

She should say no. She had promised herself that she wouldn't give in to sex without a meaningful relationship with a nice man. But she could hear his need whispering in her head like a rush of air, a need that matched her own.

"I want this, too," she answered truthfully.

He undressed her with reverence until she was naked. His eyes, already darkened from a friend's death, now darkened with sensual appreciation for her. She was moved in a way she didn't entirely understand.

He kissed the dips and curves of her body, lingering over her abdomen, nipping at the delicate skin of her navel. She kneeled with him and started tugging at the fastenings of his jeans.

"Take these off," she whispered.

His chuckle was grim as he stood. When he did, she pulled the jeans down his thighs, revealing the wound that was now covered with a large square bandage instead of the pads and tape. She hesitated for a second, worried. But then he kicked his jeans away, and his erection pressed through his bright white Jockey shorts, his body hard and so strong. And she forgot about the bandage.

Passion and desire drumming through her, pushing her on, she slipped her fingers beneath the elastic band and pushed the Jockeys down around his ankles until he kicked those away, too.

"Julia," he said, his voice strained, his length jutting forward.

She kissed him in response, kissing him low on the abdomen as he had done to her. Then she kissed him along the hard length, his hands coming up to fist in her hair, his groan hoarse. And when she took him into her mouth, he cried out. She sucked him, palming and stroking. And everything became wild.

He pulled her up, taking her mouth savagely, desperately. They came together, fulfilling the promise their bodies had sensed since the day they met. He kissed her hungrily, as if he couldn't get enough. He lifted her, wrapping her legs around his waist.

Julia held on, and when his hands cupped her bottom, the tips of his fingers found the slippery heat between her legs. This time she cried out. He drew her body up, sliding her along his hard naked flesh, his body shuddering. He brought her so close to his velvety head, and just when she thought he would bring her down on him, he tore her away.

With a curse of need, he set her on her feet, then went over to the suitcase, which was still a jumble of unpacked clothes. He found what he was looking for. He ripped the condom package open with his teeth. The wetness between her thighs surged when she watched him roll the latex down his thick shaft.

She no longer felt any remnants of prim behavior. She felt wild with wanting him, wanting to slide down the impressive length with a shuddering sigh, like giving in to that decadent slice of pie she had been denying herself.

When he was done, he came toward her, her heart swelling in her throat. He easily could have picked her up. Instead he backed her toward his bed. When her thighs bumped against the mattress, he came over her, leaning her into the sheets and comforter. Then he scooped her up and pulled them both into the middle of the bed.

She felt the crisp hairs on his chest brush against her breasts, her nipples tingling.

"I can't wait," he groaned. He kissed her on the forehead. "I want you. Now, not later."

"Ben," she murmured as she ran her hands up his arms to his shoulders. Relishing the texture of hard sinew beneath her fingers, she savored his jagged intake of breath.

Supporting his weight on his forearms, he framed her face with his hands. Their eyes met, locked, and they never looked away as he nudged her knees apart. Then he reached between them, guiding his length to her. His hips arched, and his shaft slipped inside just a bit. He was big, and she drew in her breath as he filled her as he had promised, as she had dreamed about. He never looked away.

She took him completely, raising her knees, inhaling a shuddering breath when he sank to the hilt.

Then he began to move, slowly at first because she was so tight. "Mmm," she whispered on a sigh. "Yes," she said, closing her eyes, her body beginning to move in tandem with his.

Soon they were both moving together, hard and fast.

"Yes," she cried out.

He buried his face in her neck, calling out her name as he gave in to the primal, base, instinctual need. He thrust inside her, again and again. "Come on, baby."

And she did. When he cupped her hips, pulling her body up to meet his bold, fevered thrusts, her body exploded with sensation. She thrust her pelvis against him as she climaxed, her spine arching off the mattress, taking him even more deeply. She clinched around him, and he gave one final thrust. "Julia." Her name was torn from his throat as his body convulsed in a long shuddering explosion.

They held on to each other, panting, reeling. They didn't move, didn't speak. When they finally fell apart, Julia lay back, suspended, floating, feeling drained and empty. But more than that she felt shock—shock at what had happened. Never, in any of the times she had experienced passion, had she felt anything close to this. It was a life-altering feeling of falling and flying, contracting and exploding.

When the sensation settled, her limbs felt luxuriously weak, and she stretched like a cat, feeling sexy and fulfilled. And it wasn't until then, as her mind settled down from an amazing passion, that she wondered what the hell she had just done.

Julia bit her lip and wrinkled her nose. "Oops," she whispered.

Thankfully, Ben had already fallen asleep.

en woke with a start.

Darkness surrounded him and his heart beat hard. But it wasn't with the anger or futility that he woke so often with these past two months. Something was different, he realized as he shook off the last remnants of sleep.

Without so much as moving a muscle, he took in his environment as his eyes adjusted. The furniture, the bed, the pressure against his chest.

Julia.

They were naked in his bed, the tangle of sheets doing little to cover her as she slept curled against his side. A shiver of awareness passed through him as he remembered what had happened last night. This woman. The way she hadn't let him turn away. Then their bodies coming together in a way that left him wanting her even more. As his heart settled, Ben could hardly believe the release he felt—a release that was well beyond the physical.

He stroked her arm, wanting to wake her gently. He ran his finger along the line of her ear, then her jaw. She murmured, but only curled closer.

"Good morning," he said, kissing her brow.

She mumbled something from that place halfway between sleep and being awake. He laughed softly, and kissed her again.

The sun was rising, coming in through the crack in the heavy velvet draperies. He stoked her hair, the strands like silk. Finally she stretched and rolled onto her back, the sheet only hiding her in places. What he could see sent blood surging through his body. What he couldn't see, his hands and mind remembered.

He kissed her again, his lips trailing along her collarbone.

It took her a while to figure out where she was. He wasn't sure what she'd do when reality registered on her brain. When he saw those violet eyes flicker with understanding, he couldn't make out her expression. Concern? Regret?

"Good morning," he said.

"Ah, good morning." She sat up, tugging more of the sheets around her. "I meant to leave."

"Leave?"

"Ah, yeah."

He could tell she was embarrassed, or maybe the red in her cheeks was frustration with herself that she was still there. Only Julia could be upset that she had had sex, then fallen asleep without leaving.

He smiled at her and wanted to pull her close.

She scrambled away. "Ah, well, it's good to see you're back to a hundred percent."

"Who says I am?"

"Last night told the tale." Then she blushed again, though this time there was no doubt that it was embarrassment.

"I was impressive, huh," he joked.

She scooted to the edge of the bed.

"Julia?"

"Look at the time. I'm running late. Today's my big day for getting shots for the opening segment of *Primal Guy*." She hopped off the mattress awkwardly as she tried to keep the sheets around her without tripping and falling. "I hope you're feeling better about Henry."

So much for his good mood. He instantly tensed.

"Great," she said with a groan. "You're not feeling better about it, and I shouldn't have brought it up."

"I won't feel better about it until I find out who killed him. I owe him that."

"Fine, then I'll help."

As only Julia could, she went from piqued that she had been foolish enough not to leave his bed after sex, to wanting to help someone with a problem.

"You are not going to help with this," he stated ominously. He rolled off the bed, walked naked over to the chair, and pulled on his jeans.

"You said he was killed in an alleyway," she continued as if he hadn't said a word. "You've never told me why he was there."

"Julia—"

"Ben"—she rolled her eyes—"just tell me."

He eyed her, then said, "The department believes he was there on a drug bust."

"But you think there was more to it."

"Maybe. There's word on the street that it wasn't a

drug bust. That it had something to do with Henry and a woman."

He saw the way her body tensed.

"A woman?" she asked.

"What is it?"

"Well, something Todd said about how his parents fought all the time."

"Todd told you that?"

"Yes. Then later, when I told him he should talk to you or his mom about it, he said no way he could talk to his mother about his parents fighting over hookers."

"What?" Ben bit out in surprise.

She held her arms up in surrender. "Don't kill the messenger. I'm just telling you what Todd told me."

Ben started to pace. His brain spun with questions and a flare of recognizable anger. "Tell me exactly what he said."

She did, recounting first the conversation they'd had in her entry hall, then the second conversation they'd had in Rocco's bathroom. "I told him all parents fight. But he said yeah, maybe, but his fought all the time. About hookers."

"Damn it." Ben dragged his hands through his hair. He didn't understand the fury he felt, the anger and frustration. At Julia. "Why didn't you tell me this earlier?"

Julia wasn't intimidated. "I only heard about it yesterday afternoon. Plus, if you must know, he said his mother would be furious if he talked to you about it. Besides," she added with her own anger, "it didn't come up in the middle of sex last night. I'm telling you now."

"Fuck."

"One of these days you might want to expand your vocabulary."

Then she turned on her heel and left.

Ben watched her go, then pounded across the room and went to the computer. With dread and denial filling him, he started surfing escort services. Had that been the missing piece? Had Henry found hookers on the Internet, not just a date or even drugs?

The truth was, Henry had been acting oddly before he was killed. He had been edgy, quick tempered, and a real pain in the ass. Wasn't that really why Ben hadn't answered the phone? He had been sick and tired of Henry's constant moods. One minute wanting to fight, the next apologizing on the verge of tears.

Ben had told him to see the department shrink. But he hadn't done any more to help him.

The all-too-familiar guilt shot through him at one fact that wouldn't leave him alone. Ben had been pissed off at Henry for months before the night Henry was killed. Ben had been distancing himself for weeks, and the day before that horrible night, Ben had put in a request for a new partner.

Had Ben sensed that something was wrong and hadn't wanted to face the reality of a good cop gone bad?

Was that the problem? Deep down was there guilt about not having been there for his friend for the last few months—not just that one night?

With a curse, Ben Googled escort services in El Paso, Texas. He came up with a handful and he started surfing them one by one.

As he surfed, taking notes of the sites he visited, he didn't want to find anything. He wanted this avenue to turn up as a dead end, just like all the other sites had. Site by site, he checked each page, looking for something that would give him a clue. He couldn't have said exactly what he was looking for. But he would know it the minute he saw it. Something was niggling at the back of his head. Some clue or some sign that he knew he would recognize. And with each site he got through without finding anything that alerted him, he felt relief fill him a little more.

Stubbornly, he told himself that Julia was wrong.

Todd was mistaken.

Morales didn't know what he was talking about.

Henry was killed in a drug deal gone bad.

Ben closed his eyes for a second, not sure why that would be better. Though he knew. It was the difference in dying for a good cause, no matter how much of a waste it was, and dying for all the wrong reasons.

He didn't want to find anything. But on the sixth site he visited, on the contact page, the hair on the back of his neck felt like it stood on end.

Contact Lionel@lusciousladies.com.

Ben scrambled through the piles of papers he had on the desk until he came to that printout of the e-mail he had found buried deep in Henry's files. An e-mail from a TheLion@yahgoogroups.com.

The department computer whiz had searched the address, but just as with so many mailboxes at Yahgoo, it couldn't be traced. Just one more anonymous person drifting through the Internet.

Ben had no proof that this Lionel@lusciousladies.com was the same as TheLion@yahgoogroups.com, but it was the first hint of a clue he'd gotten.

He sent an e-mail to Lionel.

Anger ticked through him even harder and he started to pace. Not being able to sit back and wait, he headed out of the house, intent on finding Spazel. The low-life snitch knew just about everyone in town who was dealing on the dark side.

Ben hit the entry hall just as the doorbell rang. Yanking it open, Ben found a flower delivery guy standing there with a dozen red roses.

"For Julia Boudreaux," the kid said. "Sign here."

He heard a gasp, and when he turned around Julia was there. Foolishly, he felt his chest squeeze at the reminder that Julia had always had many men in her life. He shouldn't care that he was just one more passing through her world. And that was what it was. Just two people losing themselves in sex, he told himself firmly.

Without a word, he left the house, slamming into the Rover, then racing to the south-side bar where Spazel hung out. It was just before noon, and despite the early hour, Ben saw him the minute he walked in the door.

The skinny con man was talking to three less-than-reputable-looking men. Ben could tell he was running numbers, taking bets, earning his living as a low level criminal.

Spaz leaned close and laughed in a deep, macho tone. When he pulled back and caught a glimpse of Ben standing there, his brown eyes went wide and he sort of squeaked, ruining his macho façade.

Ben walked up to the small group. The men looked at him, got a little nervous, and couldn't get out of there fast enough.

"Hey, man!" Spaz protested. "I'm trying to make a living here—"

"Cut the crap. What do you know of some guy calling himself Lionel who's involved with an escort service called Luscious Ladies?"

"I don't know nothing about any Luscious Ladies."

"Think harder, Spaz," he stated coldly. "We both know you stay in business because I don't turn you in. Now, what do you know about a guy named Lionel?"

"I swear, I know nothing! The only thing that is close is some guy who tried to start something a few months back. He was running girls out of the Lejos alleyway—" The con man's eyes went wide. "You don't think it's the same guy, do you?"

"Why the hell didn't you mention this before?"

"The guy hasn't been around in weeks. I figured he set up shop somewhere else, or more than likely, he couldn't make it work."

"I need an address."

"I don't have one."

"Get one. Then call me." He wrote down his cell number and stuffed it in Spaz's shirt pocket. "Don't disappoint me."

To: Ben Prescott <sc123@fastmail.com>
From: j.taggart@eppd.gov
Subject: Address

Ben, I have located a Lionel Esposito. Last known address is 245 Castille Drive. Are you sure Spazel can be trusted?

Tag

To: j.taggart@eppd.gov
From: Ben Prescott <sc123@fastmail.com>
Subject: re: Address

Trust Spaz? Hard to say. But it's the first piece of hard information that we've gotten. I'll let you know when I learn more.

Ben

To: Ben Prescott <sc123@fastmail.com>
From: j.taggart@eppd.gov
Subject: re: Address

Don't do anything crazy.

T

en turned off the computer, then went to Julia's bedroom. He knocked, but didn't get an answer. When he pushed inside, she wasn't there. He knew that before he did anything else, before he searched out Lionel, he had to find her.

What the hell had he been thinking when he got pissed off at Julia when she told him what Todd said? He had taken his shock and his frustration out on her. And before he did anything else, he wanted to right that wrong.

He called the station and asked for Kate.

"I can't find Julia," he said without preamble.

"What do you mean?"

Ben heard the instant tension in Kate's voice, the concern. "Sorry. I need to find Julia, and she's not here at the house."

Sarcasm dripped into her voice. "Do you think she might not be at the house because you got upset with her when she told you what Todd said?"

He sighed. "That's probably a good bet."

The three best friends defended one another like mother hens and their chicks.

"Well, at least you admit it," Kate stated.

"How upset was she?"

"Very. But I have to tell you, I think she was upset about more than just you flying off the handle."

"What do you mean?"

"I'm not sure. She sounded like she was in a bad place. But she promised that she'd call me as soon as she finished the tram shots."

"Tram shots?"

"A friend of mine is getting her on a utility tram to get some aerial footage of the city that Andrew wants."

A bolt of concern shot through him. "Utility tram? Not the regular tram?"

"What do you mean?"

"The tourist tram is fine, but somebody's makeshift one that I've never heard of is another story. I'll head over there now. In the meantime, get her on the phone and tell her to get the footage some other way."

Back in his Rover, he headed to the address Kate provided. Regardless that he was sure Kate would call, he dialed Julia's cell phone number as well. But voice mail picked up immediately, which meant either she was on the phone, she was not answering his calls, or the phone was off.

"Don't get on that tram," he commanded into her voice mail. "I repeat, do not get on that tram."

Beeping off, he slipped his cell back into his inside coat pocket. He coasted through the stop signs, then flew onto a road that led up to the mountain.

The 4x4 came to a halt in the gravel makeshift parking lot. He saw her car immediately, along with another SUV.

Ben leaped out, grimaced when his bad leg hit the ground, then headed for the stairs to the platform. The tram was just sliding away, the operator nowhere to be seen.

"Julia!"

She was holding the video camera in a death grip, the lens pointed out toward the view. She jerked around when he called her name, her eyes wide with what he was sure was terror. He could hardly believe Julia would be afraid of anything. But even in terror she still had that camera taking in scenic shots.

"Come on, leap off."

"Are you crazy? I can't leap off! Besides, I have to get footage."

He could tell from the stubborn tilt of her chin that despite the fear in her eyes, she wasn't getting off. So when the car got close to the end of the platform, he did the only thing he could. He leaped through the opening just as the tram swung free into open air.

"What are you doing?" she demanded.

"I came to get you," he muttered, only a foot away from Julia in the cramped space.

"Why?"

"There are better ways to get footage than riding on this thing."

That got her to lower the camera, but only for a second before she whipped it back up just as the city below burst out before them. They both were in awe of the view, standing there staring, forgetting. Though they didn't forget for long when the car jarred on its track.

Julia's eyes went wider and she set the video camera

on the wooden bench top that served as both a place to sit and a top for a storage area. Ben swore.

"Good news is that I got what I came for," she stated, though her voice shook when the tram jarred again.

She grabbed the sides of the car where the Plexiglas windows met the sheet metal walls. "I guess this would be the perfect opportunity to say, *Fasten your seat belts, it's going to be a bumpy ride.*"

Her sassy voice trembled, and he cocked his head, still trying to assimilate the foreign thought of Julia Boudreaux being afraid of anything. But she was. When the tram jarred again, she gasped, her knuckles going white from holding on so tightly.

"Hey," he said softly, "it's rickety, and it breaks down, but that's it. Even if it does break down, it's just a matter of fixing it and getting the occupants out of the car. You're going to be fine."

It didn't look like she believed him.

He reached out to touch her.

"Don't," she said tightly.

Her tone raked through him because it wasn't about fear—not entirely. She was angry at him. But he knew he deserved her anger. First, he had acted badly when she told him what Todd said. Then he had acted like a jealous ass over the flowers.

"I'm sorry," he said, meaning it. "I've been acting like a jerk."

She stared out into the distance. "True."

He grimaced. "I'm getting to the bottom of what was going on with Henry."

"Glad to hear it."

"But first I had to find you to apologize."

"Fine. Now you can check that off your list."

"Julia—" But he didn't get any farther before the tram jarred again, the cables screeching to a halt.

Her pale skin blanched white.

"Damn," he muttered. "Julia, look at me."

Finally, she dragged her gaze to meet his. He saw the terror, and he knew in that second that Julia was scared at a bone-deep level.

"You're afraid of heights." He said the words with the surprise he felt.

She closed her eyes tightly.

"Then why did you get on this blasted thing in the first place?"

She still couldn't talk.

"I know," he said quietly. "Because you never allow yourself to be afraid of anything." He sighed. "Oh, Julia. You don't have to be strong every second."

With her hands still holding the edges, she sank down to the floor, her arms spread like an eagle's wings until her butt hit the bottom. Then she let go, her palms sliding down the sides. She wrapped her arms around her knees and she buried her head.

It was painful to watch, this strong woman trying to hold on but failing.

He wanted to comfort her. But first he had to make a call.

"Dispatch, this is Ben Prescott." He gave his badge number, then explained the situation.

A few instructions were exchanged, then he beeped off and crouched down in front of Julia. He touched her chin and lifted it until she had to look at him. But her eyes were closed.

"Sweetheart, look at me."

Reluctantly, she did.

"You're okay."

"Am I?" she asked.

The question was so simple, but he realized that it wasn't simple at all.

"Sure you are."

She turned her face away. "My father had no patience with fear."

"What?"

She closed her eyes again. "Philippe Boudreaux wasn't afraid of anything."

He remembered learning that her father had died while mountain climbing, about the stories of his love of adventure.

"And he expected his only child to be the same way." She looked back at him. "This is unacceptable."

"Being afraid of heights is unacceptable?" he asked incredulously.

"Being weak is unacceptable," she clarified.

"Hell, Julia. You aren't weak."

"Then why am I crouched on the floor?"

"I know big, burly cops who would walk in front of a crazed gunman without blinking an eye but who get light-headed at the mere mention of heights."

She snorted. "Thank God they didn't have to spend time around my father."

"What's this really about?" he asked gently.

She didn't answer at first, just stared at the marked and scarred tram walls without really seeing. "I'm making a mess of everything," she whispered.

"No—"

"I am. I've been tumbling out of control ever since my daddy died. I've tried to pretend everything was okay. That I was just as strong as he always expected me to be.

But the tighter I hold on, the more I try to be a better person, the worse everything gets. I don't even know who I am anymore. I feel lost."

"You're not lost, Julia. You're just finding your way in a world that changed when your dad died."

"But that's the thing. I don't feel like I'm finding my way. I feel like I'm in a holding pattern, being given a reprieve. But come this spring I have to sell my house, and by then I better have a new life—one that works."

"Hell, I'm impressed with how well you're doing since he left you in such a bad financial place. And once you sell, won't you have money to tide you over?"

She looked him straight in the eye. "Daddy mortgaged the house to the hilt to keep up appearances. I'll be lucky to walk away breaking even."

"Hell."

"I don't care about the money. I just need to know that I can succeed at something! The old me wasn't working. But the new one isn't working, either."

She inhaled sharply, her eyes boring into him.

"Something's working. You still have admirers sending you flowers. They clearly know who you are. And still want you."

The words brought the burn of tears back into her eyes. But he could see how she fought them. She wasn't about to let herself cry.

"It's my birthday," she said, her voice choked.

His brow furrowed. "Hell, I wish I had known. Happy birthday. And I was an ass for saying anything about your admirers. Of course you have plenty. And I'm glad some guy sent you flowers."

"They were from my father."

Just that, and his thoughts collided. "What the hell? Your dad is gone—" He cut himself off.

"He is," she said quietly. "For as long as I can remember, he always sent me roses for my birthday. No matter where he was, no matter what he was doing, red roses arrived. I don't even like red roses, but somehow that made it okay that he wasn't there because at least I knew he was thinking about me."

"That's great."

"Great?" She laughed bitterly. "I realize now that he wasn't thinking of me. He had a standing order with the florist so that I'd get them no matter where he was. . . . Someone else was remembering for him. And since he died unexpectedly, he hadn't canceled the order, and no one else thought to do it." She looked at him. "He didn't remember me. He never remembered me."

The tram jarred and she flattened her palms against the sides. "I've tried to be strong. I've tried to be the fun, wild woman just like all the women he loved. Then I've tried to be the good, kind, respectable woman that I thought I should be. But now all of a sudden I haven't a clue who I really am—or even who I want to be."

"You might not know who you are, but I do."

She looked at him.

"You are the strongest woman I know. Strong and smart and sexy."

She snorted. "Yeah, real strong. Cowering on the floor."

He touched her chin again. "Strong"—he kissed her on the forehead—"smart"—he kissed her on the temple—"and sexy." He lowered his mouth to hers.

Her breath sighed out of her. He kissed her softly, gently.

"Happy birthday," he whispered.

She smiled through the tears that she was fighting to hold back, the sound of sirens in the distance getting closer.

"That would be our rescuers," he said with a smile.

"What are they going to do?"

"We'll see. Hopefully they'll be able to unstick the gears."

A few minutes later a handheld bullhorn beeped on. "Prescott, are you up there?"

Ben stood and glanced down through the opening. The officer below smiled. "What the hell are you doing up in that tram?"

"Just wondering how much trouble I could cause today."

"Yeah, a real troublemaker," the man said with a chuckle. "We're going to have to use ropes and pulleys to get you down."

Julia gave a tiny cry.

Ben grimaced. "What about the gears?"

"The operator sent for a technician, but it could be hours before it's fixed. If you'd rather stay put until then . . ."

"Nope. Ropes and pulleys will have to do," he confirmed.

When he looked at Julia, she was frozen on the floor.

"It's easy, really," he promised. "And we didn't get that far along, so we're not that high up."

Trembling, she peered out, then shuddered. "I can't."

"You got a lady up there, Prescott?"

"Yep."

"You dog."

The officer's laugh in the megaphone echoed against the mountain.

"Great," Julia snapped. "He thinks I'm one in the long line of your conquests."

"That's my girl. Just keep thinking of that."

"About all your women?"

"Yeah." He smiled. "Think about the long lines."

She stood abruptly, only to get another look out, and she grabbed the sides.

Ben handed her the video camera and searched inside the bench. "Ropes and rapelling equipment," he muttered.

He got to work with the ropes and harnesses that he found in the storage bench. One long rope was secured to the tram, then tossed down to the men on the ground to keep the tram steady. Julia shook as he looped the harness between her legs. "All you have to do is hold on to the rope as I lower you."

She looked him in the eye, but when he tried to take the video camera from her, she clutched it close. "I'm not going through all of this and not get my shots of the city."

As always, she made him smile.

"All right, hold on tight."

He guided her toward the edge, and she trembled.

"Sit on the edge and let your legs hang over."

Stiff, her fear coming off her in waves, she did as he instructed. But just when he started to lower her over the side, she grabbed him in a deadly grip. "I can't, Ben," she said raggedly.

"Sure you can, sweetheart."

Her fingers curled into his jacket. "No, really. I can't."

He placed his palms on either side of her face, forcing

her to look at him. "You can. If there is anything I have learned about you these last couple of months, it is that you do whatever has to be done regardless of what it costs you. You'll do this. And I'll keep you safe. I promise."

She looked at him forever, hope and fear mixing together.

Shaking herself, as if accepting that she had to do this and refusing to be brought low by fear, she curled her newly short nails around the rope and the video camera. When she slid over the side, she gasped at that first startling moment of dangling in the air.

Both firemen and police officers held the rope steady as Ben worked to lower her. When she finally reached the bottom, she didn't grab on to anyone. She let them do their work to free her, then she leaned against an outcrop of rock while Ben secured a second harness around himself.

He'd been rapelling since he was a kid. In seconds he was over the side, slipping down in one fluid motion. The men he had worked with on a daily basis for years slapped him on the back. But Ben's only focus was on Julia.

It was like she had waited to make sure he got down safely, then she could leave. And that was what she was doing. Walking, barely steady on her feet, toward the parking lot.

"Hey, Julia," the operator said. "I'm sorry about all this."

She lifted her hand in a "don't worry" wave, as if she couldn't get the words out of her mouth.

When she got to her car, however, she went still. She jerked around. "My purse."

"As soon as the technician gets the tram working

again," the operator said, "I'll get it for you. Don't worry."

"But I don't have any keys."

"Oh, ah, well . . ." the operator stammered.

Ben could tell Julia needed to get away from there before she truly lost her composure. "I'll take you home," he said, "then we'll get your car later."

He saw relief flash across her face, but only for a second before she shook it away. Without a word, she climbed into his SUV, then stared out the window the entire way home. She only muttered and mumbled responses to his attempts at conversation. When he pulled into the driveway, she slid down from the high seat, then shuddered when she had to turn around and ask him if he had a key to the house.

He opened the back door, and she swept passed him.

"Julia—"

"I don't want to talk about it, Ben. But thanks. Thanks for getting me down. I've got to get ready for the grand finale of *Primal Guy.*"

"We really need to talk."

"No, we don't, Ben."

Then she headed out of the kitchen and closed herself inside the study.

To: Julia Boudreaux <julia@ktextv.com>
From: Andrew Folly <andrew@ktextv.com>
Subject: Scenic shots

Dear Julia:

I heard you had some trouble getting the aerial shots. A shame that you failed.

Sincerely,
Andrew Folly

Station Manager, KTEX TV, West Texas

To: Andrew Folly <andrew@ktextv.com>
From: Julia Boudreaux <julia@ktextv.com>
Subject: re: Scenic shots

Dear Folly:

So sorry to disappoint, but I got plenty of footage. If I were you,
I'd be careful not to underestimate my ability to get what I want.

Julia Scarlet Boudreaux

To: Julia Boudreaux <julia@ktextv.com>
From: Katherine Bloom <katherine@ktextv.com>
Subject: Wow

What did you say to Andrew? He's practically spitting nails he's
so mad. I'd be careful if I were you, Jules.

Kate

Katherine C. Bloom
News Anchor, KTEX TV, West Texas

To: Katherine Bloom <katherine@ktextv.com>
From: Julia Boudreaux <julia@ktextv.com>
Subject: re: Wow

Not to worry about me, sugar. I'm back. And I don't mean simply
that I'm back from that hideous tram ride. I clearly wasn't meant
to be a good girl. I don't have a clue who Julia Boudreaux really
is, but whoever I was has to be good enough.

Watch out, West Texas.

xo, j

To: Julia Boudreaux <julia@ktextv.com>
From: Katherine Bloom <katherine@ktextv.com>
Subject: Oh dear

What do you mean, Watch out, West Texas? Don't tell me you're going to do something crazy.

Though I have to admit, I miss the old Julia. But whoever you are, or whoever you want to be, you know I love you.

Kate

p.s. Seeing Folly spit nails is the happiest I've seen this office since the day he arrived.

To: Katherine Bloom <katherine@ktextv.com>
From: Julia Boudreaux <julia@ktextv.com>
Subject: Born to serve

I'm happy to oblige and offer a bit of relief for the staff at KTEX TV. I miss them all. And hopefully as soon as I finish this show I'll be back, installed in my old office. He better not have messed with my purple leopard-print sofa.

Julia—back and better than ever at 28.

To: Julia Boudreaux <julia@ktextv.com>
    Katherine Bloom <katherine@ktextv.com>
From: Chloe Sinclair <chloe@ktextv.com>
Subject: Should be shot

Julia, I can't believe we forgot your birthday!!

HAPPY HAPPY HAPPY BIRTHDAY!!! As soon as I get back, we'll have a huge celebration!

Lots of love,
Chloe

To: Julia Boudreaux <julia@ktextv.com>
    Chloe Sinclair <chloe@ktextv.com>
From: Katherine Bloom <katherine@ktextv.com>
Subject: re: Should be shot

Julia, I have no excuse! I'm here in town and forgot. The only thing I can say is that I've been dealing with an assortment of jealous females. It's disconcerting, all the women who throw themselves at Jesse—regardless of the fact that I'm standing right there, and frequently he's holding my hand!

But I'll make it up to you! Promise.

K

To: Chloe Sinclair <chloe@ktextv.com>
    Katherine Bloom <katherine@ktextv.com>
From: Julia Boudreaux <julia@ktextv.com>
Subject: No problem

Don't give it another thought. I know you both adore me. And when you get back, I promise we're going to have more to celebrate than just my birthday. I'm just about finished with my show. It's going to be great.

As to jealous women, forget them. Jesse loves you. He married you. Not any of those groupies.

xo, j

To: Julia Boudreaux <julia@ktextv.com>
　　Chloe Sinclair <chloe@ktextv.com>
From: Katherine Bloom <katherine@ktextv.com>
Subject: Never fail

You always know what to say. Thanks!

Love,
K

p.s. are you coming over tomorrow for Thanksgiving dinner?

To: Katherine Bloom <katherine@ktextv.com>
From: Julia Boudreaux <julia@ktextv.com>
Subject: Thanksgiving

Thanks for the invite. But I already have plans.

xo, j

chapter nineteen

Right or wrong, good or bad, Julia Boudreaux was back.

With purpose ticking through her, she pulled on a leopard-print wrap dress that outlined her breasts, and fell over her hips like a sensual caress. She added a pair of four-inch come-fuck-me pumps.

She was finished with trying to be someone she wasn't. If she was going to fail, she was going to fail in the style she had always lived.

Putting on a pair of glittery earrings, Julia acknowledged that she had been avoiding Ben for the last two days. She hadn't a clue what he had done for Thanksgiving, and she felt a tad guilty that he either had to fend for himself or had to make do with a meal at some place like Luby's Cafeteria. But she hadn't been able to take on both Ben and the first holiday she had spent without her father. Too much emotion—and she was tired of emotion.

She shuddered. Julia Boudreaux, the woman who had

always been the picture of strength and resolve . . . had been an emotional basket case. In front of Ben. Worse, she had told him her secrets, too—all because she had gotten stuck on a tram.

Julia scoffed at herself when she remembered, embarrassment burning through her cheeks. But the embarrassment went beyond that single incident. She had been weak for nearly a month now. It was time it stopped.

She smoothed her dress and breathed deeply. Yes, Julia Boudreaux was back.

Adrenaline coursed through her as if she had to make up for lost time. She had to make sure everything was in order to tape the final segment of *Primal Guy*. She was going to blow Andrew Folly's socks off.

Rob and Todd were ready. Rocco was ready. His house was as good as it was going to get. And she had contacted the woman he wanted to ask out. When Julia had said she was calling for Rocco Russo, the woman had started to hang up. But Julia had acted quickly, promising that the man had changed. It hadn't been easy, but by the end of the conversation Fiona Branch had been intrigued enough with the promise of a changed man who adored her to give in and say yes.

On the day of the final taping, Todd was waiting for her in the kitchen when she entered.

Ben was waiting, too.

"Good morning," he said, turning away from the stove, a skillet in his hand as he looked at her.

The darkness of his eyes sent a shiver of longing through her. They'd had wild, passionate sex just as each of them knew they would one day. And that was all it was. Mad, wild, uncommitted sex.

Which made her heart twist.

That was the thing. When she was up in that idiotic tram, she'd had the bone chilling realization that she was falling for Ben Prescott. Falling hard. She felt vulnerable and needy, and she suddenly had an appreciation for all those women who called, desperate to speak to Ben. She had become one of those women—or rather, she was concerned that she could be. And that she wouldn't let happen.

She also refused to let him know more about her than he already did. She had never admitted to Chloe or Kate her fear of heights. Or her fear that her father would think she was boring or weak. In a course of a few minutes she had spilled her secrets to this man. And it really ticked her off.

Ben looked her up and down, taking in the sexy dress and high-heeled shoes. She could tell from his expression that he instantly got what was going on.

"Welcome back," he said, his full lips quirking at one corner.

It wasn't until then that she noticed Todd was taping the whole thing.

"Todd, really. Don't waste the tape."

"What do you mean? Ben, in an apron, cooking is a first ever. I have to get this down as proof. No one would believe me otherwise."

"Okay, wise guy," Ben said with a fond laugh. "Turn it off."

Todd chuckled as he backed away, heading for the door.

Ben started serving onto plates. It wasn't until then that she noticed the kitchen table was set with fresh fruit, toast, orange juice that she could tell was fresh squeezed, and bacon. Her stomach grumbled.

"Have a seat," he said, holding out a chair for her.

They stood close, their eyes locked, before she blinked. "Thanks, but I don't have time."

The disappointment on his face nearly made her reconsider. But she couldn't afford to reconsider. She had to shore up her defenses. And before she could change her mind, she grabbed up the purse and keys that had been delivered to her the day before, along with her car.

"Come on, Todd. Let's go meet Rob at Rocco's house."

They arrived at Rocco's little cottage in the neighborhood called Kern Place. Driving up, Julia felt some of her trepidation ease. The flowers and plants gave the house a different look. As soon as she stepped inside, she was pleased that Rocco had kept everything clean.

On top of that, the table was set with china and fresh flowers. The kitchen was filled with the aroma of cooking. Rocco had taken the groceries she had bought the day before, along with all her detailed instructions and recipes, and had already started preparing a feast. He'd even gone out and gotten a bottle of champagne that he had chilling in a bucket.

A sigh of relief passed through her that she hadn't been wrong about him. He did want this to work as badly as she did.

"Hi!" she said.

Rocco's head jerked up like he hadn't heard her walk in. When he glanced at her, he looked nervous.

"Fiona should be here any minute," she said.

He grunted. "Yeah."

"What?"

"Ah, umm, yes." He shook himself, like he was shaking away the old caveman.

But Julia couldn't tamp down the jab of fear that followed in the wake of her short-lived relief. Something felt wrong.

"Is everything okay?" she asked.

"Yes, Julia. Everything is wonderful."

She didn't believe him, and her concern spiked when the doorbell rang. Julia took a deep breath and stood back as Rob taped Rocco opening the door.

"Fiona," her Primal Guy said.

Julia hoped the camera caught the look of surprise on the woman's face, her blue eyes lighting up, her lips parting.

"Rocco?"

The Primal Guy smiled beautifully and held out his arms. "Surprise."

"Oh, my gosh! You look amazing!"

Rocco dipped his head, almost a shy gesture, his blond hair falling forward. "Do you think?"

He opened the door wider and his date stepped inside. That's when Fiona noticed the camera.

"Oh," she squeaked, her hand immediately coming up to smooth her hair.

That would have to be edited out.

"I forgot that there would be cameras," she added.

"Rob, cut." Julia stepped forward. "Hi, Fiona. I'm Julia Boudreaux. We spoke on the phone."

"Sure, I remember. Hi."

"As awkward as it might be, if you could just pretend the camera isn't there, that would be great."

"Of course. I wasn't thinking."

"Let's just reshoot from when you walk in the door."

They did, and this time it was perfect.

The whole shoot went great from there, everything from the way Rocco took Fiona's coat, to this once rough-around-the-edges man offering his date a glass of champagne. He held her chair, stood when she stood, served her plate, and by the end of the evening, Fiona actually took a bite of the chocolate mousse from the spoon Rocco offered. It was sweet and endearing and the perfect finale to show the successful journey Rocco Russo had made from primal guy to sweetie pie.

Giddy excitement pushed at concern. She had footage she believed she could make into a show. She was back as the woman she knew. She wanted to laugh and dance around the room at the thought that just when she thought things were falling apart, they were actually working out.

By the time she and her crew wrapped up and were ready to leave, Fiona was smiling like a smitten school-girl. Julia had worried for no reason.

It was six o'clock in the evening when Julia, Todd, and Rob stood out by their cars.

"Wow, that was cool," the teenager enthused.

"You've got some great footage to work with," Rob added.

"I know. Now we just need to do the final edit. We'll start first thing tomorrow morning and work through the weekend."

"Awesome," Todd said.

"I'm game," Rob added.

Julia wanted to do the work over the weekend when the staff, most especially Folly, wasn't there. As an added bonus, working at the station provided her with a means to avoid Ben.

So she worked. Up early Saturday morning until late Sunday night with Rob and Todd at her side. Ben clearly was busy as well, since when she did come home, always late, he wasn't there. Good, she told herself firmly.

They finished late Sunday night, and Julia took the morning off the next day to get ready to return to KTEX with her product in hand. When she walked into the station Monday afternoon, she had the final version of *Primal Guy* in her hand.

"Julia!" several people called out.

It was good to be back. Nothing looked different, and if she blocked out the thought of Andrew Folly taking over her office, for a few blissful seconds she could pretend that nothing had changed. Her life was still as it should be.

But it wasn't.

Fortunately, she was excited to show Kate the pilot episode of her show. When she walked into the TV host's office, Kate leaped out of her chair and flew around the desk.

"Jules!" she cried, hugging her close. "Finally!"

"You're acting like you haven't seen me in ages," Julia stated over the lump in her throat.

"Don't act all distant. I know it's just an act. Besides, it isn't the same when you aren't coming into the office. I've missed you around here."

"I've missed you, too."

When the women settled into chairs, Kate looked her up and down. "What happened to the blouses and wool pants?"

She smoothed another of her favorite wrap dresses. "I guess you could say it's hard to teach an old dog new tricks. But that's the least of my concerns." Julia held up the videocassette.

"Your show?" Kate asked with a gasp.

"It is."

Kate grabbed the tape and Julia's hand and dragged her off to the screening room.

"I can't wait to see what you have!"

The curly-headed brunette popped the tape in, then sat back as the show came to life.

Julia's image came into focus on the screen. She hardly recognized herself in the cashmere sweater set and fine wool slacks she had borrowed from Kate. Staring at her reflection, she couldn't believe she had ever thought that changing her clothes would do anything to change who she really was.

Then her voice filled the room.

"*I'm Julia Boudreaux, and like so many women out there, I've had it up to here with bad boys. You know the type, ladies. Those men who have movie-star good looks, and the manners of a caveman who thinks grunts are conversation. The fact is, mothers, sisters, girlfriends, and wives have been trying to fix these guys since the Stone Age. But mothers, sisters, girlfriends, and wives can't tell a man she loves what's really wrong with him—at least tell him and not have to live with the consequences. That, however, isn't my problem. I don't care if these guys like me or not. So I'll tell them what others won't. I'll tell them the barefaced truth.*

"*So sit back and hold on. I'm going to do women everywhere a favor. I'm going to . . . Turn That Primal Guy into a Sweetie Pie.*"

Kate swiveled her head. "Julia!" She burst out laughing. "What a great title!"

"But can she pull it off?"

They jerked around in their seats to find Andrew standing in the doorway. He wore a banker's suit with a blue shirt and white collar. His red power tie was so bright it practically blinked like a traffic signal.

"Andrew," Kate said, pressing the OFF button. "You've met Julia, haven't you?"

He grimaced as if remembering. Julia fought between a cringe of embarrassment and a shiver of pleasure when she remembered the day they had met. It was still hard to believe the things Ben had the ability to make her feel, do, and say.

"Yes, we've met," he said, the words clipped. "Now it's time I see what you've been working on these last few weeks."

He walked farther into the room, took the remote from Kate, and pressed PLAY.

"Let's continue, shall we?" he said.

Julia felt confident about the product. But still, her nerves were on edge. It was like she was exposing herself, and she didn't have a clue what anyone would say. Had she been delusional, or was it as good as she thought?

She sat perfectly quiet as the remainder of the forty-four minutes of tape ran. They watched the sweeping shots of El Paso, then the melting away into the introduction of Rocco. The tape rolled as Julia cleaned the Primal Guy up, had his hair cut, and taught him the nicer ways of life. Andrew sat forward when they got to the part where Julia transformed Rocco's house.

Andrew glanced over and raised an eyebrow. Julia couldn't tell if he was impressed or disgusted.

Then came the final date, the niceties, the meal, the pure romance of the moment.

"Wow!" Kate enthused as the credits rolled. She turned to Julia and leaned forward. "That was great!"

They both looked at Andrew. He fussed with the crease in his pant leg.

"Come on, Andrew," Kate said, "what did you think?"

He shrugged, then sniffed. "I thought it was . . . okay."

Julia felt as if he had stabbed her in the heart.

"Okay?!" Kate demanded. "It was great. Audiences are going to be wowed. Admit it."

He sniffed again. "Fine. It was good."

Julia couldn't figure out what was going on. Then he shrugged.

"All right, I admit it. As much as I never thought you could put something together that would be any good, *Primal Guy* works."

"Yippee!" Kate cried out.

She leaped up and took Julia by the hands and twirled her around. "I knew all along you could do it! And you did! It's Must See TV, Jules. I can't wait for Chloe and Sterling to get back in town. They're going to be as thrilled as I am!"

It was all Julia could do not to sag against her friend in relief.

"You look exhausted," Kate said.

"Rob, Todd, and I have been editing all weekend."

"Todd?"

"The guy who assisted Rob with the footage. Some of the sequences were his."

"Guy?" Kate raised a brow.

"A sixteen-year-old guy."

"You had a kid help with this?" Andrew demanded.

"Yep. Do you have a problem with that?"

"Actually, no. What a great angle. A kid who helped with the show. We can get coverage on MTV. We'll be able to shoot for that huge eighteen-to-thirty-four demographic that pays so well. This is great!"

Now Folly was excited. It was like her life had turned on a dime.

"Go home and get some rest," Kate said. "You deserve it. We'll take care of everything else on this end."

Now that the hard part was over, Julia wanted a break. She wanted to get away. But the thought of going home held no appeal. It was Monday evening, and Bobby's Place would be filled with men there to watch Monday Night Football.

Men who would adore her.

Men who weren't Ben.

The old Julia surged through her, and when she slid into her car, she headed toward the bar that had been a favorite hangout for her and the girls.

She felt wild and on the edge. It was like the act of keeping busy had kept the wildness at bay. And now that the job was done, the wildness surged back like a tidal wave, overtaking her.

She drove fast, pulling into the lot and throwing the car into park. The minute she walked into Bobby's Place, heads turned. She absorbed the appreciative murmurs. The smiles of promise.

She walked to the bar and took a stool that some big, brawny man vacated for her.

"Thank you," she purred.

But her heart pounded. She couldn't find the joy the attention used to bring her.

Determined, she told herself she just had to try harder.

When a strapping man next to her offered to buy her a drink, she accepted.

"A cosmo, thank you."

It was all she could do not to suck the whole thing down in one gulp in hopes of finding the ease, the power, she'd always found when she was surrounded by men.

She felt a shiver of concern that she wouldn't be able to find her way back to being a bad girl. She had always been the woman that men sought out and couldn't have—unless she wanted them. And then only for a little while. She didn't believe in commitment. She didn't want anything long term.

Long term never worked out.

She had seen that again and again with her father.

She refused to be like one of the many women he discarded when he was bored. She did the discarding.

But tonight, with handsome, interested men circling her, she couldn't find the power in her lifelong philosophy.

She must not be trying hard enough.

With the determination of a warrior going into battle, she reached under the bar and placed her hand on the man's thigh. She saw the start of surprise, followed quickly by the desire that flared even brighter in his eyes, the way the pulse in his neck beat harder. Even the rise in his tight jeans. He wanted her.

But all she felt was panic. Panic that this wasn't working for her. All because she was obsessed with another man. Damn. If she was truthful with herself, she would admit that it was Ben who she wanted. Ben, who was as bad as they came. A man like her father, who would get bored easily.

She curled her fingers into the man's thigh. Harder. She concentrated. This had to work.

Somewhere in the back of her mind she sensed a change in the bar, like an energy sizzling through the space. She tried to block it out. Focused on her hand on this stranger's thigh. She could do this.

Then she felt the man tense.

"Uh, uh," he stammered.

"What's wrong?" she purred.

That's when she saw Ben.

He stood behind her, staring at her reflection in the mirrored backsplash.

"Julia," he said simply.

"Ben." She swallowed hard.

He stood like a towering wall of muscle, his hair dark, his eyes darker. His body was sleek and smooth, predatory in a way that had every man in the room stepping back. His ruggedly chiseled face was filled with danger, a warning. This was not a man to mess with—at least a sane person wouldn't.

But that was the thing. She didn't feel sane. She felt every bit as crazed and dangerous as he had been since she met him.

She held on to the man's thigh even tighter, the nails she had polished last night, her favorite hot pink, running along his stiff blue jeans.

The man was caught between desire and the need to protect. Himself.

"Hey, uh, man, if she's with you, I didn't know." He staggered off his seat.

After a second, Ben slipped onto the stool. "A draft," he ordered with quiet control. A cold mug was set before him in record time.

"So," he said, "what was that all about?"

To someone who didn't know him well, the tone would have sounded conversational. Julia knew better. Ben was mad as hell.

"I don't know what you're talking about," she said stiffly.

"Ya know," he said with a regretful sigh, "one of the things that I always admired about you was the way you weren't afraid to tell it like it was. No matter how harsh the truth, you said it. Tell me, Julia, what happened to that woman?"

She hated that the words hit their mark—a truth that went beyond wild clothes or prim clothes, overtly sexual behavior or virginal manners.

"That's none of your business."

"Maybe," he conceded. "But I want it to be my business."

Her fingers clutched the long stem of her drink tightly. "Sure you do. Now." She swiveled away, slid off the stool, and went in search of some man to dance with her.

Ben watched her go, and in short order she was on the dance floor, pressing close to another man who wore a cowboy hat, boots, and jeans. Ben had told himself that some good old-fashioned sex with Julia would get her out of his head. He had wanted her for weeks, and had told himself that that desire had been purely sexual. Over the last few days since that amazing night, he hadn't been able to get her out of his head.

What he had hoped would finally purge her from his thoughts had only added fuel to the fire. All he felt afterward was more intense desire. For this woman. And the episode on the tram had only proved he wanted her more.

He understood her wish not to show weakness or need. So he understood why she had been avoiding him. He had wanted to avoid her, too. But the more he tried to put her out of his head, the more he wondered what she was doing, where she was. Until he came to Bobby's Place to throw back a few in hopes of drowning out thoughts of her. Only to find her here. Putting the moves on a cowboy as if proving the wild Julia was back. With a vengeance.

He wasn't sure whom she was trying to prove that to, however. The crowd or herself. And now it was like she wanted to prove what they had shared meant nothing to her.

He didn't believe it for a second. What he believed was that she didn't *want* it to mean anything.

Pushing off the stool, he slapped down some money, then walked over to the dance floor.

"I like," Ben heard the cowboy say, the man's voice filled with sexual promise.

"So do I," Julia murmured, running her hand down his chest as they moved together in a smooth Texas two-step.

It wasn't jealousy that snaked through Ben; it was something deeper. A need to keep her safe.

"What's your name?" the cowboy asked.

"Who cares about names?" she responded with a wicked chuckle.

That's when Ben knew he was right. She was pissed off, probably at herself, and doing something stupid to prove some kind of point. He'd had enough of that.

He tapped the man's shoulder. "That's enough out of you, cowboy," Ben said, pulling him away.

The man looked surprised, then ticked off. "Hey, who the hell do you think you are?"

Ben got in his face. The cowboy didn't look like he wanted to back down, but the sheer power in Ben's gaze made him flounder.

"She came on to me, man. Who is she to you?"

"Not long ago, she said she was my wife."

Julia sputtered and looked ready to spit nails.

"Wife! Shit, man, sorry." The cowboy couldn't get away fast enough.

"That's a lie," Julia called after her retreating dance partner, then gasped as Ben ushered her out of the bar. "That is a lie," she reiterated for Ben.

"Really?" he asked. "I could get the Providence medical staff to back me up."

Blood burned through her cheeks. "Oh, that," she replied. "I should have known you'd use that against me—and there I was trying to do you a favor and make sure someone was there for you, if you woke up during the night needing something."

He realized now that it had to have been more than that. The two of them had been resisting each other since the day they met. Not because they didn't like each other, but because they felt an attraction that neither of them wanted.

"Come on," he said simply.

She was spluttering with indignation when he lifted her up into the driver's side of his truck. When she scrambled over the gearshift, getting tangled up in the long thin shoulder strap of her tiny purse, then reached for the passenger's door, he caught her and clamped his hand around her wrist.

"Don't even think about it."

"Where are you taking me?" she demanded, held captive in the passenger seat.

"Home."

"What about my car?"

"We'll get it tomorrow."

"Why is it that my car keeps getting left places whenever you're around?"

"Because I'm constantly having to save your ass from trouble."

Her mouth fell open.

"If you don't like that answer," he added, "then how about, I owe you. You saved my ass. Now it's my turn to save yours."

"Go play Dudley Do-Right with someone else."

He chuckled ominously, but didn't respond. He accelerated down Mesa toward the Valley, steering with one hand, the other still attached to her. He didn't say another word. He drove until he wheeled into the driveway and braked.

Julia leaped out of the SUV and raced for the back door. He caught her with the keys in the lock. He pulled her around.

"I'm not Dudley Do-Right. Hell, we both know that I do more wrong than right when it comes to you. As to saving someone else, like I told you before, I want only you." He circled her wrist and forced her to look in his eyes. "I just didn't realize that I wanted more from you than sex."

"What?"

"Believe me, I'm not a whole lot happier about this than you. My life is fucked up enough already without falling for a woman who hasn't a clue what she really wants."

Her head jerked back and her eyes narrowed. "I know what I want. I want you to leave me alone."

She fumbled with the lock. Ben took the keys, and she breezed past him with her own inventive curse once the door was open. He watched her set her purse down, then disappear. For a second he debated. But only for a second. He locked the door, then followed her.

He caught up to her at the door to her bedroom. "Julia," he said, without touching her.

"Now what?"

Sarcasm laced the words, but Ben could tell it wasn't heartfelt. "Tell me what happened in the tram. Why do you keep trying so hard to change?"

"I'm not talking about this, okay? I've told you more than enough already."

"You haven't told me enough," he persisted. "Why do you want to cut the ties to who you've always been?"

She froze, her jaw thrusting forward. At first he didn't think she would answer. Then she looked at him. When she spoke, she was frustrated.

"You want to know? Fine. It's because I felt tied down by who I was. Tied down to a personality that I didn't know if I had created because that's who I am, or because that's who I thought would get my father's attention. I've been trying to change, to do things differently, because I wanted to find out who I had the potential to be."

He wanted to touch her, hold her, be there for her. The thought was as foreign as it was a recognition of the truth.

Unable to hold back any longer, he reached out and ran his finger along her jaw. The minute their bodies touched, he could feel the shift in her. The fight flared, but it was a different kind of battle. When he pulled her close, she went, but she stood stiffly against him, every muscle tense, her hands fisted at her sides.

"You have more potential in your little finger than most people have in their entire body. You can be anyone you want to be. But you don't need to be anyone other than yourself." He chuckled into her hair. "You're great just as you are."

He could feel her tense even more, then all of a sudden she groaned. The minute the sound left her throat, she clung to him. She held on as if she were afraid to let go.

"What's happening to me?" she whispered raggedly into his chest, her fingers fisting into his shirt beneath the leather jacket. "Why do I feel so untethered?"

"Because you're starting a new life. No one ever said that was easy."

"I know. I keep telling myself that. And I kept telling myself to stay the course and it will get easier. But it isn't getting easier. Like with you! I tell myself that you are everything I don't want. But all I can do is think about you," she finally said, her voice broken.

The shift caught him off balance.

"Since the first time I saw you," she stated, "all the rules I had made regarding men wanted to fly out the window. With just one look from you!"

Quickly, she pushed away and started to pace.

"Julia."

"Can you believe it? Me. Falling for some caveman on first sight. I mean, really falling. Not just wanting to have sex. Not just wanting to fool around. When I saw you, it was different. I couldn't believe it. So I've denied it every day since. And it makes me crazy."

"Stop," he said, the word dragged out of him. "Come here."

She stopped in her tracks and looked at him warily.

"Please," he added.

"Why?" she asked hesitantly.

"Come here," he repeated softly.

A wealth of emotion burned inside him.

"What's wrong?" she asked suspiciously.

"You're not in my arms."

Her mouth opened, but he didn't give her a chance to say anything else. He took the steps that separated them and crushed her to his chest.

"Julia," he whispered, kissing her and kissing her. Cheeks, temples, jaw, her ear.

Then, finally, his mouth slanted over hers.

The moan seeped up and slipped out from deep inside her. When she clung to him, she felt the rise of hardness against her abdomen, and she felt wild with wanting him.

He touched her all over, as if he needed to prove that she was really there.

"Julia," he repeated raggedly with each kiss, with each touch.

He kissed her slowly, then deeply, groaning against her as his hands ran down her sides, cupping her bottom and pulling her up against him.

A sigh winged out of her. That was all it took before he swept her up in his arms.

"Ben, no."

He stopped and looked at her. He wouldn't do anything she didn't want.

"I can't take having sex with you again if it isn't more than just sex."

"This is more than sex, Julia."

"Are you sure?"

"The only thing I'm sure about in this world is that I love you."

Denial flashed in her eyes. "Don't say that."

"It's true. You are the most beautiful woman I have ever met."

She tried to move away, and he could see the anger and tears mixed in her eyes.

"But," he added, forcing her to stay still, "it has never been your beauty that drew me."

She looked at him through narrowed eyes.

"If anything, your beauty kept me away." His fingers drifted along the shell of her ear. "I didn't need a spoiled, beautiful woman who believed the world should revolve around her. I didn't want that." He ran his knuckles along her jaw. "But I realize now that you aren't interested in your beauty—which I hardly understood at first."

She bit her lip.

"Once I realized you didn't care about that, really didn't care, I thought you just wanted to have fun, no responsibilities." He ran his forefinger over the seam of her mouth. "But I was wrong about that, too."

"You were?" Their words trembled.

"Yep. All you want is someone who sees you for who you really are—all the good, all the bad—and still loves you."

A chill shot through her.

"I finally realized that you exaggerate everything. In your own way making everything about you larger than life—so no one can miss your traits."

"Faults."

"Not faults. All the bits and pieces that make up a wonderfully giving and complicated Julia Boudreaux."

"I don't care what people think of me."

"Sure you do," he said with a wealth of patience. "You care more than anyone realizes. Including your friends. I realized that in the days after we got off that tram."

"My friends know me really well."

"Agreed. But you never let them see that you aren't always strong. Plenty of the time you're strong, sure. Hell, you spend most of your time taking care of other people, never letting people take care of you."

"I don't like needy."

"No, your father didn't want you to be needy."

She pressed her eyes closed.

"Everyone needs someone at some time. And that's okay."

"No—"

"Yes." He leaned down and kissed her again, lifting her up and carrying her to her bed.

chapter twenty

Ben laid Julia on the bed, then came over her, supporting his weight on one elbow. She knew he was going to kiss her. She wanted to feel his lips on hers. She wanted to feel the way he always managed to take her breath away, as if he alone had the ability to steal what she didn't want to give.

She couldn't help it when her lips parted, couldn't help it when her chin came up to meet him. The touch was electric, jolting down to the hot center of her. And she was hot. Hot and wet and wanting him. Need curled inside her, making her dizzy with longing.

With an expert's skill, he brushed his lips back and forth across her mouth. She felt his tongue graze her flesh, his teeth nipping as he drifted lower. Then she moaned and ran her palms down his shoulders to his arms.

He ran his finger along her hairline to her jaw, then over to her mouth. The minute the tip of his finger touched her lips, she took it in her mouth. He moaned as he captured her wrists and pulled them over her head. She had the thought that if he'd had some lengths of ribbon, he would have tied her up. Instead he bound her with one strong hand, then he bound her with sensation when he spread open the edges of her dress, as if he were unwrapping a precious gift.

She could see the appreciation on his face when he looked at her. She could feel the tremor that raced along his skin. He wanted her. He wanted to savor her and make her yearn for his touch.

With his free hand, he unclasped the snap between her breasts, loosening the mounds from the sheer, lacy bra. The minute he looked at her, she felt her nipples pull tight with anticipation.

A groan of pure masculine lust sounded deep in his chest before he gave in and kissed first one breast, then the other.

He pressed his lips to the soft underswell of flesh, then rose higher, and her eyes fluttered closed. When he took one nipple in his mouth, she arched up to him, her hands still caught, her body straining toward him.

He meant to be in control, and he was. But she knew that at some level it was costing him. She could feel the hard bulge of him straining against his jeans, pressing into her thigh. When she moved against him, his groan became feral and he pressed their bodies together. He planted his face in her hair and breathed her in, as if he could breathe in the strength to resist her. Then he pulled back and tugged her from the bed.

"What are you doing?"

He didn't answer with words. She inhaled sharply when inch by inch, piece by piece, he removed her cloth-

ing. When she finally stood before him, naked except for
her heels, his breath shuddered through him.

"God, you're amazing."

He took his fill and murmured his approval when her
nipples tingled without him ever touching her. He could
tell she wanted him.

He dipped his head and brushed her neck with his lips
before his tongue slid up to her ear. He took the lobe
gently between his teeth. His breath grew short when
she groaned and her hands came up and clasped his
forearms.

As always, her beauty stirred him. Though it was not
an ordinary beauty—rather a beauty of the wild prairies
or the majestic heights of the Rocky Mountains, beauty
that a man could not capture or hold, only delight in,
taking it in and savoring it. Her beauty was not just that
of face and body, but of mind and soul as well.

And he realized that that was where they had been
headed since the day he met her. For this moment it was
beyond pleasure. It was about love.

He loved Julia. He loved everything about her, from
her competent sexiness, to her deeply hidden vulnera-
bilities. And he wanted her to love him, too.

But how to prove to her that they were meant to be
together, that it wasn't just about the tease and sensation
and playful one-upmanship?

He didn't know.

All he knew was that this wasn't just about sex. He
wanted to make love to her.

As if reading his thoughts, she reached out and began
to tug at his T-shirt. When he ripped it over his head, she
pressed her palms to his chest. His breathing was rapid
as he let her touch her fill. He wanted her, in his arms

and by his side. He wanted her with an ache so intense that he thought he would burst, right there, right then, as he merely looked at her.

He bent his head to capture her lips in a barely perceptible caress. Only to taste. But his body began to burn, slowly, intensely. His mind reeled. He kissed her again, this time harder. She sought the pressure. Desire surged through him uncontrollably, turning his kiss into a demand until he had ripped the rest of his clothes free.

Then he kissed her again.

He pulled her close, crushing her to him. Lowering his head to hers, he captured her lips in a punishing embrace. With one hand at her back, he traced a path down her spine, pressing their bodies together.

She returned his embrace uninhibitedly, the touch of her tongue showing just how much she wanted him. He couldn't believe that it had taken so long before he had given in and kissed her on the mouth. Now he couldn't get enough.

He nipped at the corner of her lips. His tongue sought entrance to her mouth. At the touch of tongue on tongue, Ben forgot everything, his only thought being Julia, her feel, her warmth. Julia, his mind repeated over and over, matching the thrusting of his tongue, slowly, languidly.

He groaned as he trailed his lips down her neck. She shuddered when he ran his tongue along the pulse. Very slowly he returned to her mouth, kissing her in a sensual dance of lips and tongue, tantalizing, tempting.

He felt her answering moan deep inside him when she encircled his shoulders, clinging with a fierceness that amazed him. Their mouths slanted together desperately, then she opened to him.

"Julia," he whispered, his voice thick with passion, gravelly and rough.

And she said one word. "*Ben.*"

His body shuddered as his control snapped. He laid her back again. And this time he did find something to bind her with. Her entire body trembled when he found two silk scarves and loosely tied her hands to the curlicues of her wrought-iron headboard. She could have broken free, but didn't. Didn't want to. It wasn't until he opened her legs and bound her feet to the footboard that she felt a little nervous.

"Ben?" she asked.

"The minute you want me to stop, just say so," he promised.

"Are you trying to prove that I'm not a good girl?"

That made him go still, and he looked at her in surprise. "I want you to feel. I want you to feel what it's like for someone to give entirely to you, without taking for themselves. But if you think this is about me proving you wrong—"

"Touch me." It was the only way she knew how to really get his attention.

He looked at her forever, as if debating the wisdom of continuing down this path.

"Please," she added.

And he gave in.

He slid his arm under her back, arching her as his palm pushed first one breast high, then the other. He groaned into her neck, his mouth tantalizing her throat, then sliding low to close over first one nipple, sucking, teasing, then the other, pulling it deep into his mouth making her breath come out in tiny pants.

She gasped as his hand drifted low, over her ribs, then still lower. She held her breath. The tips of his fingers grazed a line down the center of her torso.

She felt primal and ravenous. He did this to her. Part of her understood that he was experienced at making women want him, and another part didn't care. She wanted to be with this man, whatever the reasons were.

Without thinking, she tried to touch him, only to tug against the silken bonds.

"Oh," she whispered, and he caught the sound in his mouth when he leaned over and kissed her again.

Her body reached out to him as he kissed her all over. First on her brow, then on her nose. Chin, collarbone. Lower and lower, his lips following his hands, until his fingers expertly found the curls between her spread legs.

A slow, deep moan escaped her when he parted her with the calloused pad of his thumb.

"You're wet," he murmured, his voice filled with awe and appreciation.

She was. She felt on fire from the lean, sculpted heat of him. Then her body rocked when he ran his tongue around her navel, then dipped into the shallow hole at the same moment he slid one lean finger inside her.

Her hips bucked to take more of him.

"Yes," he whispered, boldly stroking, pulling out until the tip of his finger touched her most sensitive spot, circling, then slid deeper, making her body begin to move of its own volition.

He pulled free, and she cried out.

"Shhh," he murmured against her, tugging the bonds around her ankles free.

"Lift your knees," he instructed, his voice low and gruff.

She looked up at him, and his gaze burned with hunger, a predatory gleam in his eyes. Her hands were still tied, her breasts beckoning him with their taut peaks. And she lifted her knees.

His body leaped, and she could tell he was holding on to an amazing control. Then he touched her again, parting her wet folds, one finger finding the hidden sensitive nub, circling as her eyes fluttered closed and her mouth fell open in a silent cry of pleasure. Then his finger slid deeper, the palm of his hand cupping her.

Composure and common sense were lost, and all she wanted was more of what he was giving. He stroked, and when she thought she couldn't feel anything better, his mouth captured hers once again. The thrust of his tongue was carnal, propelling her higher as he slipped a second finger inside her. She squirmed and wanted.

Their kiss turned hard and rough, hot and wet. She couldn't get close enough to his heat. She wanted all of him, his hardness inside her, his strength surrounding her. She wanted to feel the solid strength of him on top of her, her arms free to explore his body.

He broke the kiss and ripped the bonds from her wrists, allowing her to throw her arms around him, holding him close, their bodies melded together.

They rolled together on the mattress, each frantic. Then they rolled again, he on top of her. He cupped her cheeks and just looked at her.

"What are you doing?" she asked, starting to squirm.

"Looking at you here, with me." He smiled, then leaned back to her.

He kissed her, cherishing every bit of her—the sides of

her breasts, the sensitive curve of her underarm, the backs of her knees, even her toes. She felt cherished and loved. Yes, loved, she realized. Not simply desired. And it amazed her.

He lowered his head to her naked breasts, and his maddening tongue laving her nipples, each lovingly attended. He whispered words of awe before he levered back.

And suddenly the warmth of him was gone, leaving her hot and cold at the same time—then only hot when he kneeled on the floor between her upraised knees. Cupping her bottom, he pulled her down to the very edge of the bed. Her heart pounded with anticipation. And when his warm palms skimmed along the inside of her thighs, her hands curled into the coverlet.

His lips scorched a path along the tender skin from her knee to the curls between her legs. With both thumbs, he gently parted her.

"I want to taste you."

Excitement rocked through her and she tilted her hips to him. She felt a puff of cool breath against her moist center, then fire at the first touch of his tongue gliding along her nether lips.

"Ben!" She clutched his head, her fingers curling into his dark hair.

He hushed her again, his broad hand splayed on her abdomen. "This is you. Fierce, uninhibited, and passionate."

And when his lips closed over the tender nub, sucking gently, she bucked even harder. She cried out for the intensity that built and grew, threatening to consume her like a white-hot fire. Sensation coiled through her, and when he lifted her hips to take her more fully, very gently he nipped at the tender bud. She nearly went over the edge. But he held her back, kissing the inside of her thigh.

She was small and light, and when he stood he brought her up with him, making her laugh breathlessly. Need thundered through him and he buried his face in her neck, pulling her up as she wrapped her legs around his waist. He wanted to plunge deep and hard. But he refused to be the primal man that she had accused him of being. Instead he cupped her bottom, his fingers gently parting her as he guided her down to his shaft. When the secret folds of her flesh touched his slick hardness, he could feel the sensation that took her breath, and she couldn't hold back the moan that started deep in her throat.

With his hands instructing her, he moved her onto him, slowly circling her hips, her mouth parting on a silent gasp as her body opened to him.

"God," he whispered on a strangled breath.

Exhaling sharply, he moved her away from him until they were nearly parted. But then he pulled her back. Over and over again, barely a movement, slowly, deliciously, until she started moving again on her own. Moving and sliding, still seeking, she demanded more with each erotic gasp.

Then he plunged deep inside her.

They both cried out, and she clung to him as they moved together, panting, seeking. His movement grew faster as he thrust inside her. They were hot and wet, and deliciously wild.

His hips arched into her, her body tilting to take him more deeply in a way that he had never penetrated a woman before. He had never felt anything so amazing.

"I can't wait," she breathed.

With furious need, his body rock hard, he groaned as they fell together onto the bed.

He raised up over her, Julia watching, her lips slightly parted, her hair cast about on the covers and sheets. "Now," she cried.

He pulled her underneath him, insinuating his powerful thighs between her legs to let his hard flesh pulse against her, rubbing erotically.

With a frustrated cry she moved against him. She reached out to him, looking up into his eyes. "Love me," she whispered.

Love me.

The words rang in his head as he came between her knees and he pinned her down. His hard shaft found the sweet heat of her, and their eyes met. He saw her desire, but there was something else. Emotion, deep and pure and much beyond simple sexual need.

With that he couldn't hold back any longer. He plunged into her, cupping her hips, pulling her body up to meet his. She clutched his shoulders, panting, needing. He thrust inside her, desire and passion racing along every nerve ending. And then it happened. He felt her body convulse with spiraling intensity, his every sense reeling and alive. Only then did he allow his body's explosive shudder to rack the hard length of him. He cried out her name, grasping her tightly to his heart as he buried his face in her hair.

Love me, she had whispered.

And he knew for certain in that moment that he did.

To: Julia Boudreaux <julia@ktextv.com>
From: Katherine Bloom <katherine@ktextv.com>
Subject: Going crazy

You'll never believe it! After just a single promo for the show, the
phone lines are ringing off the hook. All of West Texas is
intrigued with *Primal Guy*!!

K

Katherine C. Bloom
News Anchor, KTEX TV, West Texas

To: Katherine Bloom <katherine@ktextv.com>
From: Julia Boudreaux <julia@ktextv.com>
Subject: re: Going crazy

You're kidding! When did you run the promo? And when did you
schedule the show?!!!

xo, j

To: Julia Boudreaux <julia@ktextv.com>
From: Katherine Bloom <katherine@ktextv.com>
Subject: Time slot

Andrew scheduled the show to run right after the *Friends* rerun on Thursday night. For a guy who didn't like you before, he certainly has changed his tune after seeing what you put together. The slot is the best we have in the evenings. You're going to knock 'em dead!

K

p.s. We're getting several requests for interviews for you.

To: Katherine Bloom <katherine@ktextv.com>
From: Julia Boudreaux <julia@ktextv.com>
Subject: Why me

Why would anyone want to interview me? They should interview Rocco.

xo, j

To: Julia Boudreaux <julia@ktextv.com>
From: Katherine Bloom <katherine@ktextv.com>
Subject: re: Why me

Rocco's turn will come after the show airs. In the meantime, El Paso is interested in the bad girl who is making good.

K

To: Katherine Bloom <katherine@ktextv.com>
From: Julia Boudreaux <julia@ktextv.com>
Subject: Good is a relative term

I might be making good, but I'm no longer being good. In fact, last night I had the most amazing bad night of my life.

To: Julia Boudreaux <julia@ktextv.com>
From: Katherine Bloom <katherine@ktextv.com>
Subject: re: Good is a relative term

What did you do?!!!!!!!!!!!!!!! Spill, Jules.

To: Katherine Bloom <katherine@ktextv.com>
From: Julia Boudreaux <julia@ktextv.com>
Subject: Later

Details don't belong in e-mail. We'll talk later.

xo, j

Signing off e-mail, Julia felt a jumble of emotions—a heady high when she thought of Ben and a thrill of excitement that her show was working, all mixed with a knot of nerves in her stomach. She knew Ben cared about her, and she knew that he was drawn to her. But could they have something deeper than really great sex?

She didn't know. She didn't even know if he would come back. Or if she could sustain something long term with any man.

There was no way of knowing, but she wanted to try. The thought was surprising, but exciting as well. She wanted to try to make it work with Ben—not give up easily because she refused to put her heart on the line. And wasn't that what keeping a distance had always been about? Her fear of being rejected? Being afraid that all men were like her father and couldn't stay interested in a single woman after she had shown her love for the man?

Last night, when the digital clock shone 2:59 a.m.,

Julia had woken with a gasp, her skin damp with sweat. She had been certain he was gone. She knew it, every atom in her screaming that Ben had left her. When she'd finally had the nerve to roll over, he was there, sound asleep.

Sharp, hot tears had burned in her eyes. Not knowing what else to do, she had pressed her face into his neck. How could she let herself get attached?

He had woken, groggy with sleep, and said her name. Just that, slipping his arm around her body and pulling her to him, wrapping her close. "Julia," he had whispered again, like a blessing.

She held on as he settled back into sleep, watching his chest rise and fall. And she had promised herself right then that she would stop being afraid.

Now, hours later with Ben gone before she had awoken, Julia cocked her head proudly at being so mature. She would play it cool. See how things went. And she wouldn't push him away out of fear. She would be calm, cool, and collected.

The pieces of her life were falling into place, her world coming together in a way that she could have only dreamed about. But there was still that one plaguing piece that remained loose, stopping her from putting her house in order. What she had done to Sonja—even if her intentions had been good.

Julia groaned. She had tried to push Sonja and Ben together to help herself—which had nothing to do with good. It was understandable that Sonja would feel used. Julia had called, had left messages, and still hadn't heard a word back from the hairdresser. And Julia had to make things right. So if the hairdresser wouldn't return her calls, then she'd just have to apologize in person.

But thoughts of apologies and putting houses in order disappeared when she walked into the kitchen and saw the note propped up on the kitchen counter.

Her heart plummeted into her stomach. Was this one of those Dear Jane kiss-off letters?

Every ounce of maturity fled as she picked up the single sheet of paper.

My lovely Julia,

Okay, not a horrible way to start . . .

I wanted to be there when you woke up,

Then why aren't you?

but I have some business to take care of.

The business had to be Henry's murder.

"Oh, Ben," she sighed. She hated that he couldn't leave it alone, but she also understood the relentless need to do what you could for a friend.

Regardless, her stomach churned with worry. Ben had probably left early to find out what he could about the hookers that Henry had been involved with. Now she had to sit tight and wait for him to return.

In the meantime, she had one more thing to do.

Ben drove up the gently curving length of Castille Drive and stopped in front of the address that Taggart had provided. The house was small but well-kept, a nondescript brick veneer covering the bottom half like wainscoting.

He didn't hesitate. He threw the Rover into park and took the cement sidewalk up to the front door. The need to bring closure to this case ticked through him. For the past few months he'd been filled with a crazy, all-consuming need. Now the craziness had fled. He felt like a cop again, levelheaded and ready to put Henry's murder to rest, then move on in his life. He knew he'd never move completely beyond it. He would always have to live with the loss—the guilt because he hadn't answered the phone. But he realized now that the craziness was fading because ultimately he accepted that he hadn't been in that alleyway that night because Henry didn't want him there. Which made it possible to be a cop again. It was what he did. It was who he was.

And Julia had brought him back to that.

He wanted to end this so he could make a life with her. So he could show her how much he loved her.

Love.

The word caused a kick in his chest. An intense feeling that he wasn't sure how to deal with. As a cop, he had worked hard to maintain distance. As an undercover cop who was never sure if he'd come home at night, he had hated to think of what that uncertainty would do to someone who loved him. So he had kept his distance.

But Julia had turned all his rules upside down.

After ringing the bell, he stood back. No one answered. He rang the bell again. Still nothing. So he rang it again. Finally, after the forth ring, he heard movement.

The man who yanked open the door was medium height, with dark hair and dark eyes.

"What?" the man yelled, his gaze narrowing against the sun.

"Are you Lionel Esposito?"

Instantly the man's expression changed, and he started to slam the door shut. Ben flattened his palm against the hardwood, then grabbed the guy by the collar as he tried to flee.

"Argh." Lionel groaned in pain at being jerked around. "The shoulder, man. Watch out for the shoulder."

Ben pushed inside, then kicked the door shut. The small nondescript house was filled with expensive furniture—frequently a sign that money was ill-gotten. Often criminals maintained a look of normalcy on the outside, but then lined the interior with the wealth they were unable to show or risk suspicion.

There was also a smell that made the hairs on the back of Ben's neck stand on end. Sweet and feminine. Like perfume and hair spray.

Lionel tried to move, but Ben slammed him against the wall with ease as he mentally tabulated his surroundings with his old efficiency.

"Tell me everything you know about Henry Baja's murder."

"I don't know what the fuck you're talking about!"

Ben slammed him a second time.

"The shoulder," Lionel cried. "Watch out for my shoulder!"

"Okay, let's talk about that shoulder. What happened to it?"

"I fell, man."

Slam.

"Ahhhh!"

"If you want me to play nice, then you better start talking. How'd you hurt your shoulder?"

"Okay, okay, it was an accident. I was cleaning my gun and it went off."

"Interesting. All gunshot wounds have to be reported. I wonder why yours wasn't?"

"It wasn't bad enough to go to the hospital."

Slam.

Lionel was practically crying by now. "Stop, stop."

"I'll stop as soon as you tell me the truth about shooting Henry."

"I didn't shoot him, man!"

There was something in his voice that spoke of truth.

"I swear I didn't. *He* shot me!"

Ben whirled the man around. "What did you say?"

"That scuzzy Henry shot me! I knew he was bad news. I tried to keep him away. But he was determined."

"Determined to do what?"

"Mess with the girls."

"The girls?"

"Come on, man. Don't play stupid. Henry was using the girls. He was blackmailing them, and me. What was I supposed to do?"

That knot in his stomach twisted. He hated the verification that Henry had gotten sucked into the underbelly of the crime world.

"If he shot you," Ben persisted, "then why is Henry dead and you're still here?"

"All I was trying to do was scare him off. I wanted him to know that his threats weren't going to work anymore."

"What threats?"

"What threats, indeed?"

Ben jerked around to find the barrel of a gun staring him in the eyes.

Julia pulled up to the entrance of Sonja's Salon. She was a tad on the nervous side. If Sonja refused to answer her phone calls, would she refuse to accept her apology in person, too? She thought about turning around and leaving. But she couldn't do that. She had to face the music.

Back in her high heels, she found the evenly spaced stepping stones weren't as easy to traverse as they had been in her sensible heels. Julia wondered what Sonja would say at the sight of her.

She smiled. If Sonja hadn't been upset, she would probably throw back her head and laugh. If anyone could appreciate the wild clothes, it was the flamboyant hairdresser.

Julia knocked on the screen, then pulled it open. A curling iron was turned on, and a bottle of hair spray stood on the counter with the top off. A brush was tossed into the vacant chair.

Julia heard voices coming from inside the house.

"Sonja?" she called out.

No one answered.

When the voices got louder, Julia looked for the door that led into the house.

Ben stared at Sonja and shook his head. "You shot Henry, didn't you?" he said coldly.

Sonja's face was red, her eyes darting from Ben to Lionel. "If I hadn't, he would have killed Lionel instead of just wounding him."

"Start from the beginning," Ben demanded.

Sonja scoffed. "I don't have to start anywhere! I'm the one with the gun, remember."

She waved it to make her point. But he could see that her hand shook.

"True, you have the gun," he said with a negligent shrug.

She snorted. "Typical behavior from you. You're on the verge of getting a bullet between the eyes, and you act like you hold all the cards. Well, let me tell you, I hold the cards."

"Fine, you're in charge. But just want to understand why the hell you did it."

"Why I did it?" she practically screeched. "It's easy. Henry was blackmailing my girls—"

"You mean Lionel's girls."

"No, *my* girls." The worry and anger mixed with a sudden softening of her expression as she looked at the wounded man. "Lionel's my right-hand man," she said, her voice nearly a whisper.

"And you're the madam?"

"You make it sound so bad."

"Last I heard," he said, taking a step toward her, "selling women's bodies for profit didn't fall into an altruistic category."

She jerked her gaze back to him, every trace of softness gone. "A woman's got to make a living."

Ben halted. "You've got a job as a hairdresser."

"Which makes a fraction of what I do with my escort service. And then Lionel came up with the brilliant idea of putting the site on the Internet."

"And that worked."

She sniffed. "Let's just say business has been booming. Or at least it was until we had to start lying low once you started poking around." She scowled. "First Henry was blackmailing my girls, shaking them down for a percentage of their fees. Then the next thing I knew, I heard you showed up wanting to know what happened to Henry. At least you weren't like that jerk. Scaring off customers unless the girls gave him a cut, hurting them if they didn't."

The words made him reel.

"I had more girls quit on me during that four-week period than ever before. I had to do something about it, just as Lionel said."

"So you shot him because he was in your way."

"No! We just wanted to warn him off. Lionel went with the sole intent of talking to him. Let him know we weren't going to take his crap anymore. Lionel was just going to scare him. Then the next thing I know, Henry pulls out a gun and shoots. I mean just shoots," she practically wailed, still in disbelief. "No warning, no discussion. The gun comes out and he fires like a lunatic. I was waiting down the alley, and the minute I heard the shot, I came running." Sonja's voice actually started to tremble, but she held her own gun firmly. "Lionel was on the ground"—she looked at the man now with a wealth of emotion—"and Henry had the gun trained on him. If you had seen the look on that man's face, you would have known he was going to shoot to kill the next time. He wanted to shoot. What choice did I have? I fired a single bullet."

"And you hit him in the back of the head."

"That's right! And I don't regret it," she said boldly, though she didn't look as convinced as she sounded.

"So it wasn't an execution."

"What are you talking about? I didn't execute anyone. I was protecting Lionel."

Ben ran his hand over the back of his neck as if he could relieve the tension. "You dragged Lionel away, then bandaged him up yourself."

"Lionel was lucky. The bullet only grazed his shoulder." She sighed. "Everything was going great until that night you started asking questions, then got fucking shot yourself. Geez, cops were everywhere, asking questions again. All because you were trying to find out about your drug-dealing friend Henry."

He looked at her for a second, only then understanding that she didn't know Henry had been a cop.

"Why not just go to the cops and turn Henry in?" he asked. "How can a drug dealer blackmail you?"

Sonja scoffed. "What am I going to tell them? I've got a guy dipping into my prostitution profits."

"You could have done it anonymously."

"You think I didn't?" Her patience was fading. "I did turn him in. Twice. Both times he disappeared for a few days, but then he was back, mad as hell, wanting even more money. It was like he had connections on the force or something. Probably given them a cut of the profits. Finally things were going to be better. Then you come along."

"That's why you decided that you better find me," he continued.

She shrugged belligerently. "You weren't hard to find. I had an associate follow you once you were discharged from the hospital. Later, I drove by the Meadowlark Drive address to see how I might get into the house, and there was a line down the driveway of men trying out for the show. Bingo, I had my way in. I was smart enough to use the situation to my advantage. Amazing how one little thing can get out of control."

"It doesn't have to be out of control."

She cringed and shook her head. "Sure. If you had just let the Henry thing go. But no, you've been on it like a dog with a bone between its teeth. Though now you've made it easier for me by showing up here. I have a business to save." She glanced over at Lionel, who leaned against the wall, clutching his shoulder. "And I have the man I love to protect. Besides, no one's going to miss you any more than they've missed Henry. What's one or two drug dealers in the scheme of things?"

"Henry wasn't a drug dealer."

Sonja's brow furrowed.

"And neither am I."

Sonja's head jerked back, and the gun wavered. But before she could do anything a gasp shuddered through the room.

Julia stopped dead in her tracks. "What's going on here?"

Ben and Sonja whirled around. Ben saw Julia instantly, and a fierce need to protect her consumed him. He had walked into this house intent on getting the truth. He wore a wire, and backup was waiting to move in. It would have been easy even if it hadn't ended up being a clean takedown—easy until Julia walked in.

The time for answers was up.

His calm evaporated. But wild bravado wasn't going to save Julia. For weeks he hadn't cared if he was reckless in his pursuit of answers. But with Julia standing there, innocently caught in the crosshairs, long years of training took over.

Adrenaline cranked through him as his mind kicked into overdrive and he sized up the situation in a matter of seconds.

"Put the gun down, Sonja," he said, iron in his voice.

Sonja's arm jerked back and forth between Ben and Julia, the gun extended.

"Sonja? What are you doing?" Julia asked, clearly confused.

"Damn you!" Sonja screeched. "You're making me do this!"

Ben saw the moment her finger tightened on the trigger. She was going to shoot, once again feeling the need to protect Lionel and herself. The same need he felt as horror exploded through his mind.

"No!" he roared.

The word shuddered through the room, and time seemed to stop. In some recess of his mind he saw the terror that dawned on Julia's face.

Like in the replay of that night he had gone into the alleyway, chasing Nando, or all those nights in his dreams, the gun went off, the sound so achingly familiar. But this time he wasn't dreaming. He threw his body at Sonja's like a crazed animal in just that second when her finger curled around the metal trigger. The gunshot reverberated in the small house, and Julia screamed.

The force of his weight took Sonja to the ground, her body struggling against him. Every nerve in his body screamed with fury as he pinned her to the carpet, tearing the gun from her fingers just as the front door burst open and the house filled with cops.

Ben rolled away, and it was Taggart who pulled Sonja up and handcuffed her. Another officer did the same to Lionel, despite his wounded shoulder. But Ben didn't breathe again until he saw with his own eyes that Julia stood there, stunned but whole, bits of plaster from the ceiling still sprinkling down like snow from where the bullet had hit.

"I'm sorry," Sonja whispered to the man she loved. "I screwed it all up."

Julia still hadn't moved, her face white, until she blinked and tried to find words. She looked from Sonja to Ben, then finally back to Sonja.

"Help me understand," Julia said, her voice a squeak of sound.

Sonja looked at her, tears on her face as Taggart paused before taking her away.

Julia wrinkled her nose. "So you're not really mad that I set you up on a bad date with Ben?"

A moment of startled silence sizzled through the room, then Ben threw back his head and laughed. But before he could cross the room through the detectives and uniforms to pull her close and never let her go, her cell phone rang.

Julia appeared to be in shock. Her fingers trembled as she answered without seeming to realize what she was doing. "Hello?" she said.

She listened, then suddenly her shoulders stiffened. "What?"

She listened for another second, then took a staggering step back. "Oh, God, please no."

Dear Ms. Boudreaux:

I had a call from a woman who is in your reality show *Turn That Primal Guy into a Sweetie Pie,* and she is saying she was used.

Please call me at 915-555-2000 ext. 34 to discuss. I would like to present your side before I run the piece in the newspaper.

Pedro Medina

Reporter, *El Paso Tribune*

Dear Julia:

We met at a cystic fibrosis luncheon last year. I enjoyed
talking to you, which is why I am writing now to provide
you with an opportunity to respond to the word on the street
that the new show you have created took advantage of a young
woman.

Please let me know when we can set up a meeting.

Sincerely,
Sara

Sara Weston
News Director
KVSM FM news radio

To: Julia Boudreaux <julia@ktextv.com>
From: Andrew Folly <andrew@ktextv.com>
Subject: We need to talk

Julia:

Please advise when you will be available for emergency meeting
regarding *Primal Guy*.

Sincerely,
Andrew Folly
Station Manager, KTEX TV, West Texas

To: Julia Boudreaux <julia@ktextv.com>
From: Katherine Bloom <katherine@ktextv.com>
Subject: Problem

Julia: I heard this afternoon that your Primal Guy, Rocco Russo, used the techniques you taught him along with the new haircut, redecorated house, and new clothes to lure Fiona Branch in, have sex with her, then dump her the next day. Apparently the woman was so upset and angry that she went to the *El Paso Tribune*. The *El Paso Times* has gotten wind of the story as well. Sounds like she wants her own form of retribution on Rocco, and she doesn't care if you get caught up in the process.

As soon as you can, come into the office and we can work on damage control. As you can imagine, we can't run *Primal Guy* on Thursday night as planned, since we certainly can't add fuel to what can easily turn into a fire. We will run something else in its place.

I hate that this has happened. Call me as soon as you get this.

Katherine C. Bloom
News Anchor, KTEX TV, West Texas

chapter twenty-two

Julia paced back and forth across her kitchen on Meadowlark Drive. It had taken hours before she had been able to leave Sonja's house. Hours of statements and officers asking if she was all right while she stood there in shock. Ben had kept his eye on her, but he had been wrapped up in the investigation. The minute the lead detective said they didn't need her any longer, she had left without a word to Ben. He had called her cell phone, but she hadn't answered. He had left a message saying he would be home as soon as he finished up at police headquarters.

But Julia didn't want to see him. She didn't want to see anyone. She didn't want to think about or talk about the memory of staring down the barrel of that gun. She also had to sort through the staggering betrayal of what Rocco Russo had done.

Her heart raced so fast that she felt light-headed and short of breath. Her palms were clammy, her head ached, and she felt very much like she was on the verge of panicking.

But she wasn't going to panic.

"Get a grip, Julia," she chided herself.

Her head spun with what was happening. How could Rocco have been such a bastard? But she should have known. Assholes remained assholes. Leopards didn't change their spots.

She'd been a fool ever to believe she could turn a primal caveman into a sweet and sensitive guy.

Once a jerk, always a jerk.

Roses and tuxedos from a man who had been insensitive before was a ridiculous dream. Her father had proved that over and over again. And even the roses that he had sent had been a fraud. She should have known when Trisha ran over her foolishly beloved rosebush that she was headed for a fall.

Every inch of her being was on edge when the kitchen door swung open. She wheeled around.

"Whoa," Ben said, that wonderfully cocky smile tugging at the corner of his lips. "What's the wild woman look about?"

Just like a caveman to think that teasing was an appropriate way to show affection.

"Yeah, that's me," she said unkindly. "I'm a regular wild woman."

Every bit of humor evaporated and he looked at her with intensity. She expected a biting rejoinder.

"What is it?" he asked with kindness.

The simple concern just about undid her. She felt a lump form in her throat, and if she had been a weaker woman she might have thrown herself in his arms and cried.

But that was the thing. She wasn't weak. She was Julia Boudreaux, and just like it was impossible to change a primal guy into a sweetie pie, it was ridiculous to think that she could ever be a sweet, innocently blushing good girl.

Odd despair kicked at her heart. She had wasted a month of her life trying to reinvent, and all she ended up with was a worse mess than when she started.

"Julia, talk to me."

"There's nothing to talk about."

"Sure there is."

Her jaw tightened. "Fine. If you have to know, you were right about Rocco."

"The Primal Guy?"

"None other. He turned out to be trouble, just as you predicted, and more than that, he slept with his date, then dumped her the next morning." She laughed bitterly. "I didn't turn him into a sweetie pie. All I did was give him better techniques and ammunition for screwing his female conquests. God, how could I be so stupid!" She threw her arms up and started to pace again.

Ben caught her arm gently and pulled her in front of him. "You can't blame yourself for this."

"Of course I can!"

"You didn't know. And you went into this with the best of intentions."

"What's the saying about that? The road to hell is paved with good intentions?"

"Julia—"

"No!" She shook him off. "Don't you see? I was on the verge of making a new life for myself. Then wham. Folly is pulling the show. It won't even air."

"I'll find a way to make him air the show—"

"Of course they can't air the show! I can't have some woman's total embarrassment and horror displayed on television. I can't do that to her. It's my fault that it happened."

"It's Rocco's fault."

"Again," she said sarcastically, her traitorous voice breaking, "he never would have gotten a cup of coffee with her if I hadn't shown him how to be the kind of guy who could attract women. I might as well have lured her into his bed. The jerk!"

She dropped her face into her hands and tried to breathe. "And by not running the show, by putting some rerun in its place, KTEX will lose all that revenue. And KTEX can't afford that."

"Sterling can afford it." He wrapped his fingers around her upper arms. "Don't worry about that."

She jerked away. "*I* can't afford it! Don't you see? *I* have to be good enough. *I* have to succeed. I can't keep my job because the new owner is my best friend's husband. I have to succeed on my own!"

He understood the need to stand on your own two feet—to not be dependent on family or friends for self-worth. That was why he was a cop and not an employee of his family's business.

"You will succeed, Julia."

She leaped away when he tried to touch her. She headed for the back door, but he caught her again. He trapped her against the wall, his arms on either side of her head.

"This is about more than Rocco," he stated.

"You don't think betrayal is enough to get upset about?" she asked with a scathing glare.

But he didn't let her off that easily. "What else, Julia?"

She tried to look away, but he turned her chin back. Her eyes narrowed against emotion.

"Tell me," he persisted with that kindness that undid her.

"It was like you wanted to eat a bullet," she whispered, hating that her voice was betraying her.

His spine straightened. "I didn't want to eat a bullet. I knew backup was out there, and I had to get the truth about Henry. I knew what I was doing."

She snorted, though the sound came out like a choke through her tear-clogged throat.

"Everyone is safe, Julia. No one got hurt."

Tears burned in her eyes and she tried to break away. But he held her firmly.

"Talk to me, Julia."

That's when she exploded, relishing the anger that replaced the tears. "Talk to you! No one got hurt! By sheer luck, no one got hurt! You could have been killed! You always have to be the big guy who isn't afraid of anything."

"What are you talking about?"

"You're just like my dad!"

The words burst out of her, surprising him, allowing her to duck away, leaping for the doorknob.

He stood there for a second, his arms still braced on the wall, and absorbed her words. She was afraid. She had been afraid he would leave her, just as her father left her—again and again, and then for good.

"Julia," he whispered.

Then he went after her, hurtling out the back door.

She gave a startled cry when she heard his footsteps. She raced to the far side of the Lexus. The sun was going down in the distance, painting the sky with multishades of blue and purple. They stood facing each other, the car between them, like adversaries in battle.

"Julia, I'll never leave you."

"You can't say that! You don't even think about the danger you put yourself in when you go off doing what you do. You could have been shot. Again! And I don't want any part of it." She threw up her hands and groaned dramatically up to the sky. "Who am I trying to kid! Sure I say I don't want any part of it. But the fact is, despite my best intentions, I've fallen in love with a crazy guy who is determined to eat a bullet!"

His breath snagged in his throat and his heart froze. "What did you say?"

She glared at him. "That you are trying to get yourself killed."

"Before that," he said with a laugh that was bubbling up inside him.

"I'm not sure eating bullets is something that should make you laugh."

"Not that part. The part about you loving me."

Instantly, she wrinkled her nose, but her glare didn't soften. "That just kind of came out."

"So you don't mean it?"

She sniffed, disgruntled. "Yes, I mean it. For all the good it does me!"

He started toward her, never taking his eyes off her. She stood there, watching him as he came around the front grille, and he could see the pulse beat in her neck. And the minute he got to her side she bolted. But he was ready for her.

He leaped back around the opposite direction and caught her against the trunk, pinning her there.

"I love that you love me," he whispered, pressing a

soft, fleeting kiss to her brow. "And I promise never to leave you."

She tried to free herself, but he wouldn't let her go.

"I want you, Julia. I want you as I've never wanted another woman. And I'll be here until the day you tell me that you want me to leave."

He dipped his head and brushed her neck with his lips before his tongue slid up to her ear. He took the lobe gently between his teeth. His breath grew short when she groaned and her hands came up and clasped his forearms. But she wouldn't give in.

"I love you," he stated, his voice deep and gruff as he stood back to take in the sight of her. "And I'll do whatever I have to do to prove it."

She stared at him forever. He saw her doubt—or maybe it was deeper than that. An inability to believe that he could love her enough.

"I have to go to the station," she said quietly, "to see what I can do to minimize this mess."

Ben realized that she wasn't ready yet to accept what they had. He was naïve to think that his simple declaration was enough. So he nodded, then watched her go. His mind raced as he went to her study and sat in her chair, determined to find a way to prove that she could count on him.

The desk was lined with videotapes, each marked. Clearly this was the raw footage from which they had culled the final show. Curious, he popped the first tape into the machine. Then the second. And for the next several hours he watched tape after tape, fast-forwarding in some places, repeating in others. He watched, mesmerized, as Julia danced onto the scene. Her beauty, her smile that filled his senses.

He hadn't noticed before how she took care with every single person who came in and out of her home, even the workmen at Rocco's house when they were fixing it up. He was bowled over by the sheer amount of work she had put into the Primal Guy's hideously awful place, or by the way she hadn't given up until it was perfect.

Then he saw his own image filling the screen.

Ben felt an involuntary cringe at the way he was captured on tape. Acting like some sort of wounded bear. No wonder she had thought him the perfect Primal Guy. It was nearly embarrassing to see his cocky smile, the way he would pull her into his arms.

But he laughed when he saw the tape Todd had caught of him making that huge breakfast. Of the way he had pulled Julia close when she was trying to teach Rocco to dance. Ben had danced with her. Then he remembered walking out without a word because he had been disconcerted. It had been easier to walk into Morales's compound than to face what he felt when he kissed Julia on the lips for the first time.

However, it was the tape of him teaching Trisha to drive that made his breath jar raggedly in his chest. Trisha putting the car in reverse and giving it too much gas. Todd's camera picking up Julia watching the events unfold, showing Ben how happy she was that Trisha was getting a chance to learn to drive. Then the car lurching backward.

It was the expression on Julia's face that hit him. The devastation that creased her features when he had finally pulled the car forward, no one hurt but that damned rosebush. Crumpled. Ruined. But then Julia noticed

Trisha's upset and fear. With effort, Julia had pulled on a smile.

"It's just a rosebush. Don't worry about it."

Ben remembered Julia later talking about how her father had given her that bush. And still he hadn't connected that she cared. Hell, he'd given her a glass rose as if that would replace what had to have been a cherished gift.

Julia had cared. A great deal. But she had cared more about making sure Trisha didn't experience any more trauma than she already had over the death of her father.

Julia had been holding on too tightly, trying to keep both of their lives from falling apart. Selfishly, he had thought only of himself, of his need to eradicate his guilt over Henry. But she was lost in her own way. She had lost her father, her job, and something of herself.

And what he realized, after watching hours of the tapes, was that while she fought to heal and help everyone else, no one had tried to help her.

He had given her sex, had made her feel, told her he loved her, as if simple words were enough. But he hadn't tried to truly help her.

Now he wanted to find a way to return the favor. But a viable way to do that still remained beyond reach. Though when he got to the end of the tapes it hit him.

To: Katherine Bloom <katherine@ktextv.com>
From: Ben Prescott <sc123@fastmail.com>
Subject: Favor

Dear Kate:

Hold everything. I need a favor. I know it's late notice, but can you and Rob meet me at the station in an hour?

Ben

To: Rita Holquin <rita@yahgoo.com>
From: Ben Prescott <sc123@fastmail.com>
Subject: Todd

Dear Rita: I hate to ask, but can I get Todd out of school for the afternoon?

Ben

chapter twenty-three

On Thursday morning Julia woke. It took a second before she remembered why she felt like a Mack truck had run her over.

The Primal Guy.

Plus, she had admitted that she loved Ben.

Great, just great. How was it possible that she had let her guard down and fallen for the very sort of man she wanted to avoid?

She closed her eyes, sucking in a deep breath, and remembered something else. Ben, standing there, telling her that he loved her. And she believed him. But was that enough? Could either of them commit to each other and have it work? As Chloe and Kate had said to her, she couldn't commit to a newspaper subscription, much less one man. Was Ben Prescott any different? Could he give selflessly to a relationship?

She couldn't find the answer in the jumble of her thoughts—especially when she had bigger concerns just then. Her show.

KTEX hadn't been able to do anything but yank *Primal Guy* and replace it with a second rerun of *Friends*. Advertisers had pulled their ads, and the ones who hadn't had demanded far reduced pricing for the slots they were willing to keep.

Refusing to run from responsibility, Julia had personally called Fiona to apologize. But *The Primal Guy*'s date had been too upset to talk.

Rocco had been another story.

He was talking to everyone who would listen. He felt like a major stud, as if breaking a woman's heart deserved a gold medal.

As far as Julia was concerned, he was a gold medal jerk.

She groaned into the pillow, then forced herself out of bed.

She didn't want to look at the morning papers or turn on the news. Her only consolation was that reporters and viewers would never really understand the entirety of the debacle since the show wouldn't run. A story of a man breaking a woman's heart was one thing. But to see him woo her on television—with Julia's tutelage—then to read about how he screwed her and dumped her in a single evening, brought a much more vivid and damaging image to mind.

For Fiona. And for the station.

Just then, that was all Julia cared about.

She showered and dressed. By the time she got to the kitchen, Ben was gone. In fact, she had to wonder if he had even slept there.

She felt a jab of regret that for the two of them, love might not be enough. But she couldn't think about that now.

Julia made breakfast, while doing everything she could to keep busy by trying to come up with a new profession.

What could she do?

How could she earn a living if not in television?

It didn't matter that several other programming ideas had popped into her mind, even ideas as to how to do *Primal Guy* better, because she knew she wouldn't get a second chance.

By noon, there was still no sign of Ben, and she was all too aware that the minutes were ticking down until the moment when her show wouldn't run.

Reporters and viewers were waiting. And she could imagine the slew of hate mail that she and the station would receive when the much-anticipated show didn't materialize on screen.

By five until seven, her stomach was in knots—both because of the show and because she still hadn't heard a word from Ben. She leaped out of her skin when the back door opened and banged shut.

Ben raced in looking wonderful and disreputably bad as always. She hated the kick of relief that she felt against her ribs.

"Quick, turn on the TV," he said excitedly, ripping off his leather jacket.

"Hello! You're forgetting. *Primal Guy* isn't running."

He winked at her and dragged her across the house to the family room, planted her on the couch, then turned on the set. He dropped down next to her just as the last ad ran before her seven o'clock show was supposed to appear.

"What is going on?" she asked, and even she could hear the tremble in her voice.

"You'll see."

Her heart leaped into her throat. "What have you done?! Tell me you didn't go to Sterling and force him to run the show! *Primal Guy can't* run! I told you that! It'll only make things worse!"

Her stomach plummeted when she heard the soundtrack she had created for the show. "Ben, no!"

He had the audacity to flash that devilish crook of lips at her, a smile so sexy that it could make a saint want to sin.

"Have a little faith, cupcake. Would this primal guy let you down?"

Falling back against the overstuffed cushions, she stared in utter fear as her disastrous program started to run. The title, the credits. The shots of El Paso she had painstakingly managed to get that showed the beauty of the city.

Then her voice superimposed over random shots of stunning bad boys and pocket-protector geeks.

And at the last second before the first segment began, her voice saying deliciously: *"Every woman deserves the best of both worlds—to have her cake and to eat it too. A delicious primal guy who has been turned into a sweetie pie!"*

Then the show truly began.

Groaning, she buried her face in her hands. "I'm ruined. I'm ruined."

Ben chuckled and forced her to look up . . . just as his image came on the screen.

Sitting next to her, he whistled. "Not a bad-looking guy, if I do say so myself," he teased.

Gasping, Julia looked back and forth between Ben on the screen and Ben on the sofa next to her. "What have you done?"

"Sit back and enjoy the show."

Her heart beat too hard for her to find words. She stared at the screen in dread and curious fascination. "What have you done?" she repeated in a stunned whisper.

She watched, tense and breathless, as the show played. She recognized all that she and Rob and Todd had created and captured, but now the program had been edited differently.

Rocco was gone.

Ben had taken his place.

"How did you do it?" she breathed.

He shrugged. "Who knew I was caught in so much of the footage?"

And he had been.

Ben calling her cupcake. Ben the sensual bad boy he was. Ben the wounded bear. All spliced with snippets of tape of Julia instructing on what was needed for a man to be a true gentleman. The audience would never realize that she had been instructing another man.

She was amazed at how often Ben had been there, watching it all, taking it in. And then that moment where he had taken her into his arms to show Rocco how to dance with a woman. Julia gasped. And she had been involved in television long enough to know that that same gasp of awe was reverberating through El Paso right that second. Every female viewer from age eight to eighty would be swooning over what was slowly being revealed as a sensual but sensitive man.

She sat stunned through the first few commercial breaks. But finally she turned to him in awe. "How did you manage it?" she asked in wonder.

He shrugged and his lips quirked. "Todd, Kate, and I did some reediting. Even Folly helped."

"Folly?"

"You bet. He's not stupid, and he knows a good thing when he sees it."

She sat back, too moved to speak. After a second she asked, "What did you use in place of the grand finale date?"

He smiled wickedly, then gestured to the television set when *Primal Guy* came back on. "Watch and learn," he teased.

Not knowing what to say, feeling overwhelmed, she turned back to the screen. Her eyes went wide and her mouth fell open when she got her answer. Ben in the kitchen wearing an apron, serving up that gigantic breakfast, creating what appeared to be a man who was doting on Julia, and Julia moved to speechlessness.

"This was one of the toughest cuts," he explained.

"Why?"

"As you might recall," he said, one dark brow rising, "you were speechless because you weren't speaking to me, not because I had shocked the words out of you."

She laughed out loud, the horrible clamp around her heart starting to ease. Hugging her knees close to her chest, she watched the show unfold as eagerly as she knew the audience would be watching.

Just before she knew the program was going to end, she didn't have a clue how Ben would wrap it up. But seconds later she had her answer.

The tears she had been fighting back finally spilled over as the camera captured Ben as he entered the grand living room.

This Ben, the one who sat next to her on the sofa,

whispered, "You can't believe how hard it was to get that shot of me walking into the living room without you knowing. Jesse helped, and we shot it last night while you were asleep."

"Why didn't you tell me?"

"Because I wanted to make sure it would work before you got your hopes up. I didn't want you disappointed again. Besides." He took her hands and looked her in the eye. "I owed you."

"You keep saying that, and I keep saying that you don't owe me anything."

"But I did. I owed you the same kindness and consideration you gave me this entire month. You were there for me. And I wanted to return the favor."

"Ben—"

"Shhh, watch the rest of the show."

When she turned back, Ben the Primal Guy had come close to the camera, and she could see that he wore his leather jacket and looked as bad as he ever had.

The man on the screen smiled at her. *"I might not be the perfect sweetie pie—"*

Julia laughed through her tears. "Even when you were trying to help me, I couldn't get you into a tuxedo or carrying roses!"

"But you did change me," he said into the camera. *"You changed me, but more important, you saved me. Maybe I went down kicking and screaming, but you taught me how to be a better man."*

He smiled that heartbreakingly sexy smile into the camera and said, *"How about taking a chance on a primal guy who promises to work hard to be a sweetie pie?"*

On the sofa, as the music flared and the credits started

to roll, she turned to him. "Why?" she breathed. "Why did you really do it?"

He stared at her forever, taking her in, and she started to get nervous. What would this man say? That he really did just want to thank her, or that age-old excuse he used again and again that he owed her—that it was nothing more than that?

"I wanted to be your white knight."

The words sent a shiver of amazement tingling down her spine.

He took her hand. "The guy who was there when you needed him the most. I wanted you to look into my eyes with all the love you have to give and have it directed at me."

"Oh, Ben," she whispered.

"I meant it when I said I love you," he added. "And I wanted to do whatever I could to prove that."

She threw her arms around him and hugged him tight. She didn't think about being cool and elusive, wild and sexy. She just wanted to hold on to this man.

"I love you, Ben Prescott. And I love that you are my knight in shining armor and saved the day."

"Not *saved,*" he said, holding her. "I just helped. That's the thing you never understood. You don't have to do it all by yourself."

She was beginning to understand that. She realized now that she had always felt she had to be the lone ranger, helping others but not letting people truly into her heart. It had become a matter of pride to be strong and self-sufficient, to do everything her way, by herself.

But now she knew differently. She couldn't do everything herself. And it wasn't a crime to let people help. Her show's success had taken a team effort.

"Which brings me to another point," he said.

"What?"

"I wondered if you could use a partner."

"A partner?" She looked at him curiously.

"Prescott and Boudreaux. Producers."

"You mean work together?! You and me?"

"Yep."

"But you're a cop."

"Was. I'm thinking that Serpico had it right when he got out and started making movies."

She laughed again at the sheer surprise and joy of being a partner with this man. Though there was just one thing . . .

She looked at him through lowered lashes. "I think *Boudreaux* and Prescott sounds like a great team. That is, if you can take the backseat to a woman."

This time he laughed. "How about fifty-fifty?"

She nodded. "The truth is, I wouldn't want it any other way."

"Then it's a deal."

They shook hands, but when she started to pull back, he didn't let go. "I was serious," he whispered gruffly, kissing her fingertips.

"And I said yes."

"But I want more than a work partner. Will you take a chance on me?"

Her heart leaped when she realized what he was asking. "On a bad boy?" she asked, with a teasing smile.

But he didn't smile back. His expression grew fierce.

"On a man who loves you. On a man who didn't realize he had the capacity to love so much. Not until—" His voice cracked, but he forcefully shook the emotion away. "When I saw Sonja turn that gun on you . . . when I thought I might lose you—"

She pressed her palm to his cheek, cutting him off, her charm bracelet falling down her wrist, jangling just as it always had. "Just as you said to me, nothing happened. Everyone is safe. And I love you. As I have since the day I first saw you looking like the baddest bad boy I had ever seen."

He gathered her in his arms and buried his face in her hair. "Is that a yes? Will you take a chance on me?"

She pulled back enough so that she could look at him. Then did what she had wanted to do for days. She kissed him, long and deep, filled with bold passion. "Yes," she breathed against him. "If you can take a chance on a bad girl who didn't quite figure out how to be good."

epilogue

Julia sat with her best friends around the kitchen table. For a second, they were silent, comfortable and happy. In the last nine months, each of their lives had changed irrevocably. But for all the changes that had gone on during that time, a lot had stayed the same. Julia was back in her leopard pants and stiletto heels. Chloe still had her bangs framing her startling blue eyes. Kate, with her froth of curls, wore pleated pants and a prim cotton sweater set. And the men they had chosen to love adored them just as they were.

As far as Julia was concerned, everything was perfect.

When they started to talk, they all leaped into conversation at the same time.

"Has Ben asked you to marry him yet?" Chloe demanded.

Kate leaned forward. "Did he pop the question last night? Surely it happened last night. And if not, I think it's time you asked him!"

Julia took a sip of her tea and smiled at her friends. "No, he didn't ask. And no, I'm not going to ask him."

Chloe sighed her frustration. "Sorry, but I just don't get it," she stated.

Kate agreed. "It makes no sense. It's clear he adores you, and you adore him. But here it is four months later, and at night, he goes home to his apartment, and you stay here—this after he lived with you for a month! You're not engaged *and* not even living together!"

Julia smiled, and despite her leopard-print clothes, she felt amazingly shy about this discussion. "I guess this bad girl is actually an old-fashioned girl at heart."

The thought surprised her, and also sent a thrill down her spine. She loved the idea of a true period of old-fashioned dating, which was exactly what she and Ben had been doing. After they had been thrust together while Chloe and Sterling went on their honeymoon, now Ben was being the perfect gentleman, calling her up, asking her out. For candlelit dinners, horse rides along the river, picnics in the mountains. He was courting her. And she loved every minute of it.

It had been four months since the first *Primal Guy* had become a hit. Partner Productions had several promising shows in the pipeline. The second mortgage on the house was paid off. Julia had gotten her life in order.

And she had Ben by her side.

She knew in her heart they would get married. She knew he would propose. She looked forward to that day with anticipation and certainty that they had a wonderful future ahead of them. But it would happen when the time was right—not rushed or forced as they had been with each other in the beginning.

The sound of some sort of shoveling work outside caught the women's attention.

"What's that?" Kate asked.

The friends hurried to the back door. What they saw was all three of the men they loved circled around a place in Julia's yard just beyond the driveway. Ben was digging in the warm March heat. Jesse and Sterling offered unnecessary instruction.

Kate, Chloe, and Julia came outside.

"What's going on?" Chloe asked.

Sterling extended his arm, then pulled his wife to his side. Jesse took Kate's hand and curled her close.

Julia hung back, taking in the scene. Her friends and their loves. Ben digging that hole. And something wrapped in burlap sitting on the ground.

Ben straightened and leaned on the long wooden handle of the shovel skewering the ground. He looked at Julia as if there was no one else around.

"What is that?" Kate asked.

Ben looked only at Julia. "It's something I've been trying to find for months now."

"A rosebush," Julia whispered.

"It's not the original," he admitted, never looking away. "But it's closer than the glass rose I gave you before I entirely understood what that bush meant to you."

Her heart hammered in her chest and she felt tears threatening in her eyes. "You brought me a new rosebush."

"Not just any rosebush. With Jesse's help, I found the exact same grower, the same sort of bush. Just like the one your father gave you. Only this one doesn't have red blooms." He smiled at her with a wealth of love, more than she could imagine. "This one produces pink flowers instead."

"Oh, Ben," she whispered.

He dropped the shovel and reached out, taking her hand after she took the steps that separated them. Then all three women gasped when he kneeled down in front of her.

His voice was hoarse with intensity when he spoke. "I wanted to find a way to make sure I'd be able to give you a lifetime of wild pink roses."

She felt her heart expand, and she understood something then that she hadn't before. About love and giving, about understanding another person at the deepest level.

She kneeled down in front of him and placed her hands on either side of his face. "I love you, Ben."

She sensed the grip that loosened around his heart at her words, like some sort of freeing. She felt the last traces of darkness leave his face, maybe even his soul. And with a laugh filled with his joy, he pulled her to him, kissing her hair. "Will you marry me?" he asked, his voice gruff with feeling. "Will you be my wife?"

She had been waiting for this, that perfect moment when they both would know it was time. She laughed through her tears, relishing all the emotion she felt, no longer afraid of the intensity. "Yes! Yes, I'll marry you. I'll marry you because I love you, and because you love me . . . and because you really do understand me." She leaned back and smiled at him. "Besides, how can I resist the sweetest and the sexiest man I know."

**In the game of love, being shy
gets you nowhere. . . .**

Suddenly Sexy
The prequel to *Sinfully Sexy*
by Linda Francis Lee

Kate Bloom's ordered world is turned upside down when notorious bad boy and superstar athlete Jesse Chapman comes home. Seeing him again reminds Kate of all the reasons she harbored a Texas-sized crush on him back when they were kids. But she isn't a little girl anymore . . . and she's ready to show this hell-raising playboy just how sexy she can be.

After a reporter starts digging into his past, Jesse Chapman returns home looking for space. The last thing he needs is a distraction, but that's just what he gets when he sees his little Katie. Suddenly the girl next door is hot and sexy—and more than even this legendary ladies' man can handle.

Published by Ivy Books
Available wherever books are sold

**After a close encounter of the sexy kind,
Chloe discovers her wild side. . . .**

SINFULLY SEXY
The sequel to *Suddenly Sexy*
by Linda Francis Lee

Plain-Jane Chloe Sinclair has never been
bad . . . until she stumbles—literally—into
the arms of a gorgeous stranger. To make
matters worse, her world is rocked completely off its axis the morning after, when
the sensual dreamboat turns out to be the
man brought in to save the TV station
where she works.

Sterling Prescott is hard-driven, sexy as
hell, and determined to take over the
struggling KTEX TV. But all bets are off
when the shameless wildcat who disappeared on him last night walks back into
his life—acting like a squeaky-clean librar-
ian. Life gets truly complicated, however,
when Sterling decides to win more than
the station—and to show Chloe that being
sexy isn't a sin.

Published by Ivy Books
Available wherever books are sold